NOT DONE

Tina Brooks McKinney

TABOO PUBLISHING

Not Done Copyright © 2014 Tina Brooks McKinney

All rights reserved.

ISBN: 0982108990
ISBN-13: 978-0982108994

DEDICATION

This book is dedicated to my father, Ivor Brooks. He has been the rock for our entire family. For almost sixty years, he has loved and cared for my mother, Judy Brooks. He provided a roof over our heads and showed me, by example, how a woman should be treated by her mate. When I was a single parent, he helped me raise my son to be a man.

Over the last decade, our relationship changed. He is not only my father, he's my best friend. We can sit together and not even talk and that's perfectly okay. I know he loves me and I love him.

He continues to teach me every day. I hope to one day be as gregarious as he is. He doesn't know any strangers as he will talk to anyone. I honestly can't think of anyone that doesn't love my dad!

On July 14, 2014 we found out something that changed our lives. My dad was diagnosed with cancer. Nothing that I've ever cared about mattered to me any longer. Were I not more than 97% through with this book, I probably wouldn't have finished it. I am asking for your prayers for our family as we tough this out together. We are fighters!

ACKNOWLEDGMENTS

The best and the worst part of every book that I have written is the acknowledgments. I say that it's the best because I get a chance to publicly acknowledge some of the people who have shown me unconditional love and support. It is the worst as well because I invariably forget to mention someone's name. It most cases it is not intentional. I cannot possibly list all the people who have touched my heart, so if your name is not listed, please know that I'm an old bat and if I don't write it down, I'm subject to have a temporary lapse in memory.

To my best friend and husband, William McKinney, you show me every day the meaning of true love. My children Shannan and Estrell Young, my parents Ivor and Judy Brooks, you all are the fuel that keeps me going.

My road dogs, Sharon Jordan, Joyce Dickerson, sisters from another mother, thanks for putting up with my crazy behind. My best friends Angela Simpson, Valerie Chapman, and Andrea Tanner, you already know. Barbara Morgan, Kim Moss Floyd, Patrice Harlson, Muriel Bloomfield-Murry, Detris and Candice Hamm, Marvin and Sabrina Meadows, Dee Ford, Stacy Tumbling, Tra Curry, Linda Coleman, Antionette Gates, Sheila Goss, Rose of Savvy Book Club, Ricardo Mosby, Princilla Johnson, Sydney Molare', Donna Johnson, Terrance Bethea, Sharon Russ of Words of Inspiration, Bernice Bagley, Stephanie Heard, Mississippi Readers, all of you have touched my heart. Special thanks to Bev for making my words sing.

1 GINA MEADOWS

"Now breathe, you should take nice calming breaths."

"I'm going to need you to shut up," I snapped before I could stop myself. Gavin was fussing with the sheets on my bed and acting like he had a clue as to what he was doing. It wasn't like he went to any of my childbirth classes with me, so I wasn't trying to hear any of his advice.

"I'm going to let you have that one because I know you're not in your sane mind right now."

"How the hell would you know where my mind is?" My head twisted from side to side as I braced myself for another wave of pain. My contractions were coming about two minutes apart. The pain was brutal, starting from the small of my back and working its way up. Gavin walked around the bed and started fluffing up my pillows.

"Will you leave the damn pillows alone!" I said between grunts.

"I'm just trying to help. What do you want me to do?"

Really? Does he truly want me to answer that question? "Just leave it alone, damn it. These pains—" A sharp pain pierced through my abdomen and shot around to my back. I yowled loudly as the pain radiated through my body.

"It's going to be alright, Gina." Gavin wiped the perspiration from my forehead with the back of his hand.

"Will you please shut up. You are not helping me!"

"Well, damn. I asked you what you wanted me to do." Gavin's lips were pressed in a thin line. In my heart, I knew I shouldn't be taking my frustration out on him, but the pain was so intense I wasn't thinking clearly. Lashing out at Gavin was the only thing I could do.

"Just stand over there and do nothing. Just like you've been doing."

"That's not fair and you know it. I just got out of jail for Christ's sake."

The nurse came in and took my vitals. I gave Gavin a menacing look to silence him. I didn't want our business spread all over the hospital.

"I'm going to have the doctor come in and see how far along you are," the nurse said.

"You said that half an hour ago," I grunted as another pain shot through my back.

"Honey, you aren't the only person in this hospital that decided to have a baby tonight."

Oh no, she didn't! I was ready to come out of that bed. A snappy retort was ripped right out of my mouth as I stifled a scream. It felt like my baby was trying to tear its own way out of my womb. "Y'all need to give me some drugs!"

"The doctor will have to determine that," the nurse said as she stuck a thermometer in my ear.

"I'm sorry, is he having a baby too?" I angrily replied.

"Gina, this nice lady is trying to help you," Gavin interjected as he attempted to straighten the covers that had become twisted around my legs.

"How? Because last I checked, I'm the one being ripped inside out."

"Nurse, you will have to excuse my wife. She's normally not like this. She really is a sweetheart."

"I understand," the nurse said.

My head felt like it had rotated on its axis. His what? I rose up on my elbows to meet Gavin's eyes, which were averted. He looked like the liar that he was. I waited until the nurse left the room before I addressed him.

"Are you insane? Why in the hell would you tell that nurse that I'm your wife? Got me looking like a cougar and shit up in here."

"What did you expect me to call you? I can't tell her you're my stepmother, now can I?"

"Well, no…"

"I know we haven't talked about this before, but we really do need to get our stories straight. What are we going tell our child?"

I couldn't answer him right away as another pain ripped through my body. I glared at the clock as if it were the source of my pain. I had been in labor for almost ten hours and had nothing to show for it except an aching back.

"Where is that damn doctor. Can you do that for me? Find him!"

"Gina, you heard the nurse say you weren't the only one having a baby. Perhaps the other babies are coming faster than ours."

"Stop saying ours like we're in some sort of relationship. That's sick."

"I know this is a messed up situation, but it's too late for I'm sorry now. We've got to deal with it before it deals with us."

"Situation? You know what, Gavin, you need to stop talking to me right now." I gripped the bed rails and grit my teeth as a fresh pain hovered around me. The pains were coming so fast, I wasn't able to catch my breath in between them. I was tired, hungry and sleepy, and I wanted this all to be over and done with. The last thing I wanted to think about was what I was going to tell my child about its parents. That, I had time for."

"Jesus, Gina, can you cut me some slack? I told you I wanted to be a part of this child's life. What more do you want from me?"

"I want you to stop flapping your gums. Can you just be here and be supportive? Is that too much to ask? Zip it."

"Fine, I'm going to sit here and not say nothing." Gavin folded his arms across his chest and stared angrily out the window. From his profile, I couldn't help but think of how much he resembled his father, Ronald. This thought was almost as painful as my labor. I shook my head trying to get those wayward thoughts out of my head. I didn't want to focus on the circumstances of my child's conception, or the man who I wasted most of my life loving. Both were still painful subjects for me. Now that Ronald was dead, the only thing left to deal with was this baby.

"Gavin, I'm sorry. I know I'm being a bitch. It's just this pain. I never imagined it would be so bad."

"Do you think the baby is alright? Do you want me to go get the doctor? I'll drag his ass in here if I have to."

I could see the panic building in his eyes. Two of us going buck wild in a room was not a good mix. I needed him to keep it together. The last thing I wanted was for both of us to start freaking out in this hospital room.

"I'm sure everything is fine or someone would have been in here. With all these monitors they got us hooked up to, they will probably know before we do if there's a problem. We just need to be patient. I'm sure the baby will come when it gets ready." I didn't even believe my own damn self but Gavin ate it up.

"Do you really think it's a boy? I heard they make mistakes sometimes with their tests. I hope it's a boy. I can't wait to teach him how to play sports and ride a bike!"

"Gavin, you hated sports when you were growing up."

"I didn't hate them. I just wasn't as good as my brother."

His admission surprised me. Gavin almost never wanted to admit that his twin was better at something. I couldn't help but think that his time served in jail had changed him somewhat. At least I hoped it did, especially if he really planned on being a part of my child's life. Until I knew for sure, I would continue to guard my heart.

"What about twins? Do you think it's two of them in there?" His eyes were practically shining.

"What are you trying to say? You think I'm fat enough for twins?"

Gavin sucked in a breath as he shook his head back and forth. "Stop. I wasn't implying that at all. You know twins run in my family."

I laughed as if I didn't know this piece of information. Gavin had been in my life since he was about four years old. There wasn't much about him or his family that I didn't know now. The conversation did keep my mind off the pains that appeared to be coming even faster.

"If it were twins, I would know it by now. I only feel one heartbeat and one set of feet kicking the hell out of me."

"I should have bought him a football on the way over here. Just in case it really is a boy."

"The baby can learn to play football regardless of what sex it is. I just don't want my child to stay in the house watching television all damn day like you used to do."

"Our child," Gavin corrected me.

"Gavin, please—" Another pain shot through my torso cutting off my words. I tried to remember the breathing technique that I had practiced, but I felt silly doing them.

"Where is that damn doctor?" Gavin grabbed the call button and repeatedly pressed it. His eyes crinkled with worry. I had to keep reminding myself that this was his first child, too. I had to give it to him; from the moment he found out that I was in labor, he was right there standing by my side.

I sat up unexpectedly as this overwhelming urge to go to the bathroom overtook me.

"What the hell are you doing?" Gavin shouted.

"I have to go to the bathroom."

"You can't go to the bathroom. Do you see all these wires connected to you?"

"I could give two fucks about these wires—I have to pee."

"Well, wait. Let me get the nurse."

"There's no time Gavin, I have to—" Warm piss ran down between my legs as I looked up, horrified, at my stepson. It brought back memories of his pissing on the floor when he first came to my house.

"Oh, shit. That means the baby is coming!"

For someone who supposedly knew nothing about childbirth, he knew this little tidbit. All my fears and anxieties seemed to magnify in the blink of an eye as I attempted to pull the soiled garments away from my body.

"This is a fucking mess." I was mad as hell at everybody.

Gavin kept hitting the call button as if this would make them get there faster.

"Go get somebody. I can't have this baby by myself." I expected him to object, but he tore out of the room as if it were on fire. I could hear him shouting as he ran up the hall.

"Come quick. I think it's coming! Hey you, bring your ass!" If the situation weren't so critical to me, I would have laughed. My pain was constant now, and I had to struggle to keep my fears in check. As much as I wanted this shit to be over, the constant pain was wearing me down.

Gavin came back and was practically dragging the nurse into the room. She took one look at my urine on the floor and yelled, "You've got the wrong one. I can't help you. I'm just the receptionist. The doctor is right behind me."

Gavin stood in front of the door blocking her escape. One look at his face and anyone could see he meant business. Receptionist or not she was going to do something. Luckily for her, the doctor was behind her, and he tapped Gavin on the shoulder.

"Somebody having a baby in here?" Doctor Johnson said as he nudged his way past Gavin.

"It's about time you got here, Doctor. I think her water has broken."

"Nice deduction, Sherlock. Now hang back and let me have a look to make sure." He stepped to the bed and placed my ankles in stirrups. The position made me uncomfortable, and I wanted nothing more than to put my legs back down and change my damn clothes.

"Can someone please get me out of these wet clothes?" The urine had soaked the sheets and had spread up under my back and buttocks.

Doctor Johnson smiled as he took off his gloves. "You'll be out of them soon enough. We're about to deliver your baby. Let me get you a gurney." He quickly strode out of the room, but Gavin grabbed hold of his wrist.

"You're coming back, right?"

"I'm going to scrub up. You should too if you're going to be in there with your mother."

I was mortified. Gavin looked like he was ready to take a slug at the doctor.

"Man, you got me fucked up. She ain't my momma—that's my girl."

"Oh, excuse me. I wasn't trying to be disrespectful. If you would come with me, I'll show you where to change."

"But what about her?"

Gavin acted like I was legitimately his concern. For a moment, I wished it were true. That someone was willing to claim me as their own. However, reality hit and I came back to my senses. There was no way in hell I was going to live my life defending my relationship with Gavin. We were just going to have to find a way to secretly co-parent. The hardest part would be telling him. I wasn't looking forward to it either.

2 GAVIN MILLS

As I followed Doctor Johnson into the scrub area, I was shaking so badly I was trembling. I knew I wanted to be at the hospital when my child was born, but I didn't really count on actually being in the room. I assumed Gina would shut it down. I kept waiting for someone to come in the room and check me, but it didn't look like it was going to happen.

"Lord, please don't let me bitch up and pass out in this operating room." I said as I pushed open the doors. My heart was beating so loudly I thought everyone in there could hear it. Between the rapid beating of my heart and my shaking knees, I felt like a cross between the Tin Man and the Lion from the *Wizard of Oz.* A quivering, sniveling, bag of bones.

"Mr. Mills, you can stand over here until we're ready for you." The nurse pointed to Gina's side. I cocked my head to the side as I reflected on what she said. *Ready for me. To do what?*

I wasn't ready for the faster pace in the operating room. Besides the doctor, there were two nurses and an anesthesiologist who stood next to me. I stood with my hands in front of me waiting to be told what to do. Everyone had a job to do but me. For a split second, I regretted not attending any of the childbirth classes with Gina or looking this shit up on the internet. I was sure Google had enough information on it to make me delivery room ready. However, that was water under the bridge now. I was here and was going to make the most of it.

I thought I would be good as long as I didn't have to see a bunch of blood. I got squeamish when I nicked myself shaving. If all that was required of me was to hold Gina's hand, everything was gravy.

Doctor Johnson said, "Are you ready, Gina?"

Gina just grunted as she worked through what I assumed was another pain. I never gave much thought to what women went through during childbirth. I never thought about much about women period except for the obvious reasons. Seeing what she was enduring though, I was ashamed of myself for the way I'd treated them.

"Gina, at your next contraction, I want you to push as hard as you can. Bear down really, really hard, okay?"

"I can't. It feels like I have to use the bathroom."

"Don't worry about that. We've got enough stuff around you to get it up if this happens. But I need you to push."

Gina grabbed hold of my legs and pierced my skin with her fingernails. I might not have hollered a little bit had I known she was going to do it. I tried to get her fingers off my leg, but she had me in a death grip. "Shit!"

"Can you feel my pain?" Gina howled like a wounded animal.

"Yeah, I feel it. You can let me go now." I didn't want to come off sounding like no punk, but she was drawing blood.

"That was good, Gina. Now take a couple of deep breaths and get ready for the next one. I can see the head."

I expected Gina to let go of my leg but her grip was like a vice. "She got my leg," I mumbled, but no one was paying me any attention.

"Push, Gina!"

Once again, Gina's screams lit up the room as she bore down both on the baby and me. At this point, I'm trying to yank my leg from her clutches. I felt like I was being skewered, and it took everything in me not to punch her in the damn face. "Come on, Gina, let go of my leg."

"One more big push!" Doctor Johnson shouted. He was amped up, and I might have gotten excited about it if it were not for the claws in my leg. '

"I can't," Gina shouted.

It was like a needle on an old-fashioned record to me. What did she mean she couldn't. What the fuck was the alternative. She couldn't be hanging onto my leg all damn night.

"*You can do it*, baby. Just one more push," I urged as I wiggled my leg to get my circulation going again.

I watched in amazement as Gina's entire stomach moved. It was the first time I fully understood there was a human being inside of her. So when Gina screamed with her next push, my bitch ass screamed too. I wasn't sure who was more surprised, everyone else in the operating room or me. I didn't know I could hit such a high note.

"Hold on, Gina. Don't push now. Let me do the work."

His stern tone scared me, and I accidentally looked into the mirror that was positioned directly over the operating table. I was afraid that the view I got of the baby's head coming out of Gina's vagina would stay with me for the rest of my life. "Damn, that's nasty."

Gina gasped, suddenly giving me her full attention. In fact, all movement in the room stopped. Even the second hand on the clock appeared to stop moving as I tried to recover my composure. "Uh…ah…wait. I wasn't talking about you, baby."

"Grow up, Gavin," Gina snapped as she finally let go of my leg. I was ashamed for my outburst, but she didn't have the same view of this shit as I did. She didn't have the right to assume it was because I was younger. I was quite sure some older men would have been rocked by that sight as well.

"Okay, Gina. One last push."

The silence in the room was broken by the squall of my child. My heart swelled with what could only be described as love. I watched in awe as the nurse took the baby from the doctor's arms and placed him on Gina's stomach. I expected her to shout for joy or at the very least, cry, but her face looked almost frozen. Her hands gripped the sides of the table as if she was afraid of falling off.

"It's a boy, Gina," I shouted as I mentally started a list of things I wanted to get for my son.

Doctor Johnson said, "Mr. Mills, would you like to cut the cord?"

"Say what?" I gave him my get the fuck out of here look, but he didn't appear to know what it meant as he handed me the scissors. I reluctantly took them as I stepped around to the side of the table. I wasn't sure what I was supposed to do, but since all eyes were on me I had to do this. My knees were knocking again and my fingers trembled as I held the scissors.

"Just cut right here and I'll tie off the cord."

I took a deep breath. The cord was gross, but I tried not to think about it as I positioned the scissors. Gina seized. Startled, I froze as her eyes rolled up in her head and she flopped on the bed like a fish out of water.

"She's crashing!" Doctor Johnson shouted as he grabbed the scissors from my hand and pushed me aside, seemingly at the same time. I watched in horror as blood appeared to gush from Gina's vagina.

"What's wrong with her?" Panic gripped my heart.

As the doctor cut the cord, the nurse was busy pushing me out of the room. "You need to leave now Mr. Mills while we contain this situation."

"What situation? What's wrong?" I yelled, but she was intent on getting me out of the room.

"Not now, Mr. Mills. I'm needed back inside."

As much as I wanted to detain her, I also wanted her to assist Gina. If something were to happen to her, how would I be able to raise our child alone? Women did that shit all the time, and even some men, but I already knew I wasn't the one. I was in no way prepared to do this. I was neither emotionally nor financially capable of such a huge responsibility. It was a sobering thought.

I tore away the surgical gown and mask and dumped them in a hamper inside the changing area. The tiny window to the operating room was covered so I couldn't see what was going on inside. It was a very surreal feeling for me, and I wasn't sure how to process it. I didn't know anything about babies. Growing up, there were no children around me. The only kid I knew was my brother, Merlin, and he always took care of me. I didn't know any of the details of our births. It really started me to thinking, and my thoughts were all scary to me. "God, please watch over Gina."

Both my biological parents were deceased. The only family I had left, to my knowledge, was my brother, and he wasn't speaking to me. Over the years, I had heard mention of other children that my father had, but I'd never met them. Never thought much about them either up until this moment. Now, I couldn't help but be curious about them. I wondered if my father had a greater presence in their lives than he did in mine. The fucked-up part about it was that everyone who I could have asked about it, was gone. I didn't even know if we had any grandparents or aunts and uncles. I never felt so alone in my life.

Thinking about my brother depressed me. I couldn't blame him for hating me. I ruined his marriage and made his life miserable. Now, more than ever, I wanted an opportunity to make things right, but my transgressions against him couldn't be undone. It pained me to know that I couldn't even share my news of fatherhood with him. He wouldn't understand. I didn't think anyone would.

Technically, Gina was our stepmother even though she never married our father. She raised my brother and I and was the only mother we ever knew. I got with her while we were both drunk. She had passed out on the sofa, half naked, and I took advantage of it. To this day, she hadn't admitted to remembering the night she conceived. It was a night neither one of us wanted to talk about. For me, it was a new low. I had never snuck some pussy before. I might have gotten away with it too had she not turned up pregnant.

As I paced the waiting room floor, it was a struggle to remain composed. I was terrified that Gina wasn't going to pull through. She wasn't exactly a spring chicken, and had already been warned that this was a high-risk pregnancy because of her age. Personally, I didn't think forty was old, but in terms of childbearing she was considered ancient. It warmed my heart that she would risk her life to have my child. While I wasn't kidding myself into believing she did it for me, I was still grateful.

For as long as I could remember Gina wanted a child of her own, and for whatever reason, my dad refused to let her have one. It was ironic that I was able to give her something that he would not. Regardless of whether Gina would accept me as her man or not, I was determined to be there for my child. If it could be helped, I wasn't going to make the same mistakes my father did.

■■■

Doctor Johnson entered the waiting room and looked around as if he didn't recognize me. "Mr. Mills?"

"Yeah." I couldn't tell from the expression on his face whether he was about to tell me good news or bad.

"I just wanted to let you know your baby is in the nursery and doing fine. You can go see him anytime you want."

"Great. What about my girl? She alright?"

"She's stable." He looked away.

"What the hell does that mean?" I felt the icy fingers of panic grip my heart. I asked him a direct question, and I didn't appreciate his veiled answer.

"We've transferred her to ICU. The next forty-eight hours will define her prognosis."

"I don't mean no harm, Doctor, but you are going to have to break this down for me. What happened to her? She was fine during all that pushing and shit."

"Mrs. uh, Meadows experienced post-natal bleeding and several severe tears to her uterus and cervix. We've stopped the bleeding but…"

"But what?" I demanded.

"Unfortunately, her placenta didn't come out as expected. We believe we have it all, but these things sometimes happen when we deal with these…uh…older patients…"

It seemed to me as if he were looking for an excuse to cover his shoddy work, and I wasn't trying to hear it. "How come you don't know? It's your job to know." I started pacing the room again as my anger escalated. "Fuck that. She just turned forty, man. She ain't that old."

"Mr. Mills, you can't talk to me like that especially since I'm trying to help you. Now, it's unfortunate that this has happened to your…um…girl."

"Why you keep stuttering when you say my girl? You got a problem with my liking a more seasoned woman?"

"Uh, no."

"You get your mind right. Is she awake? Can I see her?" As much as I wanted to see my son, Gina was more important right now. I was going to make sure she knew I was going to be there, no matter what."

"You can see her, but she's sedated. Like I said, the next forty-eight hours will tell the story. If she remains stable without infection, I think we'll be out of the danger zone."

I hated it when motherfuckers used the term *we*, as if they were walking in my footsteps. He didn't know my struggles or my pain. He was lucky I wasn't the same man that I was a few years ago. "Where is she?" I asked dismissively. He wasn't worth my freedom. Making that choice to walk away was growth for me.

"Fourth floor. Room 421."

3 COJO MILLS

Leaving Atlanta wasn't a difficult decision for me. Everything that I once cared about no longer existed. My marriage to Merlin Mills was over. Without so much as a telephone call, I received the papers in the mail that would end our seven-year marriage. Merlin didn't want to see me, but I couldn't blame him. I betrayed him in the worst possible way when I slept with his brother. We might have survived the first incident because I was duped into doing it, but the rest of those times when Merlin was feeling insecure, it was all me. He tried to forgive me, he really did, but I didn't deserve it.

Not only did I lose my marriage, I lost the baby I so desperately wanted. This was the final straw for Merlin. He was willing to accept the baby even though he knew there was a good possibility he wasn't the father. And even though the doctor told me it was a slim chance that his twin had fathered the child, I had my doubts. Merlin and I never used birth control, and we never had one scare, but one night with Gavin and I ended up pregnant. It would have been different if it had ended there, but I continued to lust after his brother. Lust was the only reasonable excuse I had to explain why I went to see Gavin while he was in jail, violating my own restraining order.

Gavin was the proverbial bad seed. According to his stepmother, Gina, he never cared about anything or anybody but himself. So when he started spending an inordinate amount of his attention on me, I was flattered. Scratch that, I was more than flattered, I was sprung. He consumed my thoughts so much, that my husband didn't have a chance of keeping my interest.

I shook off those thoughts of my past as I pulled up behind the moving truck that was hauling my stuff from Atlanta. If someone had ever told me I would be returning to Opelika, Alabama, I would have called them a liar. But, here I was, about to turn down Railroad and 7th Street on my way back to the apartment building my mother and I used to live in.

It wasn't in the most affluent part of town, but it was clean and affordable. It was also close to the only friend whom I had left in this town, Roslyn Lewis. She and I went to the same high school. As a military brat, I moved a lot. When my mom and I moved to Atlanta, she was the only one who bothered to stay in contact with me. She would send cards on all the major holidays, including my birthday, even though I rarely sent one back.

When I decided to move, she was the first person I thought of. After my divorce, staying in Atlanta wasn't an option I entertained. The possibly of running into Merlin again after all I put him through was too much. He deserved better than what I did to him.

Moving wouldn't have been so emotionally draining if my mother were still living in Alabama. When I got married, she decided to join my father in Italy for his final tour. They liked it so much, they decided to stay once the tour was over. Even though I wanted nothing more than to lose myself in my mother's loving arms, I couldn't bear to tell her what I had done to ruin my marriage.

I got out of the car and ran into the rental office to sign my lease and get the keys while the movers prepared to unload the truck. Merlin gave me all of our household furnishings. Obviously, he didn't want anything to remind himself of me. I didn't necessarily need the constant reminders either, but a sista was trying to conserve her funds. I never had to depend solely on myself before, and it was a little scary.

When I came out of the rental office, Rozz was standing outside my car. Seeing her brought an immediate smile to my face. "Girl, you look exactly the same! Were you window stalking me waiting for the truck to show up?

"Yes. Now come over here and give me a hug. I haven't seen you in what feels like ages."

I couldn't believe how good something so simple as a hug could feel. Especially coming from someone who appeared to love me in spite of my faults.

"I really have missed you. Thanks so much for all your cards. They really made me feel good."

"They did? I'm glad. I wasn't sure you were getting them since you never bothered to pick up the phone and call."

She was taking a jab at me, and it was justified, so there was no point in my trying to deny it. I sucked at letter writing and things like that. "I know, girl, and I'm so sorry. There is no excuse for my laziness. I'm surprised you continued to do it after all these years."

"Sending cards is a southern thing. I think I do it more for me than the people I'm sending them to. But if these postal rates keep going up, I'm going to have to whittle down my list or start using email to send my greetings. Now that you're here, that's one less card I'll have to mail."

We both chuckled.

"Are you going to stick around and help or are you going to observe from the window?"

"I think I'm going to watch from the window until they get the big stuff in. I don't mind helping you unpack the little stuff later if you want me to."

"That sounds like a plan. Thanks. I'll call you when they're done." I ran up the stairs and opened the door to my apartment. I wanted to get the movers on the way since they were charging by the hour.

■■■

"Rozz, thanks so much for coming down to help me unpack. Without your help, this would have taken at least two days." We were resting in the living room after we'd unpacked the last of the boxes for the kitchen and dining area. I still had to unpack my clothes, but I wasn't in any rush to do it.

"It's okay. You know there ain't much to do around here anyway."

"I know, tell me about it. Do you want some more wine?"

"I'm good. I'm supposed to go to bible study later tonight, and I don't want to show up not only smelling like a distillery, but stumbling, too."

"You still doing that? You were doing bible study when I left, what eight or nine years ago. You should have finished the bible by now."

"Girl, stop. You know bible study ain't like that. We use the bible to figure out life. This new pastor makes it fun, too."

"Y'all got a new pastor? What happened to the old one?"

"He got real sick and died last year."

"I'm sorry to hear that." I didn't really want to talk about her church, or to be honest, her pastor. The last thing I needed for her to do was start trying to recruit me to the misery loves company club. I preferred to be miserable alone.

"Don't be sorry, he lived a good life. He's in a much better place now."

"Hey, I didn't get a chance to thank you for hooking me up with the job at the IRS. I know I wouldn't have been able to get in without your help."

"Girl, please. They always need people. They have so many seasonal people it isn't even funny. The trick is to get yourself noticed, in a good way, so that you can stay year round."

"And how do you propose I do that?" I said, laughing.

"Hard work will do it every time. The problem with most of the seasonal people is that they're just biding their time for a paycheck. If you're truly dedicated to doing a good job, it will show. Of course, having me as your coach won't hurt you either. They won't let me be your direct supervisor, but I will have some influence in any long-term decisions for the department."

"Thank God. I could use all the help I can get. You don't have to worry about my working hard. One thing that I'm not afraid of is a little hard work. Once I learn the ropes, you won't have to hold my hand either. I'm an independent thinker and can do things on my own without having to be told."

"Then it's all gravy. I'll show you who the gossip girls are too so you can avoid them. They thrive on chaos. If they were to put the same amount of energy into their job, they'd be awesome."

"I know that's right. I definitely don't want to get mixed up with the wrong crowd. I'm tired of having my name on people's lips." I immediately regretted saying this, because I had opened a door I wanted to keep firmly closed.

"Well, now that you mentioned it…you know I'm curious about what the hell happened to you in Atlanta which has you hiding out here."

"I'm not hiding out. Can't a girl come back home without people thinking they're running away from something?"

"They can't if their face was plastered all over the local news."

"Are you kidding me? It made the news here, too?" My heart sank deep inside my chest. I wanted to put my past behind me, not relive it. It was bad enough the first time around.

"Yeah, girl. We don't have enough stories of our own to fill up the news hour. We regurgitate other people's news, but this one especially had people talking because you used to live here."

"Shit." I couldn't get mad at anyone but myself for not testing the waters before I dove in. Had I known I would be a local celebrity, I wouldn't have come. I would have kept my black ass in Atlanta.

"Maybe they won't put two and two together. The reason I chose Alabama over anywhere else was because I knew you were here."

"That's so sweet of you to say. Are you planning on staying here or is this just a pit stop until you get yourself together?"

"I'm here to stay." Even as I said it, I didn't know if I was being honest with myself. After living in Atlanta, I was afraid I might have outgrown Alabama.

"If you don't want to talk about what happened, I understand. I wasn't trying to get all up in your business."

Rozz drained her glass of wine while I poured myself another. It wasn't that I didn't trust her; I just didn't want her to think any less of me. I couldn't bear going to work with her every day thinking she was looking down on me.

"It was so complicated. I don't even know where to begin." This was not necessarily true either. My dilemma was how much I was willing to admit.

"Why not start at the beginning?"

I sighed. "Don't judge me, okay?"

"I would never do that."

"I sure hope you feel the same way once I tell you the real deal."

"I'm sure I will."

I took another deep breath and a big gulp of wine. I pointed the bottle at Rozz, but she waved it off. This was good because I had a feeling I was going to need the rest of it myself.

"I met my husband in high school. He was the captain of the football team and a total geek. All the girls were drooling over him, and I'm told he didn't pay any of them any attention. We met at a party, and I'm telling you it was love at first sight. "

"Ah, puppy love."

I smiled. "Yes, indeed. For me, there was no other man like him, and I knew he was the one. We spent all of our time together, and we became each other's first." I sighed. Those were the good old days.

"Aww, how sweet. Girl, I'm still waiting for my mister right. At this point, he might need to wear a sign so I can identify him."

"You're still a virgin?" I didn't mean to sound so surprised, but I was. She was kicking thirty in the ass. I thought thirty-year-old virgins were like fairy tales our mothers made up to keep our legs crossed.

"Trust me, it's not by choice. I'm like Beyoncé; somebody got to put a ring on it first."

"I guess I felt the same way, too. Somehow I knew Merlin would make it happen. He was that kind of guy."

Rozz sniffled. "I don't know why I get choked up when I hear love stories."

"Just don't forget you promised not to judge me."

"Will you stop; it can't be that bad."

"Oh, it's bad. Real bad and I can't believe I'm about to tell you about it."

"You've really got my curiosity going now. How did you get along with his family?"

"At first, horribly. His stepmother hated me with a purple passion. She damn near ruined my wedding, but believe it or not, we became friends."

"Wait, please tell me she didn't show her behind at your wedding!"

"Yes, she did. Tore my dress and everything. It was crazy."

"Wow. I don't mean no harm, but I would have loved to see it," Rozz said, laughing.

"Trust and believe it wasn't funny at the time. She came in late, drunk and loud. The kicker was she thought I was trying to take her man, and she was ready to fight me for him."

"Say what? Ooh girl, why was she so confused?"

"Merlin looks so much like his father, she was looking at him through liquor-colored lenses that had her showing out in that church."

"How in the world did you two make up after that? I might still be mad, especially if she tore my gown."

"Merlin did it. I was prepared to hate her for life. I was done."

"He does seem like a nice guy. Does he have any brothers?"

I was instantly irritated with her. Unknowingly, she'd gotten too close to the truth. I didn't need her to remind me how badly I screwed up. "You know what, I don't think I can do this. This is all too fresh." I got up and went into the kitchen and opened another bottle of wine.

"I understand. Sometimes it does help to talk about it though."

I thought I was ready, but I really wasn't. I felt the sting of tears in the back of my eyes, but I refused to cry anymore. I had shed enough tears over all of this. My tears didn't change a damn thing. "You sure you don't want some of this wine?"

"I do, but I got bible study, remember? You should come on and go with me. It might do you some good."

"Girl, I can't expect God to forgive me when I haven't forgiven myself."

"This sounds so serious. God forgives everybody if their heart is sincere."

"I can't. I would be afraid the building would burst into flames if I were to walk inside."

"You're still a mess. If God forgave Eve for taking a bite of the forbidden fruit, or Peter for betraying him that night in the garden, I'm sure he will forgive you. You just have to ask Him."

"That's easy for you to say; you haven't heard the rest of the story."

"I'm still listening..."

I exhaled. It was a real quandary for me. If I told her everything and she lost her respect for me, I would be devastated. I didn't have any friends left. I couldn't afford to lose her.

"Merlin was away on deployment. When he came home, it was on like popcorn. We must have had sex in every room in our apartment."

"TMI. TMI. Didn't I tell you I was a virgin!"

I was in the zone, so I didn't hear her warning me to pump my brakes. "But it wasn't him; it was his twin brother. The brother I didn't even know he had."

"Shut up! Are you telling me that you couldn't tell them apart?" She looked at me skeptically.

"The physical resemblance was uncanny. There were differences sexually, but I didn't think about it at the time. I attributed those differences to the fact that he'd been away for so long. He was more aggressive and confident than my husband. He was also very vocal with it. I didn't even know that turned me on until he did it to me."

"Oh, I can understand that."

I couldn't help but wonder if she were saying this because she really felt this way, or was trying to make me feel better. "When my husband found out, we had a terrible fight, but it wasn't my fault. He never told me he had a twin!"

"Then he shouldn't have been mad at you especially if they look just alike. He should have been mad at his brother."

"He was at him, too. Turns out his brother used to do this same type of shit when they were younger. As bad as this is, that's not the worst part of this story." I turned up my glass and drained it. I was beginning to feel the effects of the wine, but it didn't stop me from pouring another.

"Oh, Lord. I'm afraid to ask."

"I know, and I'm ashamed to tell you this, but I enjoyed being with his brother more. He was everything I didn't need in my life, but I couldn't get him out of my head. It was like he stamped his imprint on me."

"Shoot, girl. You about to get to start cussing. Let me get some of that wine. The Lord is going to have to take me as I am today."

I snickered. She was feeling my pain. I waited for her to take several sips before I resumed telling my story. I went into much more detail than I originally planned on doing. It actually felt good to be honest about it. "His brother's name is Gavin, and he was the exact opposite of my husband. I mean ex-husband."

"Damn."

"I'm not going to lie; he turned me out. He had me thinking and feeling things I never felt before. It was scary because I still loved my husband, but I was in love with his brother."

"On the news they said the brother kidnapped you. Is that true?"

"He did, but it was more complicated. See, I found out I was pregnant, and he believed it was his child."

"Oh, my God." Rozz clutched her pearls like a true southern belle. "Was it his baby?" she gushed.

"To be honest, I don't know. Since they were twins, I would have never been able to know with complete certainty. The doctor said it probably wasn't, but I still had my doubts. Merlin and I had been married for seven years and I always got my period on time. One night with Gavin and bingo, I'm pregnant. What would you think under the same circumstances?"

"Humph, this story is better than my soap operas. You might want to write a book about it."

"That's not funny; this is my life, and it's all fucked up."

"I'm sorry. I wasn't making light of your situation, but it's full of drama and you know it sells."

"I couldn't write about this shit. I'm embarrassed enough telling you about it."

"So what happened to bring you back here?"

"Despite everything that was going on, Merlin was right there by my side. But my greedy ass wanted more. I went to see Gavin in jail and walked into the middle of a fight with two other ladies. I ended up losing the baby, and Merlin divorced me." Despite my determination not to cry, tears were flowing from my eyes.

"Oh, honey. I'm so sorry. Shame on him for divorcing you because you lost the baby."

"That's not why he did it. He did it because I had no business at the jail seeing his brother. I can't blame him; I was wrong as two left shoes."

"Oh, now I understand." Rozz got up from the sofa and went to the bathroom to get some tissues for me.

"I've made a horrible mess of my life. That one night changed everything." I angrily punched the sofa cushion.

"So you just left and moved here?"

"I couldn't stay there anymore. It was just too painful."

"I feel you. Well, nothing that you have said is so terrible that God won't forgive you. But you're right; you have to be willing to forgive yourself first."

"How do I do that? I hurt an innocent man and I lost my baby?"

"It's a process. Every day it will get easier; as long as you don't dwell on the pain, there is hope."

Hope? I had erased that word from my internal dictionary. "I think I'm going to curl up in my bed and take a nap. All the driving and moving has tuckered me out."

"Are you sure you don't want to go to church with me? It will do you some good."

"Not tonight. Maybe another time."

"Okay, get some rest, I'll check up on you tomorrow." Rozz showed herself out of my apartment. It was all I could do to drag myself off the sofa and lock the door behind her. From there, I went into the bedroom, fell across the bed and cried myself to sleep.

4 MERLIN MILLS

I threw the brown envelope down on my desk in my home office and sat down staring out the window, trying to decide how I felt about my divorce being officially final. I never thought this would be my life. I believed in the sanctity of marriage even though there were no role models of a good one in my life. Both my parents were dead. I never met my father's wife, and my maternal mother never married. At the end of the day, I couldn't fault myself for the demise of my marriage. I did everything I could to hold it together. Its failure was out of my hands.

I pushed away from my desk and walked into the living room. When I finally made the decision to leave, I thought I would never experience happiness again. However, that wasn't the case. God had already put another good woman in my life, and it took ending my marriage to see her. Candace Jamison was my captain in the army, and she was everything my wife was not. Having suffered through her own failed marriage, she seemed to cherish what we had.

Even though I knew I didn't fail in my marriage, it failed me, and was still a bitter blow to my ego. I couldn't help but wonder why any reasonable person would choose my brother over me. It couldn't be about looks, since we were identical twins. I felt like I had so much more going for myself than him. These thoughts often kept me up at night and caused undue pressure on my new relationship with Candace. Emotionally, we were both wounded soldiers.

I picked up my phone and called my boy Braxton to see if he wanted to get into something since I had the weekend off. He answered on the first ring.

"Hey, bro. I was just thinking about you."

"What's good with you? You all right?"

"It's all golden over here. What about you?"

"Got some stuff on my mind, but other than that I'm good."

"Do you want to go shoot some hoops and talk about it?"

"I was hoping you would say that. Meet me at the court in half an hour."

"All right, man. I'll see you."

I walked back into the bedroom where Candace was still napping. She had gotten up this morning and fixed us an early breakfast, but had fallen back asleep after a serious romp between the sheets. I should be lying next to her, but I had too many things on my mind. I crawled onto the bed and gave her a kiss on the cheek.

"Huh?" she responded sleepily.

"I didn't mean to wake you, hon. I'm going to meet Braxton to shoot some hoops."

"I thought we were going to sleep in today."

"I know, but I need to work off some of this home cooking you've been throwing on me. If I don't start doing a better job, my stomach is going to get all out of control."

She purred, "I think your stomach looks just fine."

"And I intend on keeping that way. We won't be long although we might stop for a drink afterwards."

"Won't that be counter-productive?"

34

"It's not like you're going home or anything. You'll still be here when I get back, won't you? If you stay, I'll let you help me work it off."

"Oh, I can do it. Believe that. We ain't got to wait till you get back, we can start right now!"

I laughed out loud at her enthusiasm and it almost made me feel *safer,* but not entirely. "I'll be back soon and I'm going to hold you to it." I kissed her gently on the lips and quickly left the room before I changed my mind. Braxton would have been pissed at me if I canceled, and I needed to vent.

■■■

"All right. Tell me what's really going on."

"Why does something have to be going on? Can't a guy just stare into a glass of brown liquor without something being wrong?"

"No. First of all, you don't really do brown liquor and secondly, if you wanted to be alone, you could have stayed at the house. Now, spill it."

"You know me too well. I guess I'm in a bit of a funk because I got my finalized divorce papers in the mail. I keep looking at them trying to figure out where it all went wrong."

"Really, dog. That ship has sailed. You and I both know you didn't do anything wrong."

"How can you be so sure when I'm not?"

"Are you kidding? You are the most upstanding guy I know. What happened between you and Cojo was fucked up. I would have bet money on your marriage making it over any other married couple I know, but it didn't. Move on, son. I'm sure she has."

"Ouch. I could have done without that last part."

"Are you for real? Don't tell me you're wasting your time worrying about who she's fucking!"

"When you say it like that it does sound stupid. Maybe I'm a dead breed, but some part of me will always consider her as my wife. Shit, man; she was my first and I was hers."

"And? Just because you were each other's first doesn't mean you were meant to be together for life. You should be happy you found out now before you had kids with her."

I cringed. "You're full of them, aren't you?"

"Damn, man. That was insensitive of me. I completely forgot that she was pregnant and lost the baby. I wasn't trying to hurt you."

"It's okay. You're right about all of this. I'm going to bounce back. I always do."

"Man, I hate to see you hurting. What's up with you and Candace?"

"Candace is a great woman. I don't know how I would have been able to get through this without her."

"Do you love her?"

I toyed with the straw beside my glass as I thought about his question. It wasn't the first time I'd pondered it, but I was no closer to an answer. "I wish I knew. I mean, I could love her, but I'm gun-shy after what happened with Cojo."

"Get out of here. One thing doesn't have anything to do with the other. Shake this shit off, man; it's not a good look."

"Who you think you're telling that? I think she's waiting for me to say it, but I can't get the words out of my mouth."

"Why do you think she's waiting on you?"

"Because she said it to me first."

"Damn." Braxton signaled the bartender to refresh our drinks.

"Now you see where I'm coming from?"

"Yes and no. There is always tension when one person professes their love and the other doesn't, but I don't think she would want you to say it unless you meant it."

"That's the thing; I just don't know. I mean, I thought I loved Cojo more than life itself. How can I be sure that what I'm feeling now is love?"

"Negro, you are barking up the wrong tree there. You don't see no ring on my finger, do you?"

"That's because your ass is trying to date the whole city instead of settling down with one person. I can't do that. After watching my dad run through all those women, I promised myself I'd never be like that."

"I hear you, bro. That's the excess baggage you've been carrying all your life. You're going to need to check them bags before you lose your damn mind."

"Damn man, that's a pretty good analogy. Did you just think that up on the fly or have you been holding it for the right moment?"

"I got skills, boy; you didn't know?"

We both laughed and for a moment it felt like old times to me. When we would get together after work and shoot the shit. Braxton was closer to me than my own brother was. I trusted him with my life. He had saved my ass once before from going to jail, and I was forever in his debt.

"Have you and Candace moved in together yet?"

"Not officially. I spend most of my time over at her house, but sometimes we mix it up and stay at my apartment. Our situation is a little complicated because she's still a ranking officer. Neither one of us want those complications so this works for us."

"Aren't you up for a promotion by now? Screwing the boss has to have its own set of benefits if you know what I mean."

"Man, I wouldn't let her do that for me. I'm getting a promotion because I earned it. She's not even handling me like that."

"That's good to know. Especially if things don't go the way you want them to. I'd hate for her to have you all hemmed up."

"I don't think she's that type of lady. She got a raw deal from her first husband, and she didn't nut up on him, and he deserved it after the stunt he pulled."

"Speaking of stunts, have you heard anything from your brother? I heard he's out of jail. That man has got a lucky horseshoe up his ass."

"I know, right. They won't keep him inside for nothing. All that stuff he did, he should be under the jail instead of walking around freely."

"Well, has he reached out to you?"

"No, I think he knows I don't have anything for him. He burnt that bridge when he kidnapped my wife." That wasn't all he did to my wife, but there was no need to enumerate them since Braxton knew most of those stories.

"I feel you. I can't believe he thought that was going to be okay."

"You know, sometimes it's hard to believe we're brothers. We don't have anything in common."

"So where do you think he got all his sense of entitlement from?"

"Beats the hell out of me. We started in the same womb, ate the same foods and shared the same ass whippings. I don't know who he thinks he is."

"What about Gina? Are y'all in touch?"

"Yeah, we still talk periodically. It's weird, man; she's having my brother's baby. I don't know how to feel about that."

"That's straight up nasty, dude. What was she thinking? I know you both look like your dad, but that's creepy."

"She didn't initiate it. From what I was told, she was passed out drunk, and Gavin and his nasty ass rolled up in her while she was sleeping."

"Damn, I ain't never been that drunk when I didn't remember fucking somebody."

"If I hadn't seen how twisted she could get, I wouldn't believe it either. The house could be burning down and Gina wouldn't move. So I do believe she slept through it, or that it was part of a dream. You know we've all had that wet dream before."

"Well, I can relate to that part. One time I had this dream that me and Janet Jackson were on this deserted beach. We'd been on a boat and we crashed losing all our clothes; she was about to—"

"Negro, please. You should have known that was a dream. When would you and Janet be on the same damn boat? Your money ain't that long."

"Hey, don't hate because I dream big."

"Go big or go home. I don't blame you."

"On the real dawg, since he stole the pussy, why didn't she just abort the baby then?"

"Because the one thing that she's always wanted, even when we were kids, was a child of her own. My dad always threatened to leave her if she got pregnant."

"That's deep. I wouldn't want to be in your shoes for nothing. How are you going to treat this child? Will you be in its life?"

"I don't know, man. I mean, it's not the child's fault that his father is a sleazy motherfucker with no morals."

"Sleazy motherfucker, that's the word I've been looking for all night. Has he always competed against you?"

"Basically, yeah. When we were growing up, we didn't have any other friends. We just had each other. We couldn't invite friends over to Gina's house, because we never knew what we were going to get with her. So he was the only one I had to play with. Whenever we would play something and he lost, he wanted to quit. So I started letting him win all the time so I wouldn't have to play all alone."

"Damn, that's messed up."

"When I think about it now, I agree. Maybe that's why he took it so badly when I started doing well in sports. He always thought he could beat me in everything, so he bugged out when I made the team and he didn't."

"Wow, all this time and I didn't know this. Now Gavin's behavior sort of makes sense. I still think he's a grimy motherfucker, but now I understand him a little more. Do you know if Gina is having a boy or a girl?"

I sighed as I finished my drink and signaled for another. "She said it was a boy."

"You know that means you're going to have to be in that child's life. She can't raise a boy to be a man, and your brother is not the perfect role model."

"I know. I keep hoping Gavin will get his shit together. I don't want to be in this position. I don't know how the hell they're going to tell that child about their relationship. That would fuck up any kid knowing they were conceived the way he was."

"Let's hope they both have sense enough not to tell him."

"I think Gina has changed. Now that my dad is gone, she doesn't have anything else to obsess over. I swear it boggles my mind sometimes when I think about how my dad had her so whipped. It's not like he was showering her with gifts or attention. He treated her like scum on the bottom of his shoe, and she kept lapping it up."

"She never stepped out on your dad?"

"Not to my knowledge. I never saw her date anyone else or even talk on the phone to another dude. She was completely faithful to him till the day he died."

"That's messed up."

"No, the messed up part is that I probably have brothers and sisters all over Atlanta, and I don't even know them. Hell, I didn't find out who my mother was until I was a grown man. Luckily, I knew who she was as she was a friend to Gina, but it makes me wonder what my dad said to her to make her keep her identity a secret all those years. My biological mom probably knew more about my dad than Gina did, and now that she's dead too, I can't even ask her."

"Boy, you got a lot on your plate. What are you going to do?"

Before I could answer Braxton, my phone rang. I pulled it out of my pocket thinking it might be Candace checking in with me. It wasn't—it was Gavin. "Damn."

"Who is it?"

"We have talked this motherfucker up. I don't have nothing to say to him right now. He's going to kill my buzz."

"I feel you, but if he hasn't called you in all this time it must be important."

I thought about it for another second or two, but by the time I answered it, he had already hung up. A few seconds later I got a notification of a new voicemail. I took a deep breath and called my voicemail number.

"Shit, I got to go. Gina's in the hospital. He said it wasn't good." I signaled the bartender to settle the bill but Braxton waved me off.

"Don't worry about this. I got it. Keep in touch and let me know what's going on."

"Thanks, man." I rushed out of the bar with conflicted emotions. Even though I didn't want to see my brother again, I had to know what was going on with Gina. I just hoped it wasn't too bad or too late.

5 COJO MILLS

My first few days on the job were spent in orientation. A process designed to bore the fuck out of you. The only thing that kept me from falling asleep was the high-octane coffee and my new coworker Natoya Taylor, who kept me entertained as she gave me her *read* on our fellow coworkers. She was hilarious. She had something to say about everyone, and I was secretly happy that she was with me, instead of against me. She was brutal.

"Do you see those soup coolers? Would you want them feasting on your hot pocket?" Natoya whispered as she tore this brown brother down who was sitting in the row in front of us.

I almost spit out the coffee I had in my mouth. "You need to quit. I almost spit coffee all over your blouse."

"I'm just saying, look at them. Those things are huge. He could cover your whole coochie with just one lip. That other one would be all up in the way."

Her comment might not have been so funny if she wasn't absolutely serious about it. She was slaying just about everyone in the room.

"If you don't stop, I'm going to have to change my seat."

"And you'll be asleep in two minutes and you know it. I'm just trying to keep it lively up in here."

"True, but you're going to get us both in trouble. If you must diss these people, you should at least warn me."

"Okay. I'll say, incoming or RA, for read alert, and then you'll know."

Technically, she wasn't actually reading anyone. A read was when you say what you had to say to a person's face in a clever way. Either way it went, I was happy she was doing it to someone other than me. As funny as her comment was, I was not about to get into a discussion about hot pockets. I didn't know her like that, but I didn't see the harm in listening.

I said, "I'm so glad this is our last day of orientation. I don't think I could take another day of this man talking to me."

"I know that's right. Can you imagine being married to him? I think he just likes the sound of his own voice."

"You ain't lying. Must he describe everything in such complete detail? Who spends fifteen minutes describing what to do in case of a fire drill? Any idiot knows to stop what they're doing and exit the building."

"And if they don't know it, they deserve to burn up."

It was a good thing we were sitting in the back of the room, or we would have surely gotten split up or excused. "I like you, Natoya. I'm glad I got to sit next to you for this dumb fest."

"Me too, you're cool. Do you want to get together after work for a drink?"

I hesitated to answer. Although I liked her, I wasn't sure I was ready to sit over truth serum with her. At the same time, I didn't want to refuse in fear of making an enemy.

"Yeah, sure." I was just going to have to curtail my appetite for liquor, which had increased over the last few months. It was one thing to get shitfaced in my own apartment; it was something else to do it out in public with a coworker.

"Cool, I'm going to put this stuff in my desk and I'll meet you in the lobby."

"Okay, I'll see you in about ten minutes." Natoya and I were not going to work in the same department. She was going through a temporary agency, hoping to gain full-time employment, while I'd already secured a slot through my friend Rozz.

Rozz hadn't been in the office this week. She was on a retreat with her church. I admired her dedication to God, but I still wasn't ready to admit I needed help living my life.

Natoya was in the lobby with a sweater slung over her shoulder. It was blazing hot outside, so I was a little bit confused as to why she'd brought along the sweater.

"Am I missing something? Did the weather suddenly change?"

"No, but I don't have any sleeves on this shirt. I refused to get all cold and have my nipples standing up waving at folks."

"Gotcha." Her explanation wasn't compelling me to go back upstairs and grab my own sweater. I could see wearing one in the office, but once I had a few drinks, keeping up with the sweater would become a pain in the ass.

"Have you ever been to Jefferson's?"

"No. When I lived here, I wasn't old enough to drink," I said, laughing.

"You'll like it. The food is good and the drinks are strong. It's right downtown. You can drive with me if you want and I'll bring you back to get your car."

"Works for me, let's go. It's hot as hell out here."

"Who you telling, my mascara is melting." We took the short walk to the parking deck and quickly found her car. I was a little surprised to see it was a brand-new Mercedes E350. I didn't know much about cars, but what I did know was this car wasn't cheap. I couldn't help but wonder how she was paying for it, when she was working with a temp agency who got a portion of her salary. No matter how curious I was about how she managed it, I was going to stay in my lane. Now, if she volunteered to tell me, that was different.

Jefferson's wasn't that far from the job. Were it not hot outside, we could have easily walked the distance. However, I wasn't complaining about the ride in the fancy car. I almost felt like I was somebody inside it. Albeit it would have been better if I were driving it, instead of riding shotgun.

"This place looks nice. What do you usually have?"

"I'm a tequila girl myself with a beer chaser."

"Oh, Lord. I don't think I can hang with you on that one."

"Are you a lightweight?" Natoya laughed as we entered the bar and took a seat at a corner table giving us the full view of the whole room.

"No, I can carry my own. Trust me on that. I just can't mix liquor and beer. The beer will have my ass in the bathroom all night long."

"That's okay, I won't hold it against you. We should try to eat something, too. I really love their burgers."

The waitress walked up and we placed our orders.

"Why do you think they scheduled orientation in the middle of the week?" I asked.

"So we could have the weekend to recover from that snooze fest, is the only reason I can think of."

"Yeah, that might be it. Whatever the reason, I'm glad it's over with."

"Do you have big plans for the weekend?"

"Not hardly. I'm still adjusting to being back in town."

"That's right. I forgot you said you came here from Atlanta. What I want to know is why?"

This was the moment that I was dreading. I couldn't blame her for wanting to know. Hell, I'd want to know too. Coming back was a bit of a culture shock. Being back in Opelika was like stepping into a land time forgot. It had most modern conveniences like toilets and running water, but the other amenities were slow to come. I had yet to see a single Wi-Fi sign. I didn't even think most of its residents knew what it was. My apartment complex didn't have high-speed internet. We were suffering with dial-up. I wasn't even going to waste my time fooling with it. I was going to have to find me a hotspot or two to hang out in.

"My marriage didn't work, so I guess you can say I came back here to lick my wounds."

"But why here? Aren't you an army brat? Haven't you been to other nice places?"

"If you have so much against this place, why are you here?"

"It's simple for me. I've never been anywhere else. I'm too much of a chicken to try someplace new."

The waitress brought our drinks over to the table. "I hear you. It's hard. I picked this place because out of all the places I lived, this was the only one that I had a small measure of independence. I was a teenager when I left. The other places I was still in grade school. Plus it's still close enough to Atlanta for me to visit, if I'm so inclined."

"You mean if your ex calls you for a booty call."

I took a big gulp of my drink. "I doubt if that would ever happen."

Natoya looked at me oddly. "If he called, would you answer?"

"To be honest, I really don't know."

"That's tough. If you're trying to get over him, you might need to get under someone else." She raised her glass in salute and killed it.

It took me a minute to understand what Natoya was saying to me. I wasn't sure how I felt about it either. I didn't know her like that. After a few seconds, I realized I was being overly sensitive. The news of my divorce wasn't sensationalized.

"I wouldn't be opposed to meeting someone else, but my circle of friends is very small. Out of all the people that I knew while I lived here, I only stayed in contact with one." It was weird that I didn't realize it before I decided to move back. But I was in so much pain in Atlanta, I just wanted to get out.

"Well, consider your circle increased by one. I'll introduce you to some of my friends, and we'll see what we can do to help you get over that cheating man of yours."

I inwardly cringed. I didn't want to malign Merlin's character, but I wasn't about to throw dirt on my own either. The likelihood of her ever meeting Merlin was slim to none. "Wow, thanks. I'll admit I'm kind of lonely right now."

"We can certainly fix that starting tonight. My friend is throwing a party. Give me your address and I'll swing by your house around ten to pick you up."

"Damn, you don't waste any time do you?"

"For what? I ain't getting any younger and neither are you!"

I couldn't argue with her there. For the first time since returning to Alabama, I had something to look forward to.

6 CANDACE JAMISON

Rather than stay in an empty bed, I drove home. I tried to stay in bed after Merlin left, but my eyes refused to stay shut. I sent him a text telling him to come over when he was done. The only time I enjoyed laying up in the bed was when he was beside me. When he wasn't there, I couldn't sleep. It was especially hard on me those nights when he didn't come over. On those nights, I tossed and turned all night.

Part of my insecurity in our relationship stemmed from the way we got together. It wasn't the typical boy meets girl, boy courts girl, type of scenario. He was an enlisted man in my unit. Under normal circumstances, his face would be just a blur in a passing uniform. I didn't even have to meet him face to face, but I made an exception for him.

From the moment I saw him walking across the quad, I was drawn to him. I broke my own rule and made it my business to find out who he was. It damn near broke my heart when I found out he was already happily married. The sanctity of marriage was a line I wasn't willing to cross. I had lived through that betrayal, so I refused to be a part of any foolishness. I resigned myself to being Merlin's friend. However, the more I got to know him, the harder it was for me to keep my resolve.

It started when I used my influence to change his orders to stateside, as opposed to another tour. My actions would have been justified if I legitimately needed the extra manpower, but in this case, I didn't need him—I wanted him, but that was before I knew he was married. I hadn't wanted anyone in a while. I didn't know what to do with those emotions.

I almost regretted my decision to manipulate his orders when I received the first phone call that he'd been arrested. Fortunately, for both of us, it turned out to be a big mistake, but it also started a chain of events that ultimately brought us together. If I had to do it all again, I would. I loved this man with all my heart. His former wife and his family caused him a lot of pain. I wanted to be the one he picked up the pieces with. I wanted a future with him in it.

After using the bathroom, I decided to do something special for Merlin. I was going to cook a sexy meal to seduce him. I quickly got dressed to go to the market. I didn't know how much time I had to get ready.

I was throwing things into my grocery cart so fast, you would think someone was chasing me. I decided on a light, almost picnic-styled meal of ginger chicken, red potato salad and fresh roasted asparagus. For dessert, iced strawberries with a side of warm melted chocolate. I also grabbed a couple of bottles of champagne. Roses would be the final touch to help me set the mood. Satisfied that I'd gotten everything on my list, I approached the register. I debated whether or not to call Merlin to make sure he didn't eat, but decided against it. I wanted this meal to take him completely by surprise.

When I got home, I quickly went about preparing our meal. Since the chicken was going to take the longest, I prepared it first, adding an extra measure of the ginger that was supposed to be a natural aphrodisiac. I also boiled my potatoes and chopped up some celery and onions. I almost left the onions out but decided to put them in at the last minute. Onions weren't that bad if both of us were eating them. Finally, I cleaned and roasted the asparagus. The entire meal took less than two hours to prepare. I would melt the chocolate in the microwave to save time.

Now, the only thing left to do was prepare the house and myself. From my living room cabinet, I grabbed every candle I had ever bought, and lined them all through the living room and some in the bedroom. It was a considerable amount of candles since they were my guilty pleasure. I spread a light blanket over the carpet and put the champagne in a bucket to chill. Lastly, I sprinkled rose petals all over the blanket and floor leading to the bedroom.

"Perfect," I purred as I went to the bathroom to take a nice long bubble bath. I eased into the hot water and sighed. I was very excited and couldn't wait to see Merlin's face. This was the first romantic overture that I had made, and I was anxious for it to go well. As much as I wanted to lounge in the tub, my anxiety wouldn't let me. If things went well, we could share a bath together—after we played in the chocolate.

I climbed out of my bath and wrapped my body in one of my oversized towels. I carefully oiled up my body and chose my sexiest teddy, a red one to match the roses, and put it on. I covered my teddy with a black silk robe. I was ready! I lay across the sofa, so I would be the first thing Merlin saw when he came in the house. All he had to do was come over.

7 ANGELA SIMPSON

The birds were singing outside my window like a free alarm clock telling me it was time to get up and busy. I carefully eased back the covers and slid my legs out of the bed. I tiptoed over to my dresser and grabbed a pair of underwear from my drawer. I looked over my shoulder to see if my movements were being detected. I paused when my eyes connected with him.

"What are you doing?" Young asked as he eyed me sleepily.

"Uh, I'm going to the bathroom."

"You need underwear to do that?" Young stretched his arms over his head. He was a sexy motherfucker and he knew it. Instead of getting into a debate with him, I went into the bathroom and closed the door. With any luck, he would roll back over and go back to sleep. I quickly got dressed in my exercise gear.

When I came back into the bedroom, Young was propped up on the bed with the sheet barely covering his sex. It was a delicious sight to behold. His brown skin stood out against my stark white bedding. One of his arms supported his head while the other clutched the headboard. For a moment, I was tempted to get out of my clothes and climb back into bed with him.

"You keep looking at me like that, I'm going to need for you to get back in bed." His speech was low. The baritone in his voice sending shivers down my spine.

"I can't; I have a kickboxing class this morning. I don't want to be late."

"Damn, Angie. Saturday mornings are supposed to be spent lying in bed with your man."

Stunned, I stopped lacing up my shoes. "Is that what you are to me?"

"Well, yeah. I don't spend the night with my booty calls. If I wake up next to you it's because I want to be with you. Why else would I be in your bed, naked, and horny as hell, if we weren't working on something?"

I laughed to hide my uneasiness. This was the first time that we'd actually put a label on our relationship. I was so pleased to be on the same page with him emotionally, I was ready to toss my clothes aside and claim my place next to my man. I liked the sound of it. Turning my back on his sexy countenance wasn't easy. I vowed to make it up to him later. "I'm sorry, boo; I signed up for this class this morning and I don't want to miss it."

"What kind of class?" Young eyed me suspiciously.

I hated when he went into interrogation mode with me; however, it was in his nature to do so. He worked as a private investigator, and sometimes he brought those skills into my home. "It's only an hour class and I should be back by eleven."

"What kind of class is it?"

I didn't want to lie even though I knew he was going to be upset. I sighed. "Kickboxing."

"Damn, Ang. What's up with all of this? We just did at least ten miles on the track last night. Then you got that personal trainer three times a week that I'm still trying to understand. Why you would want to have some other nigga spotting you when it should be me? What the hell are you training for?"

I could tell he was upset because Young almost never cussed at me. I couldn't understand why my wanting to stay in shape upset him? It almost seemed as if he were jealous. The thought was so preposterous I burst out laughing.

"Am I a joke to you?" he flung off the sheet and stood by the bed. I swear that man would make a great statue. His muscles were chiseled to perfection. I couldn't tear my eyes away from his body until he spoke again.

"Hello? I'm talking to you." He angrily grabbed his shorts off the floor and slid into them. I couldn't believe we were about to have an argument about exercise.

"Babe, I'm sorry. I got lost in your, uh…"

"Nice try, but if my uh, was all that, you would be in the bed next to me instead of trying to slip out the door undetected."

"I wasn't trying to slip out the door. I just wanted you to get some more rest."

"If I wanted to sleep alone, I would have stayed at my house."

There was no denying it—he was pissed. Young and I started dating a little over two months ago, and I was still learning this complicated man. I had been fighting a battle with myself not to get too clingy with him. "Young, please. If I knew this was going to be such a big deal, I wouldn't have signed up for the class." I wasn't being completely honest. If I told him the real reason why I was doing so much, he wouldn't approve.

Young exhaled deeply. I couldn't tell if he were trying to take a step back from me or his irritation. Either way, I was scared. The good thing about him was that he always said what he meant. The bad thing was that sometimes I felt as if he were setting a trap, and my dumb ass was about to fall into it.

"Forget it, Angela. I need to be getting home anyway. You go ahead and do you."

I felt myself getting angry. I didn't have time for this silly argument this early in the morning. "Are we fighting over my getting some exercise? You know I want to work off this fat from my failed pregnancy."

"Have you looked in the mirror lately? You don't have one ounce of fat on your body. Except maybe between your ears." He slipped on his jeans and sat down on the bed to put on his shoes and socks.

"Whoa, hold on a minute. This is getting ridiculous. Why are you so upset?"

"I told you why I was upset. Weren't you listening?"

"You're mad because I'm leaving you in my bed?" I could not believe this. It wasn't like I was running off to be with someone else. I was exercising for goodness sake. He should have been glad I cared about how I looked. I was a reflection of him.

"First of all, I'm not mad. I'm upset that you can't see what I see when I look at you. If you want to have more muscles than a linebacker, that's on you. Just so you know, I don't intend to be sleeping with someone who has more muscles in her back than I do."

I drew back as if he had slapped me. Tears stung my eyes, but I refused to let them fall. Despite my anger at him, I heard some truth in his words. I did have self-esteem issues. I took offense because he knew this about me before we started messing around.

"I can't help that, and you know it."

"That's where you're wrong, sweetheart. If you exercised your mind as much as you do your body, you could change it."

"Are you calling me stupid?" I was past outdone—I was livid. I could take a lot of things, but I wasn't about to take that. I stood with my hands on my hips ready to punch him if I had to.

Young threw his hands up in the air in obvious frustration. I glanced at the clock hanging over my bed. If I didn't leave now, I was going to be late. This only irritated Young more.

"I can't deal with this. Like I said, do you and I'm going to do me." He had finished dressing and was sticking his wallet and keys in his pockets. My heart felt cold and lumpy inside my chest. As mad as I was with him, I didn't want to lose him, especially over something so stupid as a kickboxing class.

"Fine, I won't go." I slipped off my shoes and pulled my shirt over my head, tossing it to the floor.

"No, please. Don't let me stop you from doing what you want to do. You'll get what I'm saying to you one day."

His face was hard and solemn. I called it his courtroom face. I hated it when he used it on me. It made me feel like I was a little kid again and had disappointed my parents. "Estrell, please. Can we talk about this?" I knew using his first name would get his attention and possibly break through the wall he'd put up. He rarely used his government name and very few people even knew it.

He sighed again, but he didn't leave the room. Instead, he sat down on the bed. The mattress barely moved under his weight. This was a sign of a good mattress. No matter how much we shook that baby, it didn't move.

"What time is your class?"

"I don't care about that class. I care about you!"

"I can't tell."

I was certain I was hearing jealousy in his voice now. There could be no other reason for him to be upset with me. I realized I was going to have to be a little more open with Young about my motivations, or I was going to lose out on a potentially good thing.

"Listen, I know you don't understand what's going on with me. I barely understand it myself, but you haven't been where I have emotionally. A man tried to kill me. He set me on fire and left me for dead. That did something to me."

"Angie, I get all of that. I promise you I do. That's why I think you should continue going to counseling to deal with those emotions."

Instinctively, I blew off his suggestion. I wasn't going to sit around in those classes again with a bunch of strangers. I tried counseling before, after the fire, when I learned I was pregnant. My mother insisted I carry his child as a reminder of my sins. Now that the child was gone, I saw no need to subject myself to that humiliation again. "Those sessions are a waste of time. Working out and building muscle makes me feel better about myself. I can't and *won't* be a victim again." This was as close to stating my real motivation as I was going to get.

Young's face softened. "Is that what this is about?"

I nodded my head unable to speak.

"Why didn't you say that in the first place? I was thinking you were becoming anorexic or some shit like that. I didn't know it was because you wanted to be able to defend yourself. I can get with that, all you had to do was tell me."

I was relieved. I felt like I had just dodged a bullet. "I was afraid you were going to say I was being silly."

"Haven't you learned by now that I'm not like them other dudes you were dealing with? I think everyone needs to know how to protect themselves. I think it's especially important for women. Haven't I been trying to take you to the gun range to learn how to shoot?"

"Yeah, but I don't want to use a gun. There's too much that can go wrong when you carry a gun. What if I get into a fight with someone, and they take my gun and shoot me with it? I need to be able to defend myself without it, and if I can't stop them, at least I may be able to slow them down enough for me to get away."

"If that's what makes you comfortable, then I will support you. Hell, there might come a time when I'll need you to kick someone's ass for me."

I laughed out loud. I couldn't imagine a situation where that would actually be necessary. I was just glad I'd defused the situation before it had gotten totally out of control. There was growth in this for me. The old me would have cussed him the fuck out and threw him out of my apartment without a second thought. "I've got your back, Young." I flexed my muscles to prove it.

"Maybe I need to sign up for this class too just in case you start getting ideas about beating a brother into submission."

"The only thing I want you to submit to is this kitty cat. Do you think you can do that?"

He pulled his shirt over his head and threw it in the corner. "I can show you better than I can tell you." My eyes grew in size as I watched the rest of his clothes follow suit. I quickly got out of the rest of mine and scrambled under the covers as he crawled in next to me. Who needed a kickboxing class when I had the perfect workout right next to me?

"So where was I?" he growled. I could only purr in contentment as he nestled down between my thighs.

8 GAVIN MILLS

I slipped out of Gina's room and went down to the cafeteria to get myself some coffee. I had been sucking on vending machine coffee for the last twelve hours. The coffee was weak and wasn't helping to keep me alert. So I decided to try some fresh brew from the cafeteria hoping it would be more effective. In all honesty, I probably should have laid off the caffeine altogether. I was already wound up enough from the birth of the baby and Gina's precarious medical condition.

The decision to call my brother was a hard one to make. I knew he didn't want anything to do with me, but he had a right to know about Gina's health. If something were to happen to her and I didn't let him know, there would be hell to pay. He would make it personal when it wasn't. Still, knowing it was the right thing to do, didn't make making the call any easier. My call went straight to voicemail, which didn't surprise me. I kept my message to him short and to the point. I let him know up front the call wasn't about me. If he deleted the message without listening to it, the very least I could say was I tried.

I was really in my own thoughts as I wandered down the hall to the elevator. Gina had been in an induced coma for over twenty-four hours. The doctors said her condition was stable, but we weren't out of the woods yet. I passed a man pushing a cart. I assumed he was a nurse. He stopped walking as our eyes made contact. The guy looked familiar, but I couldn't place him. For a moment, I thought he rolled his eyes at me, but I wasn't certain so I let it go. I got on the elevator and quickly forgot about him.

I got my coffee and took a satisfying sip. My thoughts were filled with Gina and our child as I walked back to the elevator. I wanted her to wake up so we could give our child a name. We never got around to discussing what we would put on his birth certificate, and I was sick of the nurses asking me about it. For now, he was known as Baby Meadows. I didn't like that shit one bit. I wanted my son to at least have my last name, if not my first. I was so into my head, I didn't realize that someone else was in the elevator until the doors closed. I noticed the white shoes first, and my eyes traveled up until they rested on the face of the same man I had seen pushing the cart. Once again, I had a flash of recognition. Something about the man was definitely familiar, but I couldn't put my finger on it. He smiled, and it sent a chill down my spine. I turned and pushed my floor choosing to ignore him rather than engage in polite conversation.

All of a sudden, I felt this horrendous pain in the back of my head. I dropped my coffee and fell to my knees, grabbing my head. My fingers became immersed in blood. My blood. "What the fuck?" My eyes were playing tricks on me as I tried to focus on the man. He appeared to be moving in and out of my line of vision. I fell forward as the elevator came to a stop.

"Next time I see your ass, I'm going to need for you to remember my name." He kicked me viciously in the side with his white shoes, which may have been designed for their comfort but still packed a wallop when used just right.

"And that's for drugging me and saying I had a little dick, you fucker! Small world, ain't it?"

I remembered who he was. The dude stepped over my prone body and exited the elevator. The blow to my head brought clarity to my mind for a brief moment before I passed out. Wayne was someone I was going to rob, but didn't. Fuck! My past was catching up with me and winning.

■■■

"Mr. Mills, can you hear me? Mr. Mills, can you hear me?"

I could feel someone touching my hand, but it felt strange to me. In addition, her voice was muffled. I attempted to get up but was pushed back down.

"He's coming around," the voice said.

I slowly opened my eyes. The bright light caused my head to hurt. I cringed and shut them again. I was hoping this was a bad dream, but something told me it wasn't. "Where am I?"

"You're in the hospital, Mr. Mills."

"What the hell happened to me? I feel like I'm about to throw up, and my head is killing me."

"We were hoping you would tell us what happened to you. We found you unconscious in the elevator. The doctors had to stitch up your head."

"I feel sick," I repeated. My stomach was churning, and I needed to lift up my head for fear I would choke to death if I did throw up.

"I'm going to give you something for nausea."

I couldn't wait for whatever she was going to give me. I needed to throw up right now. I lifted up my head and turned it just enough so as my vomit wouldn't run back down my throat.

"That's okay. Nausea is common for head injuries. Can you tell us what happened?" the nurse asked after I got myself together.

I didn't even have to think hard about my answer. "I don't know. I remember going for some coffee. That's the last thing I remember. How long was I out?" There was no way in the world I was going to explain to anyone why I was laying on that elevator floor. Karma was a bitch, and it had just caught up with me. I couldn't be mad about it.

"I have some paperwork I need you to fill out."

"Seriously, now? I have to get back to my wife." I attempted to sit up again and I immediately felt dizzy.

"Mr. Mills, I wouldn't advise your going anywhere. You may feel dizzy for a while, and of course, your headache will get worse once the medicine we gave you wears off."

"Whatever you gave me isn't working. I already have a headache, but I need to get to my wife."

"I could call the pharmacy to see…"

"No," I shouted a little too loudly. If Wayne were the pharmacist as I now suspected, there would be no telling what he would prescribe for me.

"I can give you some Tylenol, that might help."

"Fine. Can you wheel me to my wife's room and give it to me there? I'll fill out your paperwork then." I didn't know what I was going to put on the paperwork. It wasn't like I had any insurance, but what were they going to do, take the stitches out?

"I guess that will be okay. Let me get a chair and the pills for you and I'll be right back."

The nurse was cute, but I had no desire to push up on her. I didn't know if it was because of the whack to my head, or my newly developed commitment to Gina. Under normal circumstances, I would have used this opportunity as a chance to get in the girl's pants. The fact that I didn't even try it spoke volumes for me. For once, I really wanted to do the right thing.

■■■

My day went from very bad to hell in a hand basket. During my absence, Merlin had arrived. He was sitting next to Gina's bed when the nurse wheeled me into the room. This was the first time I had seen him since I was taken away in handcuffs for attempting to kidnap his wife. Seeing him again was the most awkward feeling in the world. I could feel the heat emanating from his stare.

"What happened to you?" His voice was devoid of any compassion. He might as well have been talking to a stranger instead of someone who had shared his mother's womb. I did that to him and I regretted it.

"I fell in the elevator," I replied as the nurse put the paperwork in my lap. I almost asked her to take me with her rather than face my brother. I wasn't up for fighting with him, too.

The nurse looked between me and my brother. "Oh, my. You two look just alike." Neither one of us bothered to acknowledge her remarks.

"Where did you fall, down the shaft?" Merlin chuckled. He was obviously getting pleasure out of my pain. I had no choice but to suck it up. I hadn't been the best brother.

"Has she woken up yet?" I wheeled closer to Gina's bed. She looked like she was just sleeping peacefully.

"No, she hasn't. What's wrong with her?" I finally detected some emotion in his voice. I couldn't help but feel a little envious. Gina wasn't his real mother, but he was certainly acting like she was.

"There were some complications with the baby. The doctor said if she remains stable, there is a good chance she can come out of this okay. We just have to wait it out."

"How long has she been like this?"

"This is the second day."

"Fuck, man. Why did you wait so long to call me?"

"Because there wasn't anything that you could do. Besides, I didn't think you would come if I called you. I was going to let Gina call and tell you about the baby."

I saw Merlin flinch at the mention of my baby. I hadn't given much thought as to how he would react to the baby. He told me he didn't want to have anything to do with me, so I assumed the same went for my child. It was sad really. To my knowledge, he was the only family that I had left, and he hated me.

"Do you want me to stay with her while you go home and get some rest?"

"I'm not leaving her side," I firmly replied.

"Well, I'm not either."

"Then I guess we'll both be sitting here."

"I guess so," he vehemently responded.

I had never been so uncomfortable in my life. As if the situation weren't bad enough in itself, my raging headache made matters worse. I really wanted the opportunity to apologize sincerely for the damage I had inflicted into my brother's life, but I couldn't think of the words that would adequately describe how I felt.

My last time in jail changed me. I knew I didn't have another get out of jail card in me. I had no other choice but to change. My brother wouldn't believe my words. I had to show him I had changed. It was the only way.

9 COJO MILLS

True to her word, Natoya picked me up at my apartment at ten o'clock. I didn't allow myself time to think of an excuse not to go. Truth was I needed to get out of the house and have some fun. I couldn't remember the last time I had gone out with friends. By the time we got to the party, we were both buzzing. Had I been thinking more clearly, I might have thought twice before getting into the car with her. It wasn't that I thought I could do any better than she could under the circumstances, I just might have stayed home—period.

"I've got a surprise for you," Natoya said after we'd gotten inside.

"Oh, yeah? What is it?"

She looked around expectantly. "I don't see him."

"Him? What are you talking about, girl?" I started feeling nervous. I didn't like the feeling one bit.

"I set up a little date for you. Just relax and be yourself."

"Natoya, no. I don't think I'm ready to start dating yet. I'm doing good just to be out of the house." All of a sudden my buzz was gone, and I wanted nothing more than to leave. This was a problem since I didn't really know the area I was in, and the fact that I didn't have my car.

"Trust me, it's going to be fine. I'll be right here if things don't go well."

I relaxed a little bit, but not too much since I didn't really know Natoya well. She was still swilling down beers like she didn't have a bottom in her stomach. Every time someone walked in the room, or came through the door, I looked at her to see if they were my date. Each time, she waved me off.

I decided to take her advice and not worry about this so-called date. I walked over to the makeshift bar and fixed myself something to drink. The party was in someone's house. There were about twenty to thirty people crowded on the dance floor. The music was good and loud. I couldn't remember the last time I danced, and it was hard for me to keep still. Merlin and I used to dance when we first started dating. Once we were married, it wasn't such a priority. I didn't realize how much I missed dancing until that moment. I waved to Natoya hoping she would come over and dance with me, but she was in a deep conversation with her friends. She obviously didn't understand my gestures or was having too deep of a conversation to be bothered with me. So, I tried to send out subliminal messages to whomever that I was looking for a partner.

My messages weren't being sent, and I started to get annoyed with Natoya for bringing me to a party and deserting me. She knew I didn't have any friends, so she should have at least tried to introduce me to them. I wandered back over to the bar and fixed myself something else to drink. Depression was descending on me fast.

When Natoya finally came back, she was trying to talk on her phone over the loud music. She pointed at me and then at the phone as if I could possibly understand what she meant. She grabbed my hand and pulled me outside even though I was still clutching my drink.

"What?' I asked when she ended the call. I was irritated, but I was doing my best to keep it under cover.

"That was my friend. He got a little hung up, so he asked us to meet him at this after-hours joint."

"Natoya, it's getting late. I think we should just go on home and maybe try this again some other time." I wasn't trying to be a stick-in-the-mud, but I wasn't feeling it.

"Aw, come on. Don't be a party pooper. You know you need to meet some new people."

I started to tell her if she was so concerned about my meeting new people, she had missed a perfect opportunity while we were inside the party. "Are you sure you're all right to drive? I know I've been drinking way too much to do it."

"Child, please, it will take a hell of a lot more than what I've had to get me drunk. We're good. Besides, it's not that far. My boo is going to meet us there, too."

I started to feel a little bit better knowing that Natoya wasn't going to leave me again. She reached over and took my glass, drained it and tossed it in the grass.

"Well, damn," I fought the urge to pick up the empty cup. I thought it was rude to litter the yard when the owners of the house were nice enough to host the party.

"You said you'd had enough to drink; I was just helping you out." She laughed loudly as we got in the car and raced to the joint. She drove so fast, I didn't have time to be worried about the date.

■■■

Thank God the place wasn't far away from the party. It wasn't as nice of a place as the bar that we'd been to earlier. It looked seedy as most after-hours spots tended to do. Natoya slammed the car in park and jumped out with a squeal. She ran over to this guy and wrapped her arms around him as they shared a juicy kiss.

"I guess that's her man," I mumbled to myself as I exited the car. Natoya needed a serious lesson in manners. I slowly walked over to the couple who were still engaged in a kiss. I cleared my throat.

Natoya slowly pulled away from her tongue swapping. "Cojo, this is my boo, Leo. Ain't he cute."

Leo nodded in my direction, "What's up?"

"Hi." I was pretty much done with all of this. The entire evening was a waste of a pretty black dress. I was more than a little irritated as I waited with them for the dude to arrive. While I believed Natoya's heart was in the right place, she didn't know me well enough to know what kind of guy I liked.

As I stood next to the couple, I couldn't help but be envious. They made such a handsome pair, and I could almost feel the physical attraction between them. I sighed and pulled my wrap closer as I tried to ward off the unpleasant thoughts that were running rampant in my head.

It had been a little over four months since I'd packed my clothes in a suitcase and fled my home in shame. At first, I stayed with my mother-in-law, but I could tell it was causing friction between Gina and Merlin. I didn't want that; I had put him through enough. I had to move on for their sakes as much as mine.

While I wasn't actively looking for a man, I would be lying if I said that I wasn't lonely. When Natoya suggested I meet her friend, I was open to the idea because it would be more like a double date, the pressure wouldn't be on me to carry the conversation.

We were standing outside the club for about fifteen minutes before this guy approached us. The blood was gushing in my veins, and for a moment I felt slightly embarrassed. I don't know why I was feeling this way, but I attributed it to the fact I wasn't used to blind dating, or any dating for that matter.

Natoya pushed me forward, and I extended my hand to the guy. He looked me up and down as I cringed. He was tall, brown-skinned and had a small earring in his left ear. I didn't get the impression that he was sizing me up, but he was more generous with his assessment of me than I was of him. I could barely meet his eyes. "Terrence Bethea, this is my friend, Cojo Mills."

"Just call me Terry," he said as he finally accepted my hand, which I felt had been hanging out there for eternity. I didn't know if I was going to get along with this man. He seemed a little full of himself, and I prayed he wasn't going to embarrass me in front of my friend.

"All right then," Natoya said.

Startled, I looked up to see she and Leo were going in the opposite direction. Confused, I started to follow them. In my haste to accept the date, I didn't even ask the details of the evening. I assumed they had everything all worked out, and I was just bringing my happy ass to the party.

"Where you going?" Terry called to me.

"I, uh, thought we were all going together," I couldn't hide the disappointment I felt in my voice. Was this it? Did they give each other some type of signal and I missed it?

"We don't need them to chaperone us, we're both grown, aren't we?"

"Yeah, but I thought…"

"What? You don't trust me?" Terry pulled back like he was offended.

I didn't know what to think, it all happened so fast. I didn't know him from a can of paint, so how could he expect me to trust him. "Well…"

"Then you must not trust your girl either. Humph. That's shady."

"I didn't say I didn't trust her. I'm just saying this is not how I thought this date was going to go."

"She called this a date?" Terry chuckled.

A growing feeling of dread developed in my stomach. What did he mean by that? I looked around, suddenly very afraid. I had no idea where I was. My black pumps seemed to grip my heels uncomfortably. If worse came to worse, I could whip one off and beat the hell out of him if I had to.

"Well, she said she wanted me to meet a friend." Not only was I beginning to distrust him, I was also second-guessing my friendship with Natoya for leaving me in this awkward situation.

"You're funny."

A light rain started to wet our bodies. Once again, the weatherman had screwed up on the forecast. I raised my clutch and tried ineffectively to protect my hair while Terry looked on with his hands in his pockets. I looked around for shelter as the cold rain sent chills down my spine. I looked with longing in the direction Natoya had gone. If the situation were reversed, I would have never left her alone.

"I don't know about you, but I would like to get out of this rain."

I exhaled as it seemed like we were about to get on the same page. "So would I." I was ready to duck inside the restaurant to wait for this summer shower to end; however, he had other ideas.

"Come on, I'm parked the other way," Terry said as he turned away, leaving me little choice but to follow him. I couldn't understand what was the point at meeting at this after-hours joint if we weren't even going to go inside. What kind of backward ass shit was this? When I saw Natoya again, I was going to give her a healthy dose of my mind.

Terry's car was less than a block away, but with the rain, it felt like a mile. My heels were slapping against my feet making me sound more like a herd of cattle than a graceful woman. My dress clung to my body like an uncomfortable sheath. As I got in the car, I wiped my hair out of my eyes. I was angry with myself for not going in the restaurant and spending some of my money on a cab.

"Whew, we made it just in time," Terry said as he slammed his door and turned on the car. The skies seemed to empty its coffers. In my haste to get out of the rain, I didn't even pay attention to what kind of car he drove. If I later had to identify it, I would be shit out of luck. My knees were shaking. Terry turned on the heat and switched on his wipers. I welcomed the heat, as I rubbed my fingers together in front of the vent.

He pulled the car out in the sparse traffic and navigated through the damp streets. I didn't know where he was going, and he didn't ask for my address. It didn't take a rocket scientist to know that this date was going nowhere fast. I obviously didn't live up to his expectations, and it left me feeling defeated. I wasn't used to being rejected. Under normal circumstances, I was known to turn a head or two when I walked into a room. But that level of confidence was missing from my steps these days. I was beaten down, and it must be showing in my walk.

We drove for several miles, but I didn't have a clue where we were. With the rain and my relative newness to the area, I was lost. He pulled up in front of a rundown house and parked the car.

I looked through the rain splattered window at the dilapidated building. "Where are we?" I tried to keep my pitch as normal as possible under the circumstances. There wasn't anything in the area that looked remotely safe if shit between Terry and I didn't work out.

"It belongs to a friend."

He said this like it was supposed to make me feel better. I could almost see the bugs on the walls, and I hadn't even walked through the door. I was dying to ask him why we were there, or why he would take me to a stranger's house when he didn't even know me himself.

"What are we doing here?" I was beginning to wish I should have put a couple more dollars on my prepaid phone.

"We can't go to your place, can we?" He got out of the car and ran up the steps to the front porch. I sat in the car trying to figure out when the discussion about where we were going to go came up. Even though I was still confused, I wasn't about to sit outside alone, in that neighborhood. I rushed out of the car to join him.

"We can go to my place if you want. I just didn't know it was on the table."

He acted like he didn't even hear me. Terry rapped on the door three times. It was opened by a thuggish young man. Things were going from sugar to shit. "What's up, man," he brushed past the guy holding the door giving him dab. My stupid ass followed him. He didn't bother to introduce me. We walked into a small bedroom where another guy was sitting on one of the two twin beds. I was really out of my element and getting more and more uncomfortable by the minute. My mind was telling me to leave, but my feet kept saying *and go where bitch*.

"Hi," I mumbled as I felt myself being scrutinized by the other young man in the room. My greeting was ignored and so was I, pretty much. I felt like a non-entity.

Terry sat down on the bed and started watching the game on television. It was crazy the way this whole thing was going down. It wasn't until a commercial break that he acknowledged me standing there clutching my purse.

"You gonna sit down?"

I felt like he didn't give me much of a choice. I would rather not sit on someone's bed that I didn't know, but there were no other chairs in the room. It would serve them right my dress was still damp from the rain. I plopped down on the bed. Despite the chill outside, it was hot as Hades in the cramped room. The only air in the room was coming from a slow-moving ceiling fan that only seemed to agitate the heat rather than help cooling it.

Terry took off his shirt displaying his rock-hard abs. His move was so unexpected, it caused my breath to catch in my throat. Any other time, I would have been impressed by his physical stature, but it felt inappropriate, especially since I didn't even know his last name.

"What are we doing here?" I hissed. I would rather take my chances with the rain than be in these cramped quarters with three strange men.

"Relax, we're just waiting for the rain to go away." He scooted back on the bed and rested against the headboard. His muscles practically glistened in the glow from the television. He didn't appear to be at all concerned that I was completely uncomfortable.

I moved over closer to him so I couldn't be overheard. "What did Natoya tell you about me?"

He nonchalantly said, "She said you needed to get laid."

My heart sank. I didn't know who I was madder with, Natoya for her blatant lie or myself for putting myself in this situation. Why I ever expected anything more from a woman I had just met at work, was beyond me. I felt so stupid.

"I never said anything like that. She volunteered to fix me up since I was new in town. I didn't say anything else that would lead her to think anything beyond that."

"Oh, so you didn't tell her that you hadn't had none since your husband divorced you?"

"I, uh…"

"I don't know why you fronting, you know you want some of this." He grabbed his dick and leaned back with a big smile on his face.

I was appalled that Natoya had betrayed my confidence, but I would be lying if I said I wasn't curious about this man's prowess. I couldn't help but wonder about his gifts from the gods. I knew where these feelings were coming from, and it made me feel sad inside. I couldn't get the thug in Gavin off my mind. The way Terry was handling me, it took me back in time.

Terry waved his hand, and his two friends left the room. I watched silently as he rolled over and pushed me back on the bed. I couldn't move because my panties were on fire. He eased my dress up to my panties exposing the red lacy material. He ran his finger through his mouth and used it to circle my clit. I felt like I had been struck by an electric current. My body jolted off the bed.

"She said you were in need of some good loving. Did she lie on you?"

"I don't even know you."

"Does that matter?" He rubbed my clit again.

I closed my eyes. He brought back so many memories. Not all of them were good. My head rolled back on my shoulders as he nuzzled my pussy with his face. This was wrong on so many levels, but it felt so right. His hot lips made my eyes pop open. This wasn't a dream—it was very real.

"Do you want me to stop?" His hooded eyes gazed up at me. His face slightly hidden by the slight rise in my stomach—evidence from my failed pregnancy. I kept meaning to work on it, but hadn't gotten around to it. Even my thighs were thicker. "No," I whispered. I was a Christian woman, and I truly believed God would forgive me in the morning.

He tugged my panties down and off in one swift motion. I allowed my head to fall back until he slid inside of me. I gasped from his length. He wasn't as full as Gavin, but where he missed out on width, he made up for in length. My pussy cried out in adulation. The fact that he slipped inside of me without the use of a condom wasn't lost on me, but it was just going to be another thing I prayed about.

"Rock on that dick, girl. Wrap your pussy around it," Terry instructed.

I had no problem following his directions. I was like a squirrel lost in his world trying to find the nut. I was so far gone, it didn't even bother me that his friends had crept back into the room and were openly gawking at us. I couldn't describe how this made me feel. It was a euphoric sensation to watch them watching me.

My climax was explosive. I came so hard, it rattled my teeth. Terry slid off me and walked into another room. His friends also slithered out of the room, as shame rose from the bottom of my feet to the tip of my head. I rolled over on my side and allowed my head to drag near the floor. I couldn't wait to go into the bathroom and wash the stench of humiliation off me. Even though I lived alone, I couldn't stand taking the smell home with me. The stench of sex and shame was a smell I didn't think I would ever get to leave my skin.

I played with the brown carpet that resembled dirt to me. The shaggy fibers were as worn as the thin mattress I was lying on. Rubbing my fingers through the coarse material occupied my mind until I heard someone come back into the room. I didn't want anyone to see me, and I thought by keeping my eyes averted they wouldn't be able to see my pain.

"You ready to go?"

I looked up quickly and I didn't even recognize the man beckoning me.

"Where's Terry?"

"Who?"

"The guy who brought me here."

He laughed. " That's the name he gave you? Niggas ain't shit. Well, he told me you needed a ride." He walked out the door.

Mortified, I grabbed my panties off the floor and rushed out the door. I was beyond humiliated. I had sunk to a new low. Wow, the nigga didn't even tell me his real name. Something about my life had to change. Immediately.

10 MERLIN MILLS

I didn't like seeing Gina in this hospital bed. It was the first time I had ever really seen anyone that I cared about sick with something other than a cold, and it frightened me. When my father was killed, I could care less about him. He died of a drug overdose so it was quick. He was like a stranger to me, so I didn't even go to the funeral. I didn't even go to my biological mother's funeral either. I was dealing with my own stuff at the time. It all happened around the same time I found out that my wife was playing me with my brother. I cut off all familial ties, even my ties with Gina.

While I wasn't mad at Gina anymore, I didn't understand how she could have a child fathered by my brother. In my opinion, it was just sick. Candace tried to get me to understand it, but it still freaked me out.

I had a lot of questions that I wanted to ask my brother, but I could hardly stand the sight of him. Every time I looked at him, the only thing I saw was a vision of him seducing my wife. It was an image I couldn't get out of my head. Some people say that time heals all things, but thus far, it hadn't done nothing for this.

Gavin was slumped over in the wheelchair as if he were asleep. I wondered what had happened to him. It was obvious to me his trauma was fresh. It made me smile to think that Gina had finally whipped his ass like she always said she was going to do.

"I ain't sleeping, nigga. I'm just thinking is all."

"I didn't say nothing to your ass."

"I know you didn't, but I could hear your thoughts. I felt those negative vibes you're throwing at me. Whether you want to admit it or not, we still got the twin thing going on."

"That's funny; I don't feel a thing."

"That's because you have hatred blocking those feelings. I can relate though; I deserve it."

"You must have really bumped your head. You've never owned up to the fucked-up things you've done in the past."

"I know. Like I said, I deserve it. I wouldn't blame you if you never spoke to me again."

"That's good, because I don't intend to. After this mess with Gina is over, I'm out."

"That's a shame. I could really use your help with raising my son. I'd hate for him to grow up not knowing his uncle. It's not like we have a whole lot of other family members left."

I couldn't believe what I was hearing. He must really have a concussion, because the brother I knew never took responsibility for anything other than himself.

"I don't know what kind of game you're trying to run now, Gavin, but whatever it is, I'm not buying it. You are a selfish son of a bitch, and I don't want to have anything to do with you."

"I agree. I was a selfish prick for most of my life, but people change. I have changed."

"I doubt it. If it's true, I'm happy for you. I have changed, too. I'm not the same sucker I used to be."

"Hmm, you weren't a sucker. You had a heart and you gave most of it to me, then I walked all over it."

"Who the fuck are you and what kind of game do you think you're running now? If you think I'm giving you something, it's not going to happen. I'm done with you."

"I'm not asking you for anything except maybe time for me to make things right with you."

"How the hell could you make things right with me? You fucked my wife and ruined my marriage! You can't take that back." I was so mad my voice was shaking. Even though I was upset, I never raised my voice because I didn't want to disturb Gina.

"Man, I'm not trying to start no shit, but did you ever consider that maybe Cojo wasn't the one for you?"

"You must want me to bash in the other side of your head, too."

Gavin chuckled which irritated me even more. I was holding on to the armrest so tightly my fingers were going numb.

"If it's going to make you feel better, do it. I'm in no position to try to stop you, but will it change anything? I didn't say that to hurt you. I said it because Cojo was your first love. Neither one of you had any experience with anyone else. Sometimes that works, other times it doesn't."

"So now you want me to believe you're a damn relationship expert? You need to kill all that noise you're talking."

The whole time Gavin was talking, his voice barely rose over a whisper. In fact, I had to lean forward to hear everything he said.

"No, I'm no expert at anything. I just had a lot of time to think about things objectively."

"If you ask me, you didn't get enough time for all the shit you did."

"That's true, too. I should be up under the jail for the things I've done. Why do you think I've had such a change of heart?"

"I don't believe you have."

"Then it's a good thing you're not the one I have to prove it to. The only one who can judge me is God. He gave me this chance to get it right."

I smiled for the first time, having figured it out. "Oh, I get it. You're another convict who found God. What, are you going to be an evangelist now? You gonna try to swindle people out of their money using God now?"

Gavin coughed. He sounded as if he was strangling. I had to stop myself from asking him if he was all right. He clutched his head, and I could tell he was in pain. Good, I thought—he deserves to hurt. I was instantly ashamed of myself for the thought.

"Man, I can honestly say for the first time in my life I'm not looking to do nothing to nobody. If my time in the joint didn't change me, that bout in the elevator did."

I was confused. Could this be true? Or did I still have jackass written on my forehead. "What about in the elevator? You mean what happened to your head?"

"Yeah, karma caught my ass slipping. That nigga could have killed me."

"Damn, I wish I could've seen that." It was my time to chuckle.

"You would have definitely got a kick out of it. He hit me with a fire extinguisher and then kicked my ass when I went down."

"Did you fuck his wife too?" I couldn't help myself.

"Jokes. Cool. At least you're talking to me. But to answer your question, no. Dude was gay. I was going to humiliate and rob his ass, but it didn't work out. I didn't do it, but he's still a little salty at me for drugging him. I have to tell you, I didn't think he had it in him. Dude surprised me."

"That just goes to show that you can't judge a book by its cover."

"I got it, bro."

"Don't call me that. We're beyond that now." He might have changed, but it still didn't alter what he did to me.

"Regardless of what I did to you, Merlin, I'm still your brother. You can't change that. You might not like me. Hell, I don't like myself either, but I really am sorry. And before you say it, I know sorry doesn't change a thing, but it's all I got right now."

I didn't reply because I didn't know what to say. He actually sounded contrite, but I was still skeptical. Gavin had deceived me before. I didn't feel like I had another comeback in me.

My stomach growled and I glanced at my watch. I was surprised to see how late it had gotten. I had been gone all day and hadn't spoken to Candace once. "Shit," I mumbled. I turned my phone back on. I had turned it off when I entered the hospital and forgotten to turn it back on.

Within seconds, I got the first text from Candace asking me if I was okay. Her second and third text had major attitude.

"Man, go on home. I got this. Sounds like you got somebody looking for you anyway. If anything changes with Gina, I'll call you."

"I don't need you telling me what to do," I snapped.

"Damn, I ain't trying to tell you what to do. I'm just saying, you don't have to stick around if you've got something to do. She won't be here alone. I got this!"

"Since when have you been such a doting son?"

"Obviously, you haven't been listening to me. If you would get your head out of your ass, you would hear me.

You weren't the only one that I fucked over. I hurt her, too. I'm just trying to do the right thing."

I was flabbergasted. "Dag, maybe I should have busted you over the head years ago, then you wouldn't have so much making up to do."

"Honestly, I doubt it would have worked then. I had to get beat all the way down before I became willing."

"Listen, I need to step out and make a phone call. When I get back, I think you need to lay out on that cot back there. You don't look so hot."

"Okay, thanks. If you see a dude pushing a cart dressed in white, watch your back! He might think you're me and whack you, too."

"All right then. Be right back." I was actually smiling when I left the room. I walked until I found the waiting room for ICU patients. Thankfully, it was empty. I took a seat close to the door.

Candace answered the phone on the second ring, and I heard the iciness in her tone immediately.

"That's some ball game."

"Look, I know you're mad. You have every right to be. After the game, Braxton and I got a couple of drinks—"

"You don't owe me any explanations. I just want to know if you're coming over tonight so I can throw away the special dinner I made for you."

"Aww, babe. I'm sorry. I honestly didn't believe I would be gone so long. My brother called and said Gina was in the hospital. I came right over here, and I've been here ever since."

"Oh, my God! Is she okay?" Her icy demeanor appeared to have evaporated.

"She looks like she's sleeping. I haven't talked to the doctors yet."

"Do you want me to come over there?"

"No, babe. They won't let you see her anyway. She's in ICU."

"Well, what if I brought you something to eat? I could pack it up and you could nuke it in the microwave."

"You are such a sweetheart, but I don't think I could eat anything right now. Gavin is here, and it's been very enlightening."

"Why do you say that?"

"I'll explain it as best I can when I see you."

"What about the baby?"

"Damn, I forgot all about it. I'm going to go by the nursery to see if I see it before I go back into her room. I really want to be here when she wakes up."

"Okay, do what you have to do. If you need me, call me. I love you."

"Thanks, I, um—"

The line went dead. I don't know why I stumbled over those three words. Candace was such a good woman, why was it taking me so long to tell her?

11 ANGELA SIMPSON

I wasn't ready to get up when the alarm clock went off. I had an early-morning meeting with a new client, and the need to get in the office early to prepare was my only motivator to move.

I was the secretary/paralegal at a law firm and most days I enjoyed my job. I worked for a quirky attorney named Meredith Bowers, who hated to lose. Meredith worked my ass over good when she represented the man who set my ass on fire. Ironically, I didn't hold it against her. She was doing her job. It was also one of the reasons why I took the job working for her. It wasn't like I needed the money.

Thanks to a rather large financial settlement from my insurance company, and an even larger inheritance from my mother's estate, I was financially straight. I wasn't *Oprah* rich, but I had enough to live reasonably well, until I figured out what I wanted to do with my life.

Perhaps that was the reason why I didn't mind working. There was a certain freedom in knowing that I didn't have to do anything unless I wanted to. If Meredith ever got out of pocket with me, I would be able to check her at the gate. She didn't mean no harm, but sometimes she tended to forget who she was talking to. We balanced each other out like a modern-day *Cagney & Lacy*. Through Meredith, I was able to keep track of my nemesis, Gavin Mills. I knew it was only a matter of time before his ratchet ass got into trouble and needed a lawyer.

"You're here early." Meredith was sitting in her office reading the newspaper.

"I could say the same thing about you. What's up with that?"

"I couldn't sleep. Don't get me wrong, I love me some summer months, but them damn birds singing outside my window have got to go."

"I hear you. I have a crew doing chorus outside my window as well. It's kind of weird, too; once you get that wake-up call, you don't really hear them for the rest of the day. I mean, where do they go?"

"Off somewhere bugging the shit out of someone else I guess. Why are you here so early?"

"Did you forget? You have an eight-thirty appointment with a new client. I wanted to make sure I had all the newbie forms ready and the coffee percolating."

"You are so efficient. What would I do without you?"

"Let's hope you never have to find out." We both laughed.

"You know, I've been dying to ask you how things are working out with you and Young. You should be a lawyer or a priest. You're so tight-lipped about everything."

"Oh, we're good. We spent the weekend together." For a moment, I almost forgot about her friendship with my boyfriend. He used to work with her when she was an assistant district attorney for Newton County.

"Please tell him I asked about him. He doesn't have to be such a stranger either."

"I'm sure you'll see him soon. He's just real busy with work."

"That's good. I actually thought he was going to take me up on my offer and come work for me. It really surprised me when he turned me down."

"You have to understand Young. He enjoys the work that he does. Those people he represents need him. He feels like people who can afford to pay for a lawyer shouldn't have got in trouble in the first place. To quote him, a poor man doesn't have to find trouble, it finds them."

"That sure does sound like Young. I'm glad you two got together."

I didn't tell her this, but I was glad, too. I could actually see a future with him. I took a moment and gathered the information I needed from the file cabinets.

"What kind of case is this today?"

"Boring. Traffic violations and outstanding warrants."

"It pays the bills."

"You got that right. My fee is going to be more than his tickets," Meredith said, laughing.

"I guess he's going to learn today. I don't understand why people put those kind of things off. It almost always makes things worse."

"I agree. I might procrastinate for a minute, but I'll always pay my ticket before its due."

"I'm just going to knock on wood because I've never gotten a ticket."

"The way you drive, it's going to happen. Just be thankful you have a good high-priced attorney as your friend."

"Who won't charge me a thing, right?"

"I know that's right. I would never charge you anything. Having you here has really been like a godsend to me. I have to thank Young for that as well." She smiled at me, and I felt her heartfelt sentiment.

When I was finished with my preparation, I went into Meredith's office and took a seat. It was rare that we had time to sit and chit-chat. I valued her opinion more and more. I felt like she was becoming a trusted friend.

"Can I be honest with you?"

"Of course."

"I think Young is an amazing man, but sometimes I don't get him."

"How so?"

"I don't know. Sometimes I feel like he's testing me. It really gets on my nerves occasionally."

"Do you think it has anything to do with how you two met?"

I lowered my head. I had walked right into a trap I'd set for myself because Meredith had gotten right to the root of my problem. I shook my head yes. "To be honest, I think it does. I was so reckless back then. I'm afraid that one day he will throw it in my face."

"Girl, please. Then you don't know Young very well at all. Don't get me wrong; he's a very deliberate man who thinks about everything before he does anything. He wouldn't have started with you unless he thought you were worthy of his time. Believe that."

"Whew. That's good to know. When you first interviewed me, you had me feeling like a whore. I wasn't sure what his intentions toward me were."

"Trust me, he didn't know the tactics I was using on you. The only thing I had him do was to serve you without your parents being around. Given your Christian background, I was banking on your wanting to settle the matter quickly."

I sighed. "My mom was using what happened to control my life. I'm not saying I'm happy that she's gone, but I'm relieved. My dad is doing better, and I'm certainly happier."

"Then, in a weird sort of way, it all worked out."

"I'm not saying all that. Even if I was acting out, I still didn't deserve to be set on fire."

"Hey, I don't condone what Gavin did. I was required to defend him because it was my job. Nowadays, I'm more selective in the types of cases I will or won't accept."

"That's good to know, because I would have to quit if a similar case came along. It's too close."

"I feel you."

The arrival of our client interrupted our conversation. All in all, it was a good talk. I got some of the answers I needed about my boyfriend, and I let my position be known about future cases. As far as Meredith knew, Gavin raped me. That was my story, and I was sticking with it.

12 CANDACE JAMISON

I had walked back out to the living room after my conversation with Merlin. On the one hand, I was glad he was okay. On the other, I wished he would have called me sooner. It made me feel like I was checking up on him, and I didn't like the feeling. Then, because I wasn't aware what he was doing, I had an attitude which I was sure he could detect.

The evidence of my romantic overture was still in the living room. I wanted him to at least see I had something in mind. Maybe then he wouldn't trip over the multiple text messages I sent him. I didn't want to come off as too clingy. The other thing bothering me was that I had told him I loved him twice, and both times he didn't respond in kind. Truth was, I'd loved him for a long time. I just couldn't tell him because he was married to someone else.

For me, it was different. My marriage had been over for years, and any love I once had was gone. My heart was ready for love, and my ears were anxious to hear it returned to me. I could tell my words made Merlin feel uncomfortable. But what's a girl supposed to do if the words just slipped out?

I crawled on the bed and turned on the television. This wasn't the way I wanted to spend my Saturday night. If

Merlin were here, we probably wouldn't have turned it on. He said the only good thing that came on was the news, and it was only good for the weather. The phone rang, and I reached for it praying that Merlin was on his way. I turned off the television.

"Hello?" I tried to sound sexy and inviting.

"Well, hello to you. Are you keeping my stuff warm?"

My blood felt like it instantly chilled. "Who is this?" I demanded even though I already knew who it was. My ex-husband, Marc, and my worst nightmare.

"Don't act like you don't know. You sound like you've been waiting for my call. Do you want me to come right over and hit that for you real quick?"

I let out a deep breath. I could not believe this man's nerve. I had made it perfectly clear to him that I didn't want to have anything else to do with him, but every blue moon he would call as if he'd just stepped out to the corner store. "For what? There isn't anything left for you over here."

Marc growled deep in his throat. "You giving it to that other nigga? Does he know he's fucking my wife?"

I felt an icy chill travel up my back. Had this nigga been watching me? I dismissed that idea almost as quickly as I thought about it. Watching me would require work and Marc had an aversion to anything remotely close to it. "Did you forget—I'm your ex-wife? What I do and who I do it with, is none of your damn business."

"Oh, that's where you're wrong, sweetness. You will always be mine. I had you first, and there's something special about your first."

I laughed out loud. This man was so full of shit, it wasn't even funny. If I were so special, he wouldn't have cheated on me. "You should have thought about it before you started sticking your dick in anything with a skirt."

"Bitch, please. You were off playing GI Jane. What was I supposed to do, jack off every night to your picture? Fuck all that."

"I was playing GI Jane because somebody had to pay the damn bills, and it certainly wasn't you."

"I provided something more valuable. Can't put a price on that."

"Are you referring to your dick? Then you might owe me some change." I was feeling empowered and bold. I wasn't going to let Marc manipulate me ever again. His reign over me was done.

"You must be riding on the fumes of a good dick that's got you talking that way. But what you don't understand is you don't have the kind of pussy which makes a nigga stay. You got rest-stop pussy, when a brother is tired. You ain't got the snatch that makes a nigga want to build a castle around it and preserve and protect the shit. You feel me?"

If Marc were an archer, he had just shot several bull's-eyes through my heart. I gasped in pain. "What do you want?"

"I want my allotment. My pockets are running on empty and I needs to fill up."

"Then I suggest you find one of those bitches you built a castle for and ask them, because my rest stop doesn't have any vacancies."

"You're a very funny lady, Candace. I wonder what those officers down at the base will think about you shacking up with an enlisted man? Do you think you will get them to laughing, too?"

My heart was beating very fast, and I started to panic. I couldn't believe that he'd been watching me. It's the only way he could have known about Merlin.

"You stay away from me, Marc. I'm not the same woman I used to be. Your threats mean nothing to me. You stole my money; I haven't forgotten it, and you're not the only one who has something to hide." I ended the call fuming. I couldn't believe his audacity. I was so mad I was shaking, but I was also afraid of what he would do. Marc didn't like to hear the word no. And he certainly wasn't used to it coming from me. I had always been his go to girl, but those days were over. While I was terrified of what he might do now that I'd said it, I could not continue to live in fear.

The phone rang again. Its ring piercing the otherwise quiet in my house. Frustrated, I snatched the phone. "What?" I shouted into the phone hoping to hurt his eardrums.

"Baby? What's wrong?"

"Mom? Oh, Mom, I'm so sorry. I thought you were someone else who was annoying me."

"Who is messing my baby? Want me to take care of them for you?"

I couldn't help but laugh. The thought of my mom fighting anyone was comical. She was the most mild-mannered person I knew.

"You don't even want to know, Mom."

"Oh lawd, please don't tell me Marc is back. What does this fool want now?"

"The same thing he always wants...money."

"Hasn't he taken enough? He wiped out all your savings, and he spent every dime you sent home while you were overseas. He's a greedy son of a bitch!"

"Mom!" I knew my mother didn't talk like that, and I didn't want my crap with Marc to change this.

"Honey, God will forgive me. He knows the devil made me do it."

Once again my mother brought a smile to my face. I needed it because before she called, I was about to dissolve into tears.

"I know that's right. What's going on with you?" I tried to push my conversation with Marc out of my mind.

"I'm thinking about having a cookout for your birthday, and I was checking to see if you'd already made plans. This would be a perfect time for you to introduce this new man of yours to the family."

"Oh, Momma. I don't know about all that. Our relationship is so new. I wouldn't want him to think I was rushing things. And you know how you and the aunts are! Y'all will be grilling him so badly, he'll think he was at an inquisition," I said, laughing.

"I can't speak for your aunts, but I will promise to be on my best behavior."

"Um hmm. We'll see. I'll run it by him when I see him."

"When you see him? I don't like the sound of that."

"Here we go. Geez, Mom, it was just an expression. Please don't try to read something into everything I say. If something is going on with me, I normally tell you. Don't I?"

"You sure do. I'm sorry, baby. I'm going take this shoe off my foot and stick it in my mouth."

"That won't be necessary. I'll talk to Merlin and get back to you in a couple of days."

"Alright, sweetie. Don't forget Momma loves you."

"I won't. I love you, too. Good night."

"Bye, baby."

13 COJO MILLS

I spent the rest of the weekend in bed. The only time I got up was to go to the bathroom. I was so ashamed of myself, I couldn't even look at myself in the mirror. Whoever this person was who was inhabiting my body, I didn't know her. More importantly—I despised her.

Over the past seven months, my life had taken a drastic change. I felt as if I were free-falling, and I couldn't grab ahold of anything to stop it. I thought making a move would give me the peace I was desperately seeking. Obviously, I was wrong. I was even more tormented here than I was in Atlanta. It was a different time and place with the same old bullshit.

I attributed my rapid downfall to Gavin Mills. To me, he was the catalyst of all my troubles. He awoke a side of me that I didn't even know existed. A wildly reckless side, which I didn't seem to be able to control. As exciting as she was at times, this person scared me.

My phone rang again, and I ignored it. I didn't really want to talk to anyone. Even though I didn't want to talk to Natoya, I expected to hear from her. I was still mad at her for setting me up. However, there was only so much blame that I could lay at her footsteps. She didn't make me do anything. I signed up for that shit on my own. I groaned loudly when the phone rang again. "Leave me alone," I shouted. My voice echoed through my apartment. I should have been up unpacking, instead of wallowing in bed feeling sorry for myself.

A series of sharp knocks shook my door. "What the fuck!" I leaped from the bed and ran to the door clutching a sheet to my body. With shaky knees, I peered through the peephole. Rozz was there holding a bag of donuts and what looked like two cups of coffee. I could care less about the donuts, but I would kill for the coffee. I swung open the door to let her in and ran back to my bedroom.

"I'll be right back. I need to get some clothes on."

"Girl, I've been calling you since yesterday. Is something wrong with your phone?"

"Uh, it's working. I just needed to take a break."

"A break from who?"

Damn, nobody could say that Rozz wasn't sharp. She honed in on my troubled soul.

"It's not a who. I'm just getting my mind right for the job." It was the first thing that came into my head, so I decided to run with it. I threw on a sundress that was reasonably presentable. I didn't bother with undergarments since I had no intention of leaving the house. Once again, I avoided the mirror as I made my way back to the coffee.

"I was trying to catch up with you to find out how the orientation went. I know it was boring as sin."

"Yes, it was. It was almost like watching paint dry. But it's all good. I know what to do in the event of a fire."

"Right. It makes you wonder how much confidence they have in you if they have to tell you such basic things. Any idiot can figure out how to get out of a building."

"Thanks so much for the coffee. I still haven't gone to the grocery store. In fact, I don't think I've even opened my refrigerator, let alone put anything in it."

"What have you been doing about eating?"

"Honestly, I haven't really thought about it. I had something—I think it was on Friday."

"Friday! What are you trying to do? You can't afford to lose no more weight, boo."

"I'm not trying to lose weight. I honestly forgot to eat."

She looked around my apartment as if she didn't see the empty or near empty bottles of booze. Her eyes told me that she had. They were full of sadness.

"I put on a pot of gumbo before I went to church. I can bring you a bowl when it's finished, or you can come over and we can eat it there."

My stomach revolted. I jumped up from the sofa and ran into the bathroom with Rozz close behind me. She grabbed my hair and held it out of my face as I began to retch. I barely made it to the toilet in time.

"Is the coffee that bad?" she joked when I'd finished and had wiped my mouth.

I pointed to my mouth. "This is what's bad. Let me brush my teeth. I'll be out in a minute." I practically shooed her out of the bathroom. I was humiliated. I couldn't believe I had done that in front of her. I felt like my life was beginning to parallel someone from my past, and the thought scared me. I didn't want to end up like Gina—drowning my sorrows in alcohol. I just couldn't do it.

Walking back into the room, I kept my head down, hoping she wouldn't see my shame.

"Are you okay?"

"I don't know what that was. It couldn't have been from something I ate."

"Maybe that's why you threw up. The body needs food." Her eyes once again took in those offending bottles. Had I known I was going to have company, I might have hidden them.

"It could be. I'm gonna tear these donuts up. What kind did you get?" I peeked into the bag as my stomach lurched again. I quickly closed the bag as the smell wafted up my nose.

"I got a little of everything."

"Maybe after I drink this coffee," I said weakly. I prayed that she wouldn't press the issue. I didn't have the fortitude to deal with it. I just wanted to get this coffee down and crawl back in bed. It was the safest place for me where I wouldn't be such a danger to myself.

"That's fine. I bought them for you since I haven't been able to spend much time with you. We had a revival at the church last week. You missed some good services, and the choirs were off the chain."

"That's nice." I knew she didn't mean no harm, but I didn't want to hear about this right now. I had already explained to Rozz that I wasn't ready, but apparently she wasn't listening. It took everything in me not to be rude to her.

"You really should come with me one day. Prayer does a body good, too."

"Damn it, Rozz. I said I'd go one day. I don't need you to keep beating me over the head. I hear you."

Rozz put her hand up to her chest as if she were offended. She probably was. Despite my desire not to be offensive, I was. "I am so sorry, Rozz. I honestly am. I know you have my best interests in your heart. That's what I love about you. I just can't submit to God right now when I know I'm not worthy."

"God doesn't want you to submit, honey. He doesn't work like that."

"Please, Rozz. Not right now."

She held up her hands again. "Okay. I got it. I know I can get caught up in His love. I'll try not to mention it again, but when you're ready, let me know."

She acted like she was going to be my personal savior. It was starting to piss me off. I took a fast swig of my coffee and burned my tongue. For as long as we were sitting there, the coffee should have cooled. "Damn it!"

"What?"

"This coffee is too hot. I burned myself."

"Really? Mine is just right." She took a sip of her coffee as if to prove me wrong. Next to her, I felt like I couldn't do anything right.

"Thanks so much for dropping by. Now that I'm moving around, I should get my stuff ready for the morning."

"Oh, okay. I thought you might want to catch a movie or something."

"Can I take a rain check? I really do need to get some of my things out of these boxes."

"Sure. If you need me, give me a call. And don't forget the gumbo. I made more than enough."

"Thanks, I will." She hesitated just outside the door like she was about to say something else, but she finally walked off. I let out a deep sigh as she moved away and I could shut the door.

I went into the kitchen and poured a generous shot of tequila into my coffee cup. I wasn't sure how it would taste, but the way my stomach was acting up, I knew I needed something. Even though I was wrong as two left shoes, it didn't stop me from doing it. Things would look better in the morning—they almost always did. I just had to get through the   day.

14 ANGELA SIMPSON

While Meredith was busy with her client, I took the opportunity I'd been waiting for to go through her files. It was something I'd wanted to do since the very first day I started working for her. I waited until now to do it because I wanted her to both trust and need me before I breached the filing system. She was such a methodical person, I didn't want to do anything to trigger her suspicions as to my reasons for being there.

We didn't get off to a good start. She represented a man who tried to kill me. For a while, I put Meredith in the same category as him. Young convinced me she was just doing her job, and deep inside she was a good person. Now that I had gotten to know her, I agreed.

I felt a little bit guilty for going behind her back to search her files. I thought it would be easier this way so there wouldn't be a conflict of interest. I wouldn't want to make her have to choose between her client's welfare and me.

It wasn't difficult locating Gavin's file. It was a thick one and took up most of the drawer. The problem I had was getting it out of there and copying it without drawing attention to it. I wasn't surprised by the girth of the file.

Something told me his incident with me wasn't his only brush with the law. Judging by the size of his file, I was right.

There was no way I was going to be able to copy the entire file. Not only would it be time consuming, I didn't need to leave a large paper trail of my deception. Young was at my house often. While I didn't think he would go snooping through my things, he was an investigator. He told me if he had to keep checking on a woman, then he didn't need her. He made that plain from the start and I appreciated it.

Three of the folders were written in Young's handwriting. I quickly removed those folders and placed the file back into the cabinet and locked it. I stuffed the folders in my desk to read later, when I was alone. Meredith's client had an arraignment in an hour. If she took the case, she would be leaving the office with him. I kept looking at her office door willing her to come out. It might have only been fifteen minutes, but it felt like two hours. When they finally came out, I breathed a sigh of blessed relief.

I pulled the three folders from my desk and placed them side by side. I decided to open the one with my name on it last. The first folder I opened was labeled Gina Meadows. Young's distinctive handwriting glared at me in his interrogation notes. Gina Meadows was Gavin's stepmother. His notes indicated he also had a twin brother. A small shudder went through my spine when I realized that his name was the same name Gavin gave me when we met. He was obviously pretending to be his brother. According to the notes, neither Merlin, his brother nor his stepmother had a good relationship with Gavin.

I finished reading the rest of the file. I wasn't surprised to learn Gavin had spent time in lockup before for manslaughter. I jotted down the name of the victim to see if I could find out more information about her.

The second folder was for Cojo Mills. Young didn't have specific notes in this file. The only thing that I saw with his handwriting other than the label of the file was the affidavit of service. Meredith's notes were not as easily deciphered. Cojo was married to Merlin Mills. What I read next caused me to choke. Gavin had abducted his own brother's wife. "Who does that?" I scoured through every scrap of paper in the file. It was certainly interesting. He appeared to be totally fixated with his sister-in-law, but what totally blew my mind was finding out she might be pregnant by him.

My hands were actually shaking when I pulled the final file toward me. I got up from the desk determined to put the file back unread, but my fingers wouldn't pick the file up. Slowly, I sank bank into the chair and opened it. The first thing that caught my eye were newspaper clippings from the fire that almost ended my life, and the car accident that freed me. The second thing I noticed was a note, addressed to me, from Meredith. It read: *We should probably talk before you read this.*

Busted! I closed the file and sat back in my chair. I looked around the office stunned. "She knew I was going to read this." I couldn't help but wonder what else she knew. I carried the folders back to the cabinet, unlocked it and placed them back in the file. I wasn't mad—I was numb.

15 GAVIN MILLS

I woke with a start and a raging headache. For a moment, I didn't know where I was, or how I got there. Thanks to Merlin, I got the chance to actually lie down. I needed it too since I'd been spending my nights in the chair next to Gina's bed. Merlin kept watch over Gina while I got some much-needed rest. Had it not been for my headache and the need to go to the bathroom, I might have slept longer. I squinted at the clock and was surprised to see I'd actually slept through the night. I pulled myself up off the bed and got back into the wheelchair. The room was spinning.

"Is everything alright?" Merlin asked. If I didn't know better, I might have thought he actually cared.

"Call the nurse."

Merlin had moved his chair closer to the head of the bed where he could see both of us.

"Why? Is something wrong?"

"Would you just call the nurse. Please." It hurt to talk, but I had an overwhelming desire.

Merlin muttered something, but I couldn't make out his words. He reached over and pressed the call button. The red light came on over the bed. I wheeled my chair closer, careful not to make any sudden movements.

"How's your head? You don't look so hot."

"I'm alright. Just got a headache. Thanks for staying."

The nurse came over the intercom. "Yes?"

"I'd like to see my son."

"Sir, your baby is in the nursery. You can go down to see him any time you want."

"I don't want to see him behind a plate of glass. I need to hold him. Could you bring him to me."

There was a moment of hesitation before she answered. "Let me see what I can do."

"Thanks." Relieved, I sank back in my chair.

"Man, what are you doing?"

"They haven't brought the baby in here one time since he was born. We're losing valuable bonding time with him. I'm not going to make him feel he's alone just because his mother is struggling."

"Are you serious? He's an infant. He won't remember any of this."

"How do you know?"

"Well, I…"

"Exactly. At the very least, I want to hold him to let him know he is loved."

"Have you ever held a baby?"

"No, but I got to start somewhere. At least if I do it here, they can show me how to do it right."

"I still think you should wait. You might even scare the baby looking like that."

My head shot up, suddenly afraid. "Like what?"

"For one, the big-ass bandage on your head and two, both of your eyes are bloodshot and blackened. You look like you could be cast on that show *The Walking Dead.*"

The nurse came in to check Gina's vitals. She didn't even look my way, and it really pissed me off. "Where is my baby?"

"Mr. Mills, I don't work in the nursery. I called them and let them know you were asking about the baby."

"Oh, I'm sorry. I didn't mean to jump on you. I have this raging headache."

The nurse finally looked at me. "Oh, dear! What happened to you?"

"I had a slight accident. Do you think I could get something for this headache?"

"Well, I'm not actually supposed to do that. I could really get into trouble."

Merlin spoke up. "Do you know what time the gift shop opens up and if they sell painkillers down there? My brother was attacked in this hospital. I would think the hospital would at least want to keep him quiet about it."

I stared at my brother in amazement. He really did sound like he cared. Even if it were a front, I appreciated his intervention.

"Let me see what I can do. I'm going to come back to change her linens and freshen her up a bit. I'll be right back."

"Thanks, man. I really needed that rest. If I could just get rid of this headache, I would be good."

Merlin waved me off as if my words meant nothing, but I knew him better than he thought I did. I was getting to him. His hard exterior was crumbling. I was determined not to use his heart against him as I'd done in the past. Whether he believed it or not, I had changed.

A nurse wheeling a bassinet came into the room. My heart rate increased. I asked for this, and now I wasn't so sure I could handle it. I fought through my doubts. "Did someone in here ask to see their baby?" She stopped in front of Merlin.

"I did. That's my baby."

"Oh, I'm sorry. This little guy is hungry, too. Did you want to feed him?"

Tears welled up in my eyes. "I'm not sure I know how, but I really would like to try." The nurse placed the baby in my arms and handed me the bottle. He was so small, I couldn't stop the tears running down my cheeks.

"Like this?"

"Yeah, you got it. Just remember to always support his head. When he finishes eating, you'll need to put him on your shoulder and gently pat his back for gas. Or, if you don't feel comfortable doing that, lay him in your lap and pat. This is very important."

"My hands are shaking."

"First time?"

"How could you tell?" I said, laughing through my tears.

"You'll be fine. I'll come back to check on you later."

I felt a moment of panic when the nurse backed out of the room, but I pulled it together. I wasn't the first man to hold a child. A slow smile spread across my face as I counted his fingers. I thought he was sleeping, but his eyes opened when I pushed the bottle to his lips.

"He's perfect," I gushed.

"Let me see. I hope he looks like me," Merlin said as he got out of his chair to come see. I had so much pride in my heart, it felt like it would explode.

"Negro, please. He looks like me. That's my boy."

"Aw, man. This is so special. Congratulations."

I looked up to see if Merlin was being sincere. One look at his grinning face told me that he was. I almost felt hopeful our relationship could be salvaged.

"Thanks, man. I appreciate it. Look at him. He's a greedy little dude."

"Yeah, he takes after his father." Merlin gently punched me in the shoulder. It felt good. It was a feeling I could get used to.

Merlin pulled out his phone and started taking pictures of me and the baby.

"Don't do that, man. I don't want my first picture with my son to look like this." As much as I appreciated his gesture, I still didn't want to explain what happened to me to my kid.

"Man, chill. Do you recall ever seeing one picture of us when we were this age? Do you remember taking any pictures at all? I don't remember a single one."

"Wow. You know—you're right. I never thought about it before."

"Then we need to do better for your child. You should take pictures during the good times and the bad. It's just another way to show him that he is loved."

"Ok, you can take some more pictures, but I want some with you in them, too."

While we were taking those pictures, Merlin seemed to forget that he didn't like me. It honestly felt good to have him smile while holding my kid.

I took the baby and laid him down on Gina's chest, gently patting the baby on his back.

"Hold up, what are you doing?" Merlin balled his fist to his side. Gone was the camaraderie we had just shared.

"The nurse said we're supposed to burp the baby."

"She said to put the baby over your shoulder or your lap."

"Gina needs some bonding time, too. The baby needs to know her scent as well."

"Well, I'll be damned. Who are you?"

I just laughed as I continued to rub my baby who was falling off to sleep.

"I saw this shit on the internet. Google and YouTube are my new best friends."

16 MERLIN MILLS

Even though I was tired when I went over to Candace's house, I was also geeked up. I rushed to the bedroom expecting Candace to still be asleep. However, the bedroom was empty. I walked over to the bathroom door thinking she might be in there. I gently knocked on the door.

"Candace?"

The silence in the apartment was deafening. Not even the sounds of a clock could be heard. This was very unusual for Candace, and I felt a prickle of fear. The scene was reminiscent of when I first discovered Cojo was missing.

"What the hell?" Fear wasn't the only emotion I was feeling; it was mixed with anger. I looked around the room for clues as to where she could have gone.

Her bed looked as if it hadn't been slept in. Then I noticed the rose petals which littered the floor and the bed. "Damn." I followed the petals back out through the living room to the picnic blanket and the empty ice bucket. Candles were on every surface. I was immediately filled with remorse. She had done all this for me, and I didn't even show up. But this still didn't answer the question of where she was. And then I saw her curled up on the sofa in a tight ball, wearing nothing more than a red teddy. Next to her was a half-eaten bowl of chocolate-covered strawberries and an empty bottle of champagne.

"Damn." She looked so vulnerable. I never wanted to be the source of someone's pain. I walked over to the couch and picked Candace up. Dried chocolate framed her lips. She didn't even stir as I carried her into the bedroom.

I quickly got out of my clothes and joined her in bed. I would have preferred to take a shower, but I wanted her to awaken in my arms. She was snoring lightly as I pulled up the covers around us. I kissed her forehead and quickly drifted off to sleep. It wasn't what I originally intended, but I was exhausted.

She later woke me with what I felt were heartfelt kisses around my face.

"Hey, you. I am so sorry about last night. I saw how much trouble you went to."

Candace pouted momentarily, losing the smile that had just been on her face. "Yeah…well…I made the best of it."

"I could tell. Did you drink the whole bottle of champagne by yourself?"

"Actually, I drank two. You were gone a long time."

"Ouch, I wish I could have seen it. I love it when you get a little tipsy."

"Tipsy wasn't the word for me last night. I was drunk. I went into the living room to blow out the candles and didn't make it back."

"Oh, so that's why you weren't in here. When I got home I walked right past you. I ain't gonna lie—it scared me because I thought something had happened to you."

"Ah, that's sweet."

Although she made it seem like all was good, I knew enough about women to know that I'd hurt her immensely.

Even though I had a legitimately good reason for not being there, it was still inconsiderate of me when I didn't call her.

"I want to do something to make this up to you. Will you let me plan a special night for you?"

"Merlin, we don't have to do a tit for tat. I did what I did out of the love I have in my heart."

I could fill in the blanks for all the things she left unsaid. I was no dummy, and I knew that if I didn't do something soon, I was going to lose a good woman.

I sat up in the bed and pulled her up beside me, so both of us had our heads resting on the headboard. "I wasn't trying to play that game with you. You didn't have to throw roses to the floor to show me how you feel about me. I see it every day when I look at you."

Candace inhaled deeply, and it seemed as if she were about to interrupt me, but I wasn't finished.

"I know you're waiting for me to tell you how I feel about you. It hurts me that I haven't said it before. But—"

At first, our shoulders were touching, but I felt Candace pull away. "Merlin, wait. I'm not trying to pressure you into saying something you don't feel."

"Woman, would you let me finish"

"I'm sorry, go ahead."

I cleared my throat. My tongue felt a little heavy and I wished for a glass of water. "The reason why I haven't expressed my feelings to you is because I'm still uncertain." I reached for her hand, and she appeared reluctant to give it to me. I grabbed it anyway and held it tightly.

"When I married Cojo, I was so sure she was the one for me. I thought we would be together forever. If I was so horribly wrong about that, how can I be sure of us?" When she didn't respond, I felt the need to continue. I wanted to get this off my chest so that we could move forward.

"I am a one-woman man. Always have been, and I don't suspect it will change. I don't take the responsibility of that lightly either. I would be a fool not to love you, but before I say it, I want to be one hundred percent certain it's true. Can you give me the time to be sure? I can't make the same mistake again."

Candace squeezed my hand. It may not be what she wanted to hear, but at least she knew I was thinking about it.

"Of course. I want you to be sure, too. You are just coming out of a relationship, whereas I've had time to think about what I want in a mate. I don't want you to make a mistake because I don't have another comeback in me either. So, I'm good."

"Whew. I don't know what I would have done if you kicked my ass out of bed."

"Don't get it twisted; I might still kick you out every now and then just to keep you on your toes," she said, laughing.

"Okay, thanks for the heads-up." I immediately felt better about the situation.

She said, "I had a very disturbing call last night."

I was about to get distracted by the sight of her plump breasts sticking up through the sheets. I was just about to reach out and touch them, but her words brought me back.

"From who?" Since we were both army, there was always a possibility of one, or both of us, getting deployed.

"My ex."

The hairs on the back of my neck started tingling. "What the hell did he want?" I was suspicious of the timing of this conversation. No man wanted to hear about another man when they're lying naked in a bed.

"Money. That's all that fool ever wants."

I breathed a sigh of relief. If she had said anything else, I would have been out. "I suspect you told him which ass cheek he could kiss."

"I sure did. Told him he could kiss the entire thing, but the disturbing part of the call was when he mentioned you."

"Me? How did that nigga know about me?" I felt myself getting angry.

"The only thing I can figure is that he's been spying on me. He must have seen you coming over here."

"And? Y'all are divorced and have been for years. You don't belong to him anymore—he fucked that up." I stopped short of telling her she belonged to me.

"He sure did and I'm quite sure that greedy motherfucker knows it. But he's threatening to expose our relationship. That's what has me worried."

"Would he do some shit like that?" My anger surged. This could throw a serious monkey wrench in our relationship.

"Honestly, I don't know."

"Maybe I need to pay this nigga a visit. I'm not trying to go through this bullshit again with another stupid ass man."

"Merlin, no. He's probably trying to scare me. He only wants money and I'm not giving him a red cent."

"Well, he's got one more time to threaten us, and then I'm going to do the talking and it won't be with my mouth."

My problems with my own brother taught me to deal with issues such as this straight up. I was going to do a little snooping of my own and find out who this nigga was and handle him accordingly.

17 GINA MEADOWS

The first thing I saw when I opened my eyes was Gavin's bowed head with a big-ass Band-Aid on it. It kind of reminded me of my earlier years with Ronald. When Ronald used to deal drugs, he struck fear in the hearts of a lot of people, but there were times when someone tried him. I didn't know which scared me the most. The ass-whipping he got, or the one he gave me in return. He didn't believe in suffering alone.

My breath caught in my chest when I noticed Gavin was cradling a sleeping baby. I thought I was dreaming as I clutched my stomach. "My baby." My voice was hoarse and barely above a whisper, but it was obviously enough to wake Gavin.

"Hey."

"Is that..." I couldn't even finish my sentence as tears flooded my eyes and flowed down my face.

Gavin smiled and nodded his head. "I think I should let the nurses know you're awake. How do you feel?"

"I want to hold him. Is he okay?"

"He's fine, Gina. Let me get the nurse."

I didn't notice he was sitting in a wheelchair until he stood up. "What the hell happened to you?"

"I'll tell you about it later." He walked over to the bed and placed my son on my chest. My heart swelled with love for this child even though he hadn't laid eyes on me.

At this moment, nothing else mattered to me. I could have died right then and been happy. Gavin returned to the room a few minutes later with a nurse in tow.

"Welcome back. You gave us all quite a scare." She took my vitals.

I looked at her, confused. I felt fine, so I wasn't sure what she was referring to. "I did?"

"I'll let the doctor explain it to you. I've already notified him that you were awake."

"How long was I out?"

Gavin spoke up then. "It's been three days."

"Three days! Who has been taking care of my baby?"

"Our baby was well taken care of."

I couldn't ignore the warning in Gavin's voice. It wasn't my intent to slight him. I just didn't know what to expect from him.

"I'm sorry, Gavin. I didn't mean it the way it sounded. I meant how was he being fed. I really wanted to breastfeed him." I wiped fresh tears from my eyes.

"Don't let yourself get upset. Let's see what the doctor says about it. I, uh—"

Gavin's face had turned red. I followed his eyes down. The sheet covering my boobs were wet. This was a clear indication to me that there was some milk in my old jugs. He went into the bathroom and brought back a towel for me to use.

"Oh, my," I said, laughing. The movement stirred the baby and caused him to whine. Gavin reached for him, but I pulled him into my chest. I needed to do this. Been wanting to do it my entire life. The feeling of contentment was unlike any feeling I had ever had before. I snuggled him with my lips against his neck. His smell wafting through my nostrils. The baby quieted down.

"What are we going to call him? Baby is getting old."

"I was thinking of Jaylen."

"That's nice. I like it. Jaylen Mills. It has a nice ring to it."

I frowned. "Gavin, you can't be serious. What would people think?"

"Think about what?"

"You know what I mean?"

"Do I look like I give two shits about what people will think? You would deny your child the right to know who his father is because of someone's thoughts? Are you kidding me?"

"I wasn't saying that you couldn't be a part of Jaylen's life. I just thought it would be better if he had my last name."

"Better for who?"

Gavin looked like he was about to bust a blood vessel.

"Well, uh—"

"Well, uh, nothing. You always said you didn't want to raise another child by yourself. Now I'm giving you a chance not to let it happen."

"I want you to be involved in our child's life."

"As what? I'm not trying to be some fake-ass uncle," he shouted loud enough for people in the hallway to hear.

"Would you please keep your voice down. You're going to wake Jaylen and bring half the staff in here."

"I'm trying so hard to give you the respect you deserve— first for raising me, and second for birthing my child, but you are testing me. This shit is ridiculous."

"No, what is ridiculous is your thinking we're going to raise this child together given our relationship."

"I didn't see you raising such a fuss when you found out it was my sperm that gave you this baby."

Gavin went straight for the jugular. I was so angry, fire should have been shooting out of my nose. Were I not in the hospital with a baby on my chest, things would have gone a lot differently. It was hard to have a full-fledged argument when you were trying to be quiet.

"That's a low blow, even for you." The dynamics of Gavin's and my relationship had changed. Now that he was the father of my child, it didn't feel right treating him like a disrespectful child. It was like all of a sudden I had to look at him on my level, and I wasn't feeling that either.

"I'm not trying to disrespect you, Gina, but you can't have it both ways."

A doctor who I had never seen before came into the room and put a temporary end to our discussion. He walked over to the sink and washed his hands. "Good morning, I just want to take a quick look at you before we send you downstairs for some tests." He turned to Gavin and pointed at Jaylen.

Gavin stepped forward and picked up the baby. I followed him with my eyes, certain he was going to do something wrong, but he surprised me with the ease of which he handled our child.

"Doctor, would it be okay if I were to breastfeed my baby?"

"Well, let's see. Give me a moment to review your chart." He carried my chart out into the hall. I assumed it was because the lighting was better. The lights in my room were dim. He came back into the room after several minutes.

"Normally, I would advise against breastfeeding because of the medications we used to stabilize your condition. However, since we stopped administering it to you yesterday, everything should be okay. To be quite honest, nursing is probably going to benefit both you and the baby."

"Really?" I was excited.

"Yes, because it actually makes the uterus constrict thereby strengthening the muscle. So, I don't see why you shouldn't do it unless you're having problems producing milk."

"Trust me, I have no problems there. I've been leaking like a sieve since I woke up."

"That's good. We're going to run some tests on you to make sure everything is healing correctly. We won't use any contrast to protect the baby."

"Is my baby okay?"

"Your baby is fine. In fact, he's ready to go home. He is just waiting on you."

"Oh, my! Then I guess I'd better get my act together, too. Thanks, Doctor."

"I'll be back later to review your results."

"Thank you."

It felt like Gavin was trying to stare a hole through me. I understood that he was upset, but I was, too. There was no easy solution to our problems, and I honestly didn't know what to do.

"Are we going to finish this conversation?"

Jaylen had awakened, and Gavin was changing his diaper. Which was something that I also wanted to do. It took everything in me to demand that he hand me my child. Despite my anger, I had to admit he was good with him.

"You look pretty comfortable doing that."

"I can do a lot of things. You'd be surprised," he answered confidently. The whole time he worked, Jaylen didn't utter a peep. Gavin finished changing him and handed him back to me.

I exhaled loudly. I was so used to doing everything by myself, it was difficult for me to accept help when it was given.

"What are we going to do, Gina? We can't have that nurse come back in here one more time, and we don't have a name for our child."

"I can't think about this now. It's too much. Just let me sleep on it for a minute. I'm very tired." I pulled my baby closer to me and pretended to drift off to sleep. I was so glad Gavin went along with my ruse.

18 ANGELA SIMPSON

I was sitting at my desk fidgeting with some papers when Meredith came back into the office about a couple of hours later. "How did it go?"

"We won, of course. I wouldn't have taken his case at the last minute like that if I didn't think I could do it."

"That's good."

Meredith glanced at the files on my desk and continued on into her office. "You ready to talk about it?"

I got up and followed her inside. Now was as good a time as any. "How did you know I was going to look?" I felt slightly ashamed of myself.

"I would have been surprised if you didn't. If I were in the same situation, I know I would have. It's human nature. I actually expected you to do it on your first day."

I laughed. "You don't know how much I wanted to, but I needed this job, and I wasn't trying to get fired on my first day."

"I wouldn't have fired you for doing something that is natural."

"Now you tell me," I said, laughing. I was trying to keep the mood light despite how I felt on the inside.

"I wanted you to do it at your own pace. Besides, I'm not proud of the tactics I used in that case. I was pretty ruthless."

"You were really hard on me. I told Young you were a bitch." I felt comfortable saying this to her now, especially since she'd already admitted to doing me dirty.

"Honey, I was a bitch. This was my last case with the DA's office, and I wanted to go out with a bang by winning a case that everyone else deemed as a loser."

"Forgive me if I don't share your enthusiasm about the win. Let's just hope he doesn't try that shit again with someone else."

"If he does, he'll be another client."

"That's cold. Someone could die in the process."

"Don't get me wrong. I have compassion for the potential victims, but I got to eat, too."

"That's a callous way to look at it considering someone could get killed."

"I can't debate you on this because it happened to you, so it's more personal. Did you read the entire file?"

"No. I didn't know how much time I had. I read a little bit about Cojo and Gina. When I got to my own file, I saw your note and stopped."

"Ah, I thought you would read yours first. Okay, let me give you the story the way I saw it. As you know, I couldn't just refuse his case because I didn't like what he did. I was obligated by law to give him the best defense possible."

"Even if he was guilty?"

"Unfortunately, in the eyes of the law, you are innocent until proven guilty. So, in essence, yes. I have to say too that this case was one of the most bizarre cases I've ever worked. Gavin had everybody pregnant."

"Wait, what? I didn't read that in the files."

"You must not have read it very closely. He had both his stepmother and his sister-in-law pregnant at the same time you were."

"Eww. That's disgusting."

"I know. Just nasty. I told him the same thing. He had earned himself a one-way ticket to hell."

"And you saved him." I couldn't help but to feel a little salty about it.

"I didn't have a choice, Angela. I wasn't proud of it."

"Well, I know what happened to the bastard I was carrying. What happened to the others?"

"Damn, girl. I know what he did to you was wrong, but these are innocent children we're talking about."

"Let a nigga set you on fire and leave you for dead, then come talk to me."

"Since you want to get all real about it. Let me say I feel you. Like I said, I never condoned what Gavin did; however, I'd be less than honest if I told you I believed your story of rape. Something about it didn't ring true with me."

I felt myself sweating, and I could swear the temperature in the room had just gotten about ten degrees warmer. "Does Young know about it?"

"No. He doesn't know all the details about the case. It wasn't necessary for him to know."

I visibly exhaled, relieved that this information wouldn't be thrown back in my face. "I'll admit the sex was consensual, but the shit that happened afterwards…"

"Gavin swore to me he didn't do anything to you, and that you were fine when he left you."

"He's a liar. We got into an argument, and I might have called him a minute-man. Needless to say, he didn't exactly like it."

"Ah, now I get it. Hell, a man will let you talk about his momma before he allows you to talk about his dick."

"Tell me about it. That nigga beat me like I was a dude."

"I'm so sorry this happened to you. You were so young, too."

"I still dream about it sometimes. I can't believe he got away with it. I should have testified against his ass."

"True. You were the last piece of the puzzle holding him in jail. The girl, Cojo, ruined her own case by visiting Gavin in jail after she'd violated her own restraining order against him. She ended up losing her child in an unrelated scuffle."

"What about the stepmother with her nasty ass?"

"Believe it or not, she was the only truly innocent one in this entire case. She didn't seduce Gavin. He actually took advantage of her while she was passed out."

"How do you sleep at night knowing that you let this man go free?"

"I didn't let anyone free. Like I said—all of you, for whatever reason, decided not to press charges. The judge had no choice but to set him free."

"That just makes my flesh crawl. I wish I would have been stronger."

"Don't be so hard on yourself. You were young, and your mother would have pinned you to a wall if this case went to trial."

"You ain't lying about that. She's the reason why I concocted the rape story in the first place."

"I could tell. You did the right thing, and if you want to know my honest opinion, Gavin is not the same man he was. I think he had a wake-up call this time. I would be real surprised if he gets in any more trouble."

"If that's supposed to make me feel any better—it ain't working. I'm still mad at that son of a bitch."

"I know that's right. I'd be mad, too. But you're going to have to eventually let go of the anger. In some ways, isn't your life better? Be honest."

I threw my hands up in the air aggravated that she would go there. "For Christ's sake. My mother is dead!"

"And you hated her evil ass. Don't front."

I sucked in a quick breath and almost choked laughing. I was busted once again.

"Maybe not hate, but I sure as hell didn't like her ass much," I said when I had gotten myself under control.

"Right. That's what you should hold on to. You got a little money out of the deal; you have your man, and your dad is happier. Those are the silver linings you should hold on to."

I nodded my head in partial agreement. She could think that shit was even if she wanted to, but I still wanted revenge.

19 COJO MILLS

I caught of glimpse of Natoya going into the bathroom at work, and I decided to follow her. It wasn't my intention to have a big blowup with her, but since she wouldn't answer any of my calls, I was going to confront her the only way I could. I just prayed the bathroom would be empty in case things got a little ugly.

Ever since the night she convinced me to hang out with her, I'd been getting the cold shoulder from her. If anyone had reason to be mad, it was me. I slowly pushed open the bathroom door. I didn't hear any voices, so I continued inside. Had there been someone else in there, I wouldn't have gone inside. She wouldn't be able to run from me forever.

"Natoya, you in here?" At first, I was going to pretend it was a coincidence we both chose to go to the bathroom at the same time, but I changed my mind when she didn't answer me. I called to her again with the same results.

"Damn girl, I can see your shoes. Why you fronting?"

Natoya flushed the toilet and came out of the stall with attitude in tow. "Damn. Can't a bitch go to the bathroom in private?"

"Good luck with that, it's a public bathroom."

"I know what it is, but you could have at least waited until I came out of the stall or something."

"What are you saying? It ain't like I peeked over the stall at you. I just asked if it was you. Why you throwing me all this shade?"

"Ain't nobody throwing you nothing. I didn't even know who it was calling my name."

"You knew somebody was calling you. You could have said then that you wanted to be alone."

"Well, it's too late now, isn't it?" She walked over to the sink and started vigorously washing her hands as if she were preparing to do surgery.

I was trying not to let her rude behavior affect me. "How have you been?"

"I'm good."

"How you liking the job?"

"It's a paycheck."

"I guess you don't want to talk."

"Did you figure it out on your own?" she answered sarcastically.

She'd pushed my last button. "What's your damn problem?"

"I ain't got no problem. Except maybe I don't like for bitches to be running me down."

I didn't know which statement to react to first. I had to remind myself where I was because I was about to go smooth off on this heifer. "I know you are not calling me a bitch, so I'm not even going to trip on that. And you don't ever have to worry about me calling on you again. I just wanted to ask you, woman to woman, why you told me you were setting me up on a date and then told the dude something else?"

"I don't know what you're talking about. I didn't tell anybody shit." She was mean mugging me in the mirror as if she were afraid to take her eyes off of me. I just didn't get it. None of it was making any sense.

"So, are you telling me he lied on you?"

"If he said I said something about you, then yes he did."

"You know what, I'm too old to be playing games of 'he said she said.' Forget I ever asked you about it."

"Naw, bitch. You come busting in the bathroom like you all that and then some. It's not over just cause you say it's over."

I did a double take. Out of all the ways that I'd played this out in my head, what was going down was never one of them. "Are you freaking kidding me? What's really going on with you?" I wasn't about to let this bitch punk my ass again.

"With me? Bitch, I ain't got no problem. You followed me! What, you want to lick this pussy or something? Is that why you're sniffing behind my ass? I heard you were a big old nasty freak."

It was like an imaginary record was scratched in my head. Was this chick bipolar? How was she gonna come at me all sideways and shit? "I'm not about to be too many more of your bitches, and I'm not about to lose my job for punching your stupid ass in the face either."

"Who you call stupid, you ratchet trick ho!"

I had just about decided to throw all caution to the wind and drown this chick in the sink, when a couple of people busted into the bathroom. Natoya looked like she'd tried to swallow a grapefruit her cheeks were puffed out so far.

"Is everything all right in here?" one of the supervisors I recognized from orientation inquired.

"Yeah, it's all good," I answered innocently, as I stepped to the sink trying to act like we weren't about to kill each other in that restroom.

Natoya swept past everyone leaving an icy chill in the air. I was going to see that bitch again, and it wouldn't be pretty. All of a sudden, this small-town life had just gotten smaller.

■■■

For the rest of the afternoon, I tried to keep my ass in my cubicle and out of the spotlight. It felt like everyone was talking about me. I wanted to concentrate on the returns I'd been assigned, even though my mind wasn't all in. I couldn't afford to lose my job over no trifling ass woman. So I just plugged in my iPod and prayed five o'clock would hurry the hell up. I was so far into my own head I didn't immediately hear Rozz when she stepped into my cubicle.

"Hello." Rozz snapped her fingers in front of my screen for me to look up.

"Oh, hey girl. I was in the zone."

"I saw that, but you know you shouldn't be plugging in like that. It's against the rules."

I didn't want to tell Rozz what I thought about the rules. Especially since she went out on a limb and got me this job.

"You know you're right. I had them on at lunch and forgot all about it." I pulled out my plugs and stuck them in my desk. I already knew this wasn't a social call since Rozz rarely came into my space.

"Did you get into a fight with someone in the bathroom?"

I expected her to beat around the bush for a few beats, but she just went right in. "I wouldn't necessarily call it a fight. It was more like a verbal altercation."

"Can you come into my office? We need to talk."

I didn't feel like this was a multiple-choice request, since she didn't even wait for me to answer before she ducked out of my stall. I felt like I was being summoned to the principal's office. It might have been better if she'd just called me to her office. That way, I wouldn't have to follow behind her like some puppy on a leash.

She stood by the door and waited until I came in and closed it behind her.

"News travels fast around here," I said with a chuckle. I wanted to make like it wasn't a big deal. Even though Rozz wasn't my direct supervisor, it wouldn't hurt to have her on my side.

"It sure does. That's why I wanted to ask you about it first."

"I appreciate it. I don't know what that girl's problem is. She was wilding out."

"Do you even know her?"

I shifted around in my seat uncomfortably. "Well, apparently not. We met during orientation and hung out after it was over with."

Rozz shook her head. Her otherwise beautiful face turned up with a frown. "She's saying some pretty nasty things about you."

"Me? Why would she be talking about me? She doesn't even know me like that."

"I don't know what's up with that. You know I don't do much for gossip, and I've been trying to stay out of it, but she's turned up the heat with this fight. Everybody is talking about it."

I felt a growing feeling of dread. My hopes of a new beginning seemed to be going up in flames. "I don't believe this bitch. What is she saying?" Rozz shook her head again. I couldn't help but feel like I'd let her down.

"She's telling everyone who will listen that you're a whore among other things."

"What other things?" I didn't want to know, but I needed to hear it from someone I at least trusted not to embellish the story.

126

"Drinking and drugging. She's really going in on you."

"I'm going to kick this bitch's ass. You wait till I catch her." I had a lot of emotions running through me all at once. The overwhelming one was rage. I wanted to kill that bitch. She took everything that had happened and turned it around on me.

"Cojo, that's not going to make things any better."

"Oh, yeah? What do you think I should do?"

"If you want to continue to work here, you might have to ride this one out with no more confrontations. Gossip tends to die quickly here as long as someone isn't sitting there fanning the fire."

She didn't ask me whether any of the things she heard were true. This hurt me more than anything because I thought she knew me better than that.

"I don't know if I can do it. After all the things I've lost, the only thing I have left is my character."

"The truth will come out in its own time. In the meantime, you have to let go and let God."

"I'll try, Rozz, because I need my job. But she's got one more time to call me out my name, and I'm going to drag this bitch all through these halls."

"At least you found out she isn't your friend."

"You got that right. I sure did."

20 GAVIN MILLS

When the nurse came to take Gina for her test, we were no closer to a resolution regarding the baby's name. She didn't want to talk about it, and I had relented. The nurse had taken Jaylen back to the nursery, so I had a chance to wash up a little in the bathroom. I desperately wanted to change clothes and take a shower, but I didn't want to leave Gina alone.

My headache was nothing more than a persistent throb. I didn't mind the pain; it helped keep my mind off my more pressing problem.

"Nurse, do you think I could get a razor?"

"Sure. I can change that headdress for you, too. It looks like some of the swelling has gone down."

"Thanks, I'd appreciate it. I'm not trying to scare my baby half to death." I smiled.

"I'll be right back."

It was a shame that I didn't have some other clothes to put on. I'd been in the same clothes for four days, and it wasn't a pleasant feeling. Had I known things were going to be this bad, I would have packed my own bag when we headed to the hospital. But there was nothing I could do about it, so I would make do.

The nurse came back, changed the dressing, and gave me the razor. "Thanks again," I said with a smile. She winked at me as she left. I wasn't blind. She was coming on to me. I felt it in the way she handled me while she changed the bandage. Under different circumstances, I might have pursued her advances.

Merlin walked in carrying balloons and a small carry-on. "Hey, where's Gina?"

"They took her for some tests." I did my best to hide my surprise at seeing my brother so soon. I sent him a text letting him know that Gina was awake, but I didn't expect him to come.

"Oh, okay. I brought these for her."

"Nice, she'll like them. She should be back soon."

"Okay, I can wait for a few. I thought you could use some clothes, too." He pushed the overnight bag at me.

"Aw, thanks, man. You read my mind. These clothes are so nasty I can't wait to get them off." If I didn't think he would slug me, I could have kissed him.

"It's no big deal. It's a good thing we wear the same size."

It might not have been a big deal to him, but it was a big deal to me. I was also glad that he was there because I wanted to talk to him. "Let me shower real quick. I'll be right back."

"Alright. I'm going to catch up on the news."

I came out of the bathroom talking. Thankfully, Gina was still out of the room. "Do you remember how we used to feel about Dad not being in the picture, and all those random chicks pretending to be our mom?"

"Uh, yeah. How could I forget? It sucked." I could see the revulsion on Merlin's face as I forged on. This wasn't something that we usually talked about.

"Me too, and I don't want that for my son."

"What are you saying, Gavin?" His brow was all wrinkled up and he suddenly looked much older.

"This situation right here is fucked-up. I know it, but I can't do anything about it. What I did to Gina was wrong, and I'll be the first one to admit it, but I don't want our baby to pay for my mistake."

"That's very big of you." There was a hint of sarcasm in his voice that I chose to ignore. I understood where it was coming from. Hell, it would have freaked me out too if the situation were reversed.

"Hear me out, please. I told Gina I want to be a part of my child's life, but she doesn't want to give the kid my last name. So what does that make me?"

"Whoa. What are you saying? You mean you want to have a real relationship with her?"

I nodded my head yes.

"Damn! I was not ready for that. What does Gina have to say about all this?"

"I haven't told her that part yet. I just thought about it myself while I was taking a shower."

"Wow. Oh wow. Man...I...uh—"

"Can you forget about the past for a moment and think about your nephew's future? The only people who knew about our previous relationship with Gina are dead. For everybody else, it would just be a matter of my dating an older woman."

"Are you serious? You must have really hit your head hard. She changed your diapers, man. That's just wrong on so many levels."

"How? She's not my biological mother. She never married our father. Hell, we spent more time with her than he did."

"Right, so that means you know how she is. How are you going to deal with that?"

"Honestly, I don't think she'll be that way now. Our dad made her miserable, and misery loves company."

"I get all that. She's a different woman when she's not boozing it up, too. But damn, man. A relationship? I can't see it."

"Why not? Gina is still a good-looking woman. I could do worse."

"Hell, don't kid yourself—she could, too."

"I can't get mad at that. I deserve it. But this ain't about me, or her for that matter. It's about our child."

"Wait. Are you talking about marrying her?"

"Yeah, I think I am."

Merlin's mouth dropped open as his eyes grew wider. I understood how he felt because I was a little overwhelmed myself now that I'd said it. Until I said the words out loud, I didn't realize I was thinking it.

"Ooh, shit! What do you think she's going to say?"

"I really don't know. She might be more receptive if you don't have a problem with it."

"Me. I ain't in this mess at all. I can't even begin to imagine how we got here."

"What mess?" Gina asked suspiciously.

Our heads swerved around when she was wheeled back into the room.

Merlin leaped forward. "Hey Gina, you're looking great. Your baby is adorable."

"You've seen him?" She appeared to blush.

"I saw him the other night. You were still out of it."

"Oh, Gavin didn't tell me." The nurse helped her back in the bed giving us both a reprieve. I waited until she left before I spoke.

"Merlin was thoughtful enough to bring me some clothes, too."

"That was sweet of him. It's good to see you two getting along."

I had to agree with her. It was rather special. "I agree. I missed him. I promise you both, I won't do anything else to fuck up our relationship."

I think I surprised them both with my announcement. I was on a roll. "While I'm on the subject of not fucking up. I was speaking to Merlin about—"

"Oh, shit." Merlin walked over to a chair in the corner and sat down.

"What?" Gina clutched her chest looking alarmed.

"I told him I wanted to ask you to marry me." My knees got weak, and I had to sit down myself. I've never uttered those words to anyone before, and it shook me.

"Boy, stop playing." She laughed somewhat nervously as her eyes darted between Merlin and me.

"It could work, Gina, and it would solve most of our problems."

"They must have slipped my ass something else when they gave me that test, because either you're talking crazy, or my butt is hallucinating."

Merlin cleared his throat. "I wasn't going to say anything, but it does kind of make sense. You two already have the baby together. Even if it were a marriage in name only, it would cut down on some of the questions people will have about the identity of the father."

"Merlin, I can't believe you even opened your mouth to say that. It's just plain silly. What can your brother do for me?"

I didn't want to get angry, but I was. "I've already done more for you than my father did in twenty-some years. I gave you a child and I'm willing to put a ring on it." *Boom.* If I had a microphone, I would have thrown it to the floor and walked the fuck out of the room. Since I didn't, I just took in the stunned expressions on both my brother's and Gina's faces.

21 MERLIN MILLS

I stood up. "You two have a lot to discuss, so I'm going to go into work. Whichever way you go with this, I'll support you." I couldn't look at either one of them as I hastily left the room. I just hoped that Gavin wasn't blowing smoke up Gina's ass. She'd been through enough with my dad. I didn't want to see her hurt again.

As much as I hated to admit it, marrying Gina was a good option from a technical standpoint. By doing it, they immediately shut down the gossipmongers. People would still talk about their apparent age difference, but Gina would be perceived as a lioness and Gavin, well, he would just be Gavin. Since he was already living with Gina, there wouldn't be much difference except maybe which bed he slept in.

I shuddered inside. Thinking about a physical relationship between them was a little nauseating to me. I couldn't do it. I doubted if my dick would even rise to the occasion. Not because she wasn't attractive, but because she would always be Mom in my book. But if she married my brother, she would be my sister-in-law. It was laughable to me that the first person Gavin brought home to meet his mom was his mom. I was sure our real mother was turning over in her grave.

I laughed out loud as I got out of the car at the base. I was a little late, but I didn't think it would be a problem. It wasn't like I did this on a regular basis. My commander only asked that I make it fair. Which meant I would stay later or work through lunch to make up my time.

"Is your name Merlin?" this dude in civilian clothes asked as he got right up in my face.

"It depends who wants to know," I answered back, even though I already knew who I was talking to. I had seen his picture a time or two when I'd been over at Candace's house.

"Nigga, I know who you are. I'm just giving you a heads-up that you're fucking around with my wife, and I'm not having it."

"Your 'wife' as you want to call her, divorced you. You should have gotten the notice in the mail by now, but in case you didn't, I'd be happy to tattoo it on your ass." I wasn't in the mood for any foolishness. This cat might have spooked Candace, but he was barking up the wrong tree with me.

"Divorced or not, her pussy belongs to me. I'd advise you to stay away from her."

I looked around for witnesses. Thankfully, there were none. "I don't know what you've been sniffing, but you've got the wrong one this time."

"We'll see what you have to say after I talk to the bigwigs inside—"

I didn't wait for him to finish his sentence before I punched him right in the mouth. He went down like he had cement in his pockets. "I said you had the wrong one." I stepped over him and onto the base without looking back. He would think twice before he ran up on me again. I was done with him. The old me might have heard him out. The new me ain't got time for that.

I went right to Candace's office to fill her in on what happened. I knew there was a possibility she would become upset with me, but whether she did or not was irrelevant. I knocked on her door frame before I stepped in. Thankfully, she was alone.

"Hey, you. Wait, what's the matter?" Candace said as she hung up the phone.

"I just had a run-in with your ex. Motherfucker was in the parking lot talking a bunch of noise."

She got up from her desk and looked out the window, which was odd to me since she couldn't possibly see the lot from her window.

"He did what? Oh no!"

"I just wanted to warn you in case he called you talking a bunch of mess."

"Are you okay?"

"Hell yeah, I'm okay. That fool will think twice before he runs up on someone else."

"Oh, no. Merlin, what did you do?"

"I laid his ass out; that's what I did. I'm not taking that mess from him or anyone else for that matter."

"But why did you have to do it here?"

"Are you kidding me? Because he showed up here. What was I supposed to do, ask him to go for coffee so I could knock him the fuck out?"

"Well, no. I mean, damn. I don't know what I mean."

"You might want to get a restraining order if this persists."

"What if he tries to file charges against you? He can be such a prick."

"I'm not worried about that fool. He can come at me again if he wants to."

"Maybe I should break down and give him some money so he can go away again."

"That's not the answer. You do that, and he'll keep coming back. His ass needs to do like the rest of us and get a damn job."

"Tell me about it. It's like he has some sort of aversion to work."

"I don't mean no harm, but how in the hell did you ever get stuck with him?"

"He wasn't like this when we first met. He had a good job and was holding it down. He had a car accident and he hasn't bounced back."

"Was he permanently disabled?"

"Not at all. He tried to milk it for a fat check which didn't happen, and I think he just got lazy."

"That's a sorry excuse for a man. Well, I doubt if he'll come around me again, but I am worried about his messing with you."

"I can take care of myself. I'll call the police if I have to. I think I need to speak to the commander about it, just in case he tries some foolishness."

"What's the commander going to say about us?"

"He shouldn't say anything. You're not a private anymore, and I'm not your commanding officer. I might not even mention your name. I may just tell him he's causing some trouble and leave it at that."

"I'll leave this to you then. Do what you think is best."

"How did it go with your family?"

I took a seat. The events of the day were finally catching up to me. "It was a trip. Let me show you something." I pulled out my phone and went to my pictures. I handed Candace the phone, grinning.

"Aw, he's adorable. Oh my god, is that how you looked as a baby?"

My smile slipped off my face. "I wouldn't know. We don't have any pictures of us when we were born." I shrugged as if it didn't mean anything to me, but in all honesty—it hurt. Our mother had given us to my dad after birth. He passed us around like pawn tickets until we went to live with Gina. We were lucky to have never been split up.

"That's terrible. I'll bet you were a cutie. How's Gina?"

"She seems good. They were running some more tests on her. I left before I got to ask if she received any results. They had some big decisions to make."

"What kind of decisions?"

"Believe it or not, Gavin wants to marry Gina."

"Shut the front door. How do you feel about that? Better yet, how does Gina feel about it?"

"At first, I was freaked out about it, but after he explained it to me, I'm okay with it. I don't know what Gina will say. I left them to handle it on their own. He's actually trying to do the right thing. He doesn't want his son to grow up feeling like we did."

"When you put it that way, it makes sense. Will it be a marriage in name only?"

"That's too much information for me. I can be okay with them trying to do better by my nephew. He didn't ask for any of this. I gotta draw the line with anything over and above that. I don't want a visual of them being intimate in my head for too long."

"Stranger things have happened. They might actually fall in love."

"You're just a hopeless romantic."

"What's wrong with it?" she asked defensively.

"I didn't say anything was wrong with it. I was only making an observation." I wasn't trying to start an argument. I still had some making up to do.

"Good, because I think it's sweet, as long as he's not just running some kind of game."

"You know I've been through my share of shit with my brother, but this time I honestly believe he's being sincere. I hope it works for both of them."

"Well, I'd better go and put this bug in the commander's ear. Keep your fingers crossed he doesn't ship one or both of us out."

I got worried for the first time. I wasn't ready to leave Atlanta, and if I were being totally honest, I didn't want to leave Candace either. "Do you think that will happen?"

"I doubt it. He's a friend, and I respect him. I'll make sure he knows we won't compromise our positions, and our judgment is sound."

"I'll wait for you to get off today. I don't want you going home alone."

"Okay. I think that's a good idea. I'll talk with you later."

"Good luck."

22 COJO MILLS

I managed to the get through the rest of the day without killing the bitch, but my anger was still on overdrive. I wanted nothing more than to find Natoya and stomp a mud hole in her ass. The only problem was I had no idea where she lived. I tried searching for her on the internet, but unless she went by another name, she wasn't socially connected. I didn't even have her phone number because she had either forgotten to pay her bill, or she'd given me the wrong damn number. I wouldn't have been surprised by either scenario.

When I got home, I fixed myself a light supper and poured myself a drink. I felt as if I were moving through a thick fog, and nothing seemed real to me. I thought I was a good judge of character, but I had completely misjudged Natoya. Her attitude and her actions baffled me. She was being shitty to me for no reason.

It bothered me there were so many rumors floating around the building about me. When Rozz told me she was saying I was a whore, I couldn't even fix my lips to deny it. "I should have said a whore gets paid," I mumbled to myself. By reacting to it, I would have been acknowledging and accepting her remarks.

I had to find a way to stop this downward spiral. I downed my drink in two large swallows. Making friends had never been easy for me, especially with a bunch of females. They seemed to keep up a lot of drama, and I wanted to be on a mess-free diet. I fixed another drink after I walked over and turned on the television. I surfed the channels until I found something to hold my interest. I lucked up and found an old episode of Snapped. I used to love the show, but it might not have been the best choice, given my circumstances. Women who killed perfectly described how I was feeling.

I was tipsy, bored and lonely. Not a good combination. Rozz mentioned dropping by after her bible study, but at the rate I was going, I wouldn't be in any shape to talk to her. She would never understand my pain anyway. Her life was perfect, albeit boring. I felt like we were much too young to spend all our time in church. I wasn't trying to do that.

The urgent knock on the door startled me. Assuming it was Rozz, I hurried to answer it ready to give her some excuse as to why I wasn't up for company. I yanked open the door, and two dudes rushed in and closed it behind them. My heart felt like it was about to burst out of my chest. This was not going to be good.

"What the hell? Get out of my house." I was trying to sound a lot braver than I felt. My whole body was shaking, and it had nothing to do with the alcohol.

"Shut it up, bitch," one of the guys said. I immediately recognized him from the night out with Natoya.

The liquor made me stupid. "I know you. What the fuck are you doing in my house?"

"Bitch, didn't I tell you to shut up?" He slapped me across the lips, dropping me to my knees. My head rocked back painfully. He'd literally smacked the taste out of my mouth.

The other guy walked over to my television and flipped it on the floor breaking it. "Ain't shit in here. This piece of shit ain't even high definition."

Was this a robbery? I didn't know. The fact that one of the faces was familiar led me to believe it had more to do with Natoya than an actual theft. The television might not have been worth much to him, but it was mine, and I resented him trashing it.

"What do you want?" I shouted mindful of his hovering hand. He snake-charmed me with it, so I didn't see his foot before it connected with my stomach sending me sprawling to the floor. I grunted in pain as the wind seemed to leave my lungs.

"What you want me to do, cuz?" the other dude asked.

"Fuck up her shit, man. Bitch got to learn to keep her mouth shut."

"Wait, why are you doing this? I didn't say nothing to nobody." I couldn't believe this was happening to me.

"You must be hard of hearing. I'm not going to tell you to shut up again."

He stomped down on my head trapping my hair beneath his feet. I wanted to scream, but I was terrified of what they would do to me. In time, I could replace my material possessions. None of them were worth my life.

I had no choice but to watch as he sliced my sofa and chair, broke my coffee table and shattered the dishes in my kitchen. The destruction, however, was limited to those two rooms.

The man holding me yanked me to my feet and placed his face very close to mine. So close, I could identify everything he'd eaten in the last twenty-four hours. His sour breath burned my nostrils. "You still got diarrhea of the mouth?"

"I told you I didn't say anything to anyone. I tried to talk to Natoya today and she went off on me."

"You got a hard head." He punched me in the mouth again with a closed fist. The only thing keeping me on my feet was his strong arms. I ran my tongue over my lips and teeth wincing in pain. My lip was busted, but it didn't feel like he'd knocked out any teeth. Blood filled my mouth, and I had no choice but to swallow it. I wished they would say what the fuck they wanted and get the hell out of my apartment. But I wasn't foolish enough to say any of this, so I waited.

"My friend doesn't want to see you anymore."

"Who? Natoya?"

His eyes flashed at me as his hand hovered once again in the air. My eyes followed it like a bouncing ball.

"We think you need to find yourself another job. You don't like it there anyway, do you?"

As much as I needed my job, I valued my life more. There was no way I could go into work looking like I'd been in a fight anyway. Quitting was my only option. I nodded my head yes.

"You like your job?" he asked menacingly.

"No, I hate it. I quit." I answered quickly.

"Good answer. I trust you will also keep word of this visit to yourself. You wouldn't want us to come back, would you?" He let go of my hair, and I slumped back to the floor.

"No," I gasped.

"Too bad, though. I was going to let you have some of this dick. Come on, man. This bitch is through."

They strolled out of my apartment like we'd been sipping tea and crumpets. I couldn't even get up to shut the door. Going back to work now wasn't an option for me. They whipped my ass when I didn't say anything. They'd probably kill me if I did. Something in my life had to change.

23 GINA MEADOWS

"I've got great news for you, Mrs. Meadows," the doctor said as he came into the room all smiles.

"Are you releasing me?"

"I sure am. Your tests are all normal, but I still want you to take it easy for a while. No heavy lifting or strenuous activity." He looked at Gavin when he said the latter part.

"Outstanding. I'm ready to go." I was both excited and nervous about it.

"The nurse will come in to remove the IV from your arm, and she'll have some paperwork for you to sign as well. Do you have any questions for me?"

"What about the baby? Are there any special instructions for him?"

"You can follow up with your pediatrician. If you don't have one already, I would be happy to give you a list."

"No, thanks. I already have one in mind. Thank you."

"It was a pleasure meeting you. I wish you both all the best."

Gavin was still mean mugging me after the doctor left. He was waiting for an answer, and I honestly didn't know what to tell him. What surprised me the most was Merlin's acceptance of the whole situation. "I've been meaning to ask you when did you and Merlin bury the hatchet? You two seemed so comfortable around each other. I thought I woke up in someone else's room."

He shrugged his shoulders. "I keep trying to tell you people change. When he first got here he still was a little mad at me, but after we talked, I think we're going to be good. Better than ever actually. It's not good to hold on to anger. It rarely helps any situation."

"Are you throwing a jab at me? Because I had every reason to hate your father. You don't know the half of the things he did to me."

"I'm not taking jabs at anyone, Gina. To each his own. I just know for me, I can't hold on to anger anymore. When I get mad, I get stupid. Do you realize I hated my brother my whole life because of jealousy? All those dumb things I did to mess him up backfired on me. It took my going to jail this last time to realize the only person getting hurt by the things I did was me."

"Well, you hurt him deeply with that mess with Cojo. Did you really care for her at all, or was that just to get at Merlin?"

"I thought I cared about her, but what did I know? I've never had anybody before. I wouldn't know what real love felt like if it slapped me in the face."

He might not have meant to hurt me, but he did. In the beginning, I tried to love them. The older they got, the harder it became. They looked so much like their father it made me crazy. "I tried to love your little bad ass, but it was never good enough."

"I understand that now. You did good to keep us with you for as long as you did. I didn't learn to appreciate what you did for me until after you had washed your hands."

Without any warning, I started bawling like a baby. I never thought I would live to see the day where Gavin appreciated anything.

"What's the matter? Should I get the doctor?" Gavin rushed to the bed with a concerned look on his face.

"No, I'm fine. Damn hormones, I guess." The nurse came in before I could say anything else. Gavin's face still looked stricken.

"Are you okay?" The nurse's head bobbled like a doll.

"Yes, I'm fine. The doctor said I'm ready to go."

"He wrote the orders, but he neglected to tell you one thing. I need for you to have a bowel movement before you go."

"What if I don't have to go?"

"Sorry, it's the rules. I don't know why the doctors don't tell patients this in the beginning. They save the dirty work for us," she said with a laugh.

I didn't see a damn thing funny. "What if I don't have to go till tomorrow? Will you keep me in here then?"

"We can give you something to help you go, but you might not like it. You've been lying in this bed for a while now. You need to get up and move around a bit. You'd be surprised what that will do for you."

"Will you take this thing out of my arm?"

"I can do that." She walked around to the side of the bed and removed the IV from my arm. I instantly felt better. Having the needle there was uncomfortable.

"Did you want me to bring you something?"

"If you give me some milk, I'm sure I can make this happen quickly." I should have felt ashamed mentioning this to a stranger, but I was so ready to go, I didn't care.

"I think we have some in our refrigerator. If not, I'll call down to the kitchen for some."

"Thanks. Can I get dressed now or should I wait?"

"I don't see why not. I'll be back."

I swung my legs over the side of the bed anxious to get up out of the bed. "Can you help me?"

Gavin reached for my arm and helped me to stand up. I felt dizzy for a few moments, but it quickly passed.

"What are you going to do?"

"I'm gonna see if I can take that shower so I'll be ready to go when I'm finished."

He pulled the back of my gown closed. Oddly, I didn't feel at all ashamed about his seeing my naked ass. After the delivery room, I didn't have anything new to show him. He passed me my clothes through the door.

"Do you need any help?"

"No, I don't think so. If I need you, I'll call you." As I was shutting the door, I saw the nurse return.

"Mrs. Meadows, I'm going to need a signature on the birth certificate," she said through the door.

"Can my fiancé fill it out? I'm about to step into the shower."

"That's fine with me but, uh—"

I was trying to hold in my laughter. I could almost see Gavin's face when he realized what I said. I knew it would have been priceless. "Uh, what?" I said between snickers.

"Well…uh…I would but I think he fainted."

I snatched open the door and sure enough Gavin was laid out. "Shit just got real to him," I said, laughing.

"I guess so. Should we get him up off the floor?" The nurse was bent over holding her stomach.

"Leave him down there. He might need a minute." I took the birth certificate from her and quickly filled it out. I laughed the entire time.

23 GAVIN MILLS

I pulled the nurse out in the hall by her arm. "Do you have a chaplain in this hospital?"

"Yes. I'm not sure of their hours, but the office is on this floor."

"Could you show me?"

"Are you sure you're all right? You hit your head a little hard."

"I slipped, but I'm okay." In less than forty-eight hours, I'd hit my head twice, but I wasn't about to let on how much pain I was in because of it.

I was slightly embarrassed when the nurse giggled, but I didn't have time to be ashamed. Gina was ready to get out of the hospital, and I wasn't leaving until we had the names on our baby's birth certificate corrected. "Didn't you hear her say yes? I need to marry this woman before she changes her mind."

"I hate to be the one that bursts your bubble, but unless you have a license, they aren't going to be able to marry you."

"Damn. What do I need to do to get a license?"

"That I don't know. I've never been married."

"Thanks. I need to think. Do you know how long it will be before we're released?"

"That depends on her. It shouldn't take too long to process her out once she actually uses the bathroom."

"Can you stall her? Give me some time to work this out? I really don't want to leave this hospital until my child's birth certificate matches mine."

"Aw, you keep this up and I'm going to cry."

"Can you do it?" I wasn't trying to tell all my business, but if it would get her to help me stall Gina, I was willing to try it.

"I can delay her for my shift, but I'm not sure how much longer after that I can hold it up."

"What time is your shift over?"

"Six o'clock. What are you going to do?"

I pulled the birth certificate from her fingers. "Can you make this go away?"

"I never saw it."

"Good. I'll be back." I rushed out the room with my phone in hand. I knew I didn't have much time. Gina was probably going to freak out when she came out of the bathroom and found I wasn't there, but it wasn't like she could go anywhere until I got back since I had her vehicle and the car seat.

I called Meredith Bowers, my former lawyer's office as I rushed to the car. I was hoping to catch her before she went to court.

"Good morning, Law Office," a cheerful voice answered.

"Miss Bowers, please."

"I'm sorry, she's not in the office. Can I take a message?"

"Do you know where she is? I really need to talk to her."

"May I ask who is calling?"

"One of her former clients, Gavin Mills."

"Is that right? Like I said, she's not here. Can I take a message?"

I noticed the change in her voice, but I thought she was being protective.

"I don't have time for messages. I need her help now."

"Mr. Mills, have you been arrested again? Do you need her to arrange bond or something?"

"Hell no, I ain't in jail! I'm trying to do the right thing for once, and twit's like you…" I felt the familiar urge to lash out building up inside. The desire to hurt someone or something burned brightly for the briefest of moments.

"Mr. Mills, if you want any help from this office, I'd advise you to change your attitude."

"You're right. I do apologize. I'm really in a bind, and I could use her immediate help."

"I can get a message to her if you'll describe the nature of the problem." The iciness in her tone wasn't imagined—it was real. I assumed she was a bitter bitch who needed to get fucked. Luckily for her, I wasn't that man anymore.

I realized there was no way getting around this woman, so I was going to have to let her in on my problem. "I need to get a marriage license, ASAP."

"Come again?"

"A license to get married. I need it right away."

"You're getting married? That's your emergency?"

"Yes. My fiancée just had a baby, and I can't let my child be a bastard. We need to fix it on the birth certificate before we leave this hospital."

"What do you expect her to do? Miss Bowers doesn't do weddings—you need a judge for that."

This lady had to be the dumbest woman on the planet, and I wished I had time to pay her a personal visit, but I didn't. I needed to get back to the hospital before Gina lost her happy mind. "I'm not asking Meredith to marry me; I need a license, and I don't know how to get it."

"You've got this office confused with Google or some other informational service. We don't provide information like that."

"If I had access to Google, I would have used it. I've been in the hospital for the last few days while my fiancée fought for her life. Now could you please show a little compassion and have Meredith call me? Unlike you, I know she will help me."

"Uh…"

I sensed her indecision. I wanted her to believe that Gina was clinging to life. She didn't need to know we were on our way home as soon as I got this matter handled.

"Please." I was hoping this single word was the extra push I needed to give her.

"You can get a license at the Clerk of the Court's office in the county you reside in. Where do you live?"

"Covington."

"That's good. If you could meet her there on Trinity Street, I'll see if she can come to you. She's already in the courthouse."

"Thanks so much for your help."

"I haven't done anything yet. I'll call you back. Is this a good number?"

"Yes, it is. Thanks again."

I ended the call and turned the car around heading for the courthouse. I knew exactly where to go, since I'd been there on more than one occasion. This would be the first time I went in when I wasn't in trouble. I then called Merlin. I wanted him to know about this before it happened.

"Hey, is everything okay?"

"I'm sorry to bother you on the job, but I wanted to let you know they're planning on releasing us sometime today."

"Good. I'm happy to hear it."

"That's not all. Gina agreed to the marriage. I'm trying to get it done before we leave the hospital, so we can have the birth certificate corrected."

"Are you serious? Wow. I don't know what to say."

"I know, right? I never thought I'd ever get married."

"Me either to be honest. I guess I should be saying congratulations."

"Thanks, man. It means a lot to me. I know we still got a long way to go, but I'm really happy you're okay with this."

"I know this ain't none of my business, but I've got to ask, do you love her like that?"

"I really don't know. It's like I told her; we didn't have any shining examples of what love was supposed to look like around us. I respect her, and I guess that's enough for now."

"Does she love you?"

"We didn't even go there. We'll have to figure this out as we go. The most important thing for both of us is our child."

"I'm proud of you, man. I really am."

"Thanks, bro. Wait, can I call you that now?"

"Yeah, you can call me that," he said, laughing.

"I won't fuck up." I was getting a little choked up.

"When y'all trying to get married?"

"Today, if I can get this license. I'm on my way to the courthouse now. My attorney is going to meet me there."

"You don't need no attorney to get a license. It's not that complicated. All you got to do is go to the clerk, pay your fee and it's done."

"Hell, I should have called you first. I had to deal with this bitch on the phone, and her attitude was way over the top."

"Who are you going to get to marry you on such short notice?"

"They got a chaplain at the hospital. That's why I'm rushing to get this done so I can get back before Gina changes her mind."

"I sure wish I could help you with this one, but I'm pretty sure you are going to have to show your license."

"I know, it would have been perfect if you could have, but I got my lawyer meeting me down there. Hopefully she can help expedite the process for me. The good thing about it is that Gina can't go anywhere until I get back since I have the car seat."

"You mean she didn't know you left the hospital? How's that?"

"She was taking a shower and I hauled ass. She should know by now."

"Then it's a good thing you do have the car seat, because the Gina I know would beat your ass to the house and have the locks changed by the time you get there."

"I know that's right. I'm at the courthouse now. I'll call you back later and let you know how it went."

"Call me later hell. I wouldn't miss this wedding for all the tea in China. I'll see you back at the hospital."

"You're coming?"

"Yeah. How often can a man say he saw his brother and mother married in the same damn day."

"Thanks, man. It will mean a lot to her, and it damn sure means a lot to me. See you later."

I rushed through the courthouse as fast as I could without drawing attention to myself. I didn't do good in places like this where a large portion of the people there carried guns. I didn't want to fuck up and make them think I was running for any other reason than I was in a hurry. I followed the signs to the clerk's office. I looked around expecting to see Meredith standing there tapping her feet impatiently, but she wasn't there. I was very disappointed, but I didn't have time to dwell on it.

"I need to get a marriage license," I said to the lady behind the counter. She looked up at the clock and rolled her eyes.

"It's my lunch hour."

The clerk put her head down like it was the end of the conversation, while I stared at her in utter disbelief. She was the only other person in the open-air office, so I didn't know what else to do. "What time is your lunch over?"

She looked at the clock again. "Two more minutes later than when you interrupted it the first time."

I was at a complete loss for words. How she managed to keep her government job was a mystery to me. Whatever happened to customer service? Jumping over the counter and choking her out wouldn't get me a license any quicker. In fact, it would send my black ass back to jail quicker than I could bat an eye. Lucky for her, I valued my freedom a little bit more today than I did yesterday.

"I'm so sorry to bother you. Is there anyone else here I could talk to?" I was doing my best not to clown and be nice.

"Do you have an appointment?"

"No."

"Pity, we only work by appointment. We have it listed on our website, too." The entire time the lady was talking to me she didn't look up from whatever she was reading at her desk.

I stood there for a few more seconds hoping that this was some sort of a joke. But if it was, it was on me. I stepped away from the counter and dialed the number to the clerk's office. The phone rang two times before the clerk picked up the phone. "You have reached the office of the clerk of the court for Newton County. Our office is closed for lunch. At the sound of the tone, please leave a message…beep."

I walked closer to the desk just to make sure I saw her lips moving. I began recording her on my phone. I couldn't believe it. She was pretending to be an answering machine. "Are you serious? You got this job now, but you won't much longer. My taxpayer dollars pays your salary."

"I don't know how many different ways I can tell you that I'm at lunch."

"Whatever. Where is your supervisor? Are they at lunch, too?" I was about to act a royal ass up in that bitch.

"Don't worry about where my supervisor is. Worry about the damn license you need so badly. That's what you should be worrying about."

I sucked so much wind up in my cheeks I could have been a helium balloon. This could not be happening at a worse possible time. I didn't have time for jail because that was surely where I was headed if I didn't walk away from that counter. I let the air out of my cheeks slowly. I had to think about my future wife and my child. Those were the only things keeping me away from the bitch behind the counter.

I pulled out my phone and dialed Meredith's office again. I might not have been able to cuss out this witch behind the desk, but I sure as hell could cuss out Meredith for not bothering to help me.

"Law Offices."

I counted to ten. The voice didn't belong to Meredith. "This is Gavin Mills again. Were you able to reach Meredith?"

"She's not in the office right now, can I take a message."

"Urgh! What the hell? Can't I get a little bit of cooperation today? Just a freaking little?"

"Mr. Mills?"

"What?"

"Turn around."

"What did you say?" I slowly turned when I realized the person on the phone wasn't the person telling me to turn around. My eyes felt like they were going to leap off my face. I couldn't believe it.

"Meredith told me you changed. I didn't believe it."

"Oh my god. I know you, don't I?"

"Yeah, the last time I saw you, you were setting my ass on fire."

"Oh shit." I looked around for a chair. I needed to sit down before I fell down.

"How do you know Meredith?" My mind was rolling at over at a hundred miles an hour. My thoughts were breezing by so fast I couldn't concentrate enough to catch one of them.

"I work for her."

"Oh, so this is fuck with Gavin day. I get it. I deserve it. After what I did to you, I'm lucky I'm not looking down the barrel of a gun."

"Don't think I didn't think about it. But I'm not trying to spend the rest of my life in jail for the likes of you."

"I know it doesn't mean much, but I am really sorry for what I did. It won't change anything, but I am so very sorry."

She looked at me very strangely. So strange that I thought she might change her mind about shooting me after all.

"Give him the license, Mary. He's not the same man I once knew."

"Huh?"

"This is my friend Mary Green. I asked her to fuck with you to see if she could push your buttons."

I was stunned. "This was all a stunt or a test?"

"Pretty much. I still don't like your ass, but I don't feel like I have to kill you today."

"I guess I should say thanks. Again, I really am sorry."

Mary came up to the desk and this time she was a lot more helpful. She got my information, and I paid the fee and rushed from the courthouse. I still didn't know how I felt about seeing Angela again and her test, but I didn't want to focus on it either.

24 COJO MILLS

The only thing I could do was lie on the floor and cry. Try as I might, I just couldn't make any sense out of what just happened. It was so unnecessary. If Natoya wanted me to stay away, a simple phone call would have done. I didn't need her goons to teach me a lesson. Now I had to come up with a plan B, since A obviously wasn't going to work. Trouble was, I didn't even know where to start.

Finding a new job was probably going to be an issue. I considered myself lucky when I was granted an interview from out of state. My move had wiped out the small financial reserves I had, and I hadn't received a full check yet from the IRS. My situation was critical, but there was no way I was going back in that building again for anything if I could help it.

My door was still standing open, and as much as I would like to stay where I was, I knew I would have to lock my door. Given all the noise my intruders made, not one of my neighbors bothered to come see if I was okay. This shouldn't have surprised me, but it did. Even if they didn't want to get involved, they could have at least phoned the police anonymously. It made me not even want to stay in the building anymore, and was a stark reminder of how alone I really was.

For the first time since my divorce, I actually considered calling my mother. She would be disappointed that my marriage had failed, but she wouldn't want me to be suffering. Regardless of how old I was, I was still their baby. My pride allowed me to forget this. While Mom might moan and groan, shouting a bunch of 'I told you it wouldn't work' with regards to my marriage, she'd be doing it as I packed. I just had to work up the nerve to tell her.

I struggled to my feet. My limbs were so heavy, I didn't know if it was because of my physical injuries, or my emotional baggage. Although the door was less than ten steps, it may as well have been the length of a football field. It seemed like it was taking forever to get there. The coppery taste of blood in my mouth was making me nauseous. I knew my lip was busted, but I believed I'd bitten my tongue as well. I only had a few steps to go when Rozz breezed through the door looking distraught. She was moving so fast she generated her own breeze.

"Oh my god! Father, Lord help."

While I appreciated her prayer, what I really needed was for her to be my crutch. "Can you help me to a chair?"

"We don't need a chair—you look like you need an ambulance. Were you robbed?"

Rozz had provided me with a perfect explanation for my appearance, and I almost took it, until I looked around. My purse was on the floor; my television and entertainment center were both smashed. It didn't look like a robbery had occurred—it looked like my spot had been vandalized. That wasn't going to work. "No."

"Do we need to call the police? Were you raped?"

I shook my head no to both questions. Tears welled in my eyes again. I didn't want to cry anymore. It hurt to cry, and it changed nothing.

"Then what in the name of Jesus happened to you?" I could tell Rozz was scared and frustrated, but I couldn't tell her what had gone down without putting her at risk too. I couldn't do that to her. "No police."

"What do you mean?" she shouted.

"They said if I reported it they would come back."

"Who is they?"

I had given her all the information I was willing to give. "I can't tell you that."

"You're going to have to tell me something." She lowered me into a chair and went to shut and lock the door.

"I would if I could, Rozz. Trust me, you don't want to know."

She looked at me suspiciously. "Are you involved with drugs?"

I laughed out loud, and it caused my stomach and mouth to hurt worse. "Ouch, that hurts. No, boo; I don't mess with drugs."

"Then I don't understand."

"To be honest, I don't either, but I'm going to take them at their word that if I go to the police, I'm going to regret it. It's bad enough that you know. I wouldn't want to do anything to endanger you, too."

"Don't worry about me; I'm covered in the blood of Jesus."

I rolled my eyes. I didn't mean to do it. Had I known it would hurt my head, I might have worked harder at stopping it. I thought I had made myself clear to her that while I had nothing against God, he hadn't been showing up and out in my life.

"I don't mean no harm, Cojo, but you've been doing things your way for a while, and it doesn't appear to be working. At this point, why not give Him a try?"

"God doesn't even know my name. He probably doesn't even know my number."

"I beg to differ. He's been calling your number, but you're obviously not picking up the phone."

I had to think about what she said for several minutes before it registered with me. Maybe God was trying to tell me something. "A simple note would have done the trick."

"Maybe that wasn't enough for you. God gives us free will and choices. He probably gave you some subtle hints." Rozz looked around innocently like she wasn't dropping pearls of wisdom on me. I followed her eyes through the destruction. It wasn't a pretty picture.

"I'm not coming back to work."

"Say what? Why not?"

I thought fast for a plausible excuse. The last thing I needed was for her to start asking me a bunch of questions. "My face. There is no way I'm going in there looking like this."

"You're choosing vanity over a paycheck? Take a few days off. Don't quit."

"I wasn't feeling it anyway. It's no big deal."

For a brief moment, I saw a fire flash in Rozz's eyes. It was the closest to anger I had ever seen her. Even though she seemed mad, her tone was even-keeled and calming. "I pulled a lot of strings to get you this job. You haven't even given it a chance."

I felt bad, like I had kicked a gift horse in the mouth, but those thugs made it real clear going back to that job wouldn't be a healthy choice. "I'm sorry; I can't. Can you see about getting my check for me? I don't want to wait for it to come in the mail."

Rozz's lips were pressed together in a thin line. Her disapproval was written all over her face. "I'll see what I can do. I'm going to need your access key to the office and parking pass, as well as your identification."

"Fine, it's in my purse." I sat waiting for her to hand it to me, but she didn't look like she was budging. The purse looked like it was so far away, even though it was actually right at my feet. Bending meant crunching my stomach muscles, and they were entirely too sore for that. I leaned back on the chair trying to get myself together. I wanted nothing more than to fix myself a drink and quietly medicate myself.

Finally, Rozz picked up my purse and placed it in my lap.

"Thanks." I rustled through it and got the items she requested and handed them to her.

"I'll let you know what they say. They may not give me your check, but I'll try my hardest."

"Thanks. I'm going to get some rest now."

She stood up to leave. Her disapproval was evident in her staunch movements. "I'll check in on you tomorrow after work."

"Okay. I'll be here. Can you also bring me a flyer from your church?"

"Of course. I can go get one right now if you want me to. We're having a revival tomorrow night."

"You can slip it under the door in the morning. I'm not making any promises, but I'll think about it."

"I hope you come. I just know you will love it like I do."

"Tomorrow is too soon. I want my face to heal first." I got up and slowly followed her out. I locked the door thinking I just might give her way a try. After all, it couldn't hurt.

25 MERLIN MILLS

I phoned Gavin to find out how he made out with the license. I was nervous, so I could only imagine how he felt. I told my commander about the wedding, and he gave me permission to attend. I wanted to see Gina's face when he told her the wedding was about to go down.

Gavin said, "I got it, bro. I'm on the way back to the hospital."

"Cool. I'm headed that way, too. If you get there before me, can you wait on me in the lobby? I want to see Gina's face."

He laughed, "It might not be pretty. She's ready to go, and I left without saying a word. Knowing her, she's cussing up a blue streak right about now."

"Not the best way to start a future together, but she'll get over it."

"Then again, she might not fuss at all. Like I said before, people change. I can't judge her by her past because she doesn't live there anymore."

"Damn, man; that's pretty profound. I'm impressed."

"I can't take credit for that one; I saw it on Facebook."

"Hell, that's growth for you. The old you wouldn't have been as honest."

"Stick around, I'm sure the best is yet to come."

He laughed again good-naturedly. It was hard to remember that he was the same man who used to torment me while we were growing up. I tried to push those thoughts out of my head. He was getting married today, and it was cause for celebration, not sadness. We didn't share too many of those moments, and I wanted to relish in them.

It was easy for me to believe that Gavin had changed, because I had, too. Mostly because of the things he'd put me through. I wanted to believe that I, too, was a better man for it. I didn't let myself dwell on the past too much because it always led me back to Cojo. She was the one who caused me the most pain. With Gavin, I knew where he was coming from. When Cojo betrayed me—it came from left field.

I was waiting for Gavin in the hospital lobby when he got back. I stood up, and he greeted me with a hug and several pats on my back. It was a great feeling. We hadn't connected like this since we were kids, and I felt my eyes getting moist. When I thought of all those wasted years, it made me sad. Had it not been for Gina's complications, we probably would have never made up.

"We couldn't have timed this any better if we'd tried. How long have you been here?"

"I actually just got here. I thought about going upstairs, but I wasn't about to let Gina cuss me out because she was mad at you for ducking out."

"I don't blame you. That woman can have a mouth on her when she gets riled up. I'm just hoping it won't be too bad, since I plan on having the chaplain come in with us. We can have him go in first, like a shield, then you with the baby and then me."

"Damn, man; this sounds just like a wedding processional to me. She can't be mad about it. Let's make it happen."

"Wait, I might not get this chance later. I just want to thank you for being here. It means the world to me."

"Means a lot to me, too. We'd better get up there before she changes her mind. You can get the chaplain while I see about getting the baby."

"Sounds good to me." I matched Gavin's long strides to the elevator. I wondered if he was as nervous as I was. "What are you going to do about a ring?"

The elevator doors opened, but he didn't move. "Fuck! I didn't even think about that shit."

"Come on, man." I tugged on his arm pulling him into the elevator.

"How could I forget a ring? Damn."

I pulled two small velvet-covered boxes from my pockets and handed them to him. "If you don't mind these hand-me-downs, you're welcome to them."

Gavin's eyes got as big as small plates. "You're giving me your wedding rings?"

"Before you get all excited, they're just bands. Never did get around to upgrading them like I wanted to."

"Aw man, I'm about to start crying like a bitch up in here. I just don't know what I've done to deserve a brother like you."

"Just don't hurt her, man. If you don't, then we good."

We stepped out of the elevator. "As nice as this is, I can't take your rings. It's too much."

"Of course you can. I don't have any use for them. They have been sitting in my desk drawer for months. If I ever get married again, I would be getting new ones anyway. I just hope you get better use out of them than I did."

"Wow! I'm going to make you proud. Just you wait and see."

I left Gavin at the chaplain's office, while I went in search of the nursery. I said a little prayer that Gina didn't already have the baby with her, thereby ruining our surprise. Thankfully, he answered my prayers. I spotted Jaylen sleeping peacefully among a row of crying babies. I motioned for the nurse to come outside and she did.

"Can I help you?"

"You sure can. My brother is about to get married in his hospital room before they take this little fellow home. We thought it would be extra special if his son were there when it happened."

"Aw, that's so sweet. But I can't let you take any of these babies out of here without written authorization from the parents."

Damn. On my way to the hospital, I had tried to think of everything, but I didn't anticipate this. I couldn't be mad at the nurse though, given some of the sick people running around in the world. It would kill Gina if something would've happened to her baby after all she'd been through. "I guess we didn't think this all the way through."

"Well, I can't let *you* take the baby, but I can bring him to the room for you. If you want me to."

"Lady, you don't know just how close you are to my kissing you right now! This will be perfect."

"Young man, if I were a little older, I would let you." She laughed loudly. I was a little puzzled by her response.

"Older?" She was already pushing fifty—it didn't make sense.

"Yeah, old women can get away with lip-locking a much younger man. Me, I'd look like a sexual predator."

I was so surprised by her response, I couldn't even laugh at it. Luckily, Gavin came down the hall with the chaplain, virtually saving me from an embarrassing moment for both of us.

Gavin said, "We good?"

He was all smiles with his chest puffed out like a proud peacock. I remembered feeling the same way when I got married. Oh, how times had changed. Ironically, Gina was right. Cojo wasn't the woman for me. I shook my head trying to clear it of those unpleasant memories.

"We sure are. This lovely young lady is going to bring the baby for us. She just couldn't let me take him, which is a good thing," I said.

"Oh, my. You two look exactly alike. You must be brothers," the nurse exclaimed.

I tensed, waiting for Gavin's reaction. He hated when people said that. It didn't bother me, but it always sent him up the wall.

Gavin laughed. "We sure are. He's older though."

"By what, two minutes? You got your nerve pointing that out like it makes a big difference."

"I'm just saying you will be eligible for AARP before I will."

"I'm going to take that from you since it's your wedding day. Speaking of which, we'd better hurry up before your bride gets mad at both of us."

"Okay, let's do this. Nurse, could you go in the room first?"

"Sure. This is so exciting. We don't get many weddings on this floor."

I gave Gavin one final hug as a single man, and I fell in line behind the nurse.

Gina was dressed and sitting up in the chair by the window when we walked into the room. "There's my baby. I was wondering when he was going to come see his momma." Her face lit up as she got up and came over to fetch the baby. She stopped when she saw me enter the room.

"Merlin, what are you doing here? We're about to go home as soon as your brother comes back. I swear I don't know where he's gotten off to."

Before I could answer her, the chaplain walked in. Gina's mouth dropped open into a big O.

"What's going on?" She looked nervous.

I said, "We thought it would be a good idea to have the baby christened before you took him home."

"We, who is we?"

The chaplain smiled and stepped out of the way to let Gavin in. I could tell he was nervous because of the circles of sweat under his arms.

"I'm we. We need to have the baby blessed after we get married."

Gina's face swiveled between us. "Wait, what? We can't get married now." She looked down at her clothes shaking her head back and forth.

"You look fine." Gavin stepped forward and took her hand and stood next to her. The way he was moving it was like he'd done this before, or at least had plotted it out in his head.

"But what about a license? We need one of those," she complained.

"Relax, I've got this."

I'd never seen Gavin like this before. He might have been a bundle of nerves before he walked into the room, but he was all poised now.

The chaplain stood in front of them and opened his bible. "Are we ready?"

"Yes," Gavin answered confidently. Gina was still stunned, and all she could do was nod her head.

I couldn't stop smiling as the chaplain performed the brief ceremony.

"Will there be an exchange of rings?"

The smile slipped off of Gina's face as she started to shake her head no. Her eyes grew wide as I pulled the two boxes out of my pocket and handed them to the chaplain. Gavin had made me his ring bearer. As Gavin placed the ring on Gina's finger, tears began to flow from her eyes. I didn't blame her as I wanted to cry a little, too. I wished them nothing but happiness. They were going to need each other.

26 ANGELA SIMPSON

Meredith was back in the office when I got there. For a second, I was nervous about what I was going to tell her about where I'd been. I was actually really proud of myself for the way I handled seeing Gavin again. I thought it was going to end very differently. My plan was to run up on him in a crowded room or some dark place, but this opportunity presented itself, and I couldn't resist. Why he thought Meredith would have been able to assist him was a mystery to me. She was a lawyer; she didn't talk to the peons who were working those offices. She spoke to the bosses, and they didn't know how to do shit.

"How did it go in court?"

"The judge rescheduled because the defense needed more time."

"That's a bummer. I know you hate it when that happens. Did they say why they weren't prepared?" I was stalling trying to avoid the inevitable.

"They said they were still trying to locate a few witnesses. It's all good. My time is still billable."

"Dag, Meredith. Have you no compassion for your client's pocketbook?"

"Look at it this way—if we don't bill, we don't eat."

"I know that's right. What was I thinking," I said, laughing.

"What did you do, take an early lunch?" Meredith was good to laugh and joke with, but she was all about the business. She wouldn't hesitate to cut me if I weren't pulling my share of the weight.

"Not exactly." I walked into her office and took a seat.

"What's that supposed to mean?"

"Well, you got a call from a former client."

"Which client?"

"Gavin Mills."

"Oh, shit. Why didn't he call me on my cell? I'm so sorry you had to hear his voice again. Are you okay?"

"I'm fine. I'm not going to lie; I was upset at first. I still wanted to hurt him like he'd hurt me."

"What did you do?"

"I didn't do anything really."

"Why don't I like the sound of that? Is someone going to come to this office and arrest you?"

"No, it was nothing like that."

"Would you please tell me before I have a panic attack or something?"

"He's getting married." I was going to enjoy this. She knew Gavin better than anyone.

"Say what? To who?" Meredith leaned forward on her chair.

"Are you ready for this? His stepmother, Gina."

"Shut the hell up! What kind of ratchet-ass foolishness are they doing?"

"I didn't believe it either, so I had to go down to the clerk's office and see it for myself."

"Wow. Well, why was he calling me?"

"He thought you could help him speed up the process. He was in a big hurry. Gina had the baby, and he intended to marry her before they left the hospital."

"Wow."

"You said that already."

"I know, but damn. I'm so shocked. Not only by his news, but your reaction to it. I would have thought you would have been pitching a fit."

"I ain't going to lie; I was thinking of ways to hurt him and get away with it the whole way over there. It's probably a good thing you and I'd talked before I had to actually deal with him, or I might have been the one calling you for bail."

"Oh yeah, how did I help you deal with it?"

"You said he'd changed and I didn't believe it. So, I had my girl fuck with him a little bit to see if he would nut up and get himself arrested."

"Fuck with him how?"

I was a little worried about how protective she was about Gavin. It sounded like she cared about him a lot more than as just a client to me.

"It wasn't that serious. She just gave him a hard time about the marriage license. He got upset, but he never raised his voice or did anything that would get him either arrested or thrown out of the courthouse."

"Why didn't you just call me to deal with it?"

"For one thing, I'm your assistant, and I'm supposed to handle the minor things and two, you said he'd changed and I had to see him for myself."

"Well, did you?"

"Yeah, I did. I no longer feel like I need to set him on fire too."

"Oh, wow. Were you really going to do that to him?"

"I was going to do something. I just didn't know what."

"I'm glad it didn't come down to that. I would hate to have to break in a new assistant."

"I actually feel good. It feels like a weight has been lifted off my shoulders."

"I'll bet you do. Carrying hatred in your soul is heavy. I'm glad it all worked out."

"Oh, I still hate the motherfucker, but I no longer have to do anything about it."

"I guess we'll just have to leave it at that. Hey, it's Friday. What do you say we knock off early today?"

"I say what are we waiting for. I'm out of here. Enjoy your weekend."

"You, too. Don't hurt nobody."

"I won't. Enjoy."

27 COJO MILLS

I had been calling Gina's house for over a week, and she hadn't been answering the phone. I didn't want to start panicking, but it was hard not to. We were both supposed to have babies around the same time. Due to her advanced age, her pregnancy held greater risks than mine. Had I not been stupid, I would have had a child and a husband. Instead, I essentially killed them both when I took a chance and visited my husband's brother in jail.

Thoughts of Gavin kept me awake at night. I hadn't forgotten the way he made me feel when he touched me. Hell, he didn't even have to touch me to make me all gushy inside. I only had to think of him and it was on. It was like I was dickmatized. Now that I wasn't working, I had a lot of time on my hands to think about where it all went wrong.

It had been two weeks since my unwanted visitors forced their way into my apartment, and I had yet to leave the house. Rozz had been a godsend running errands and making sure I had food to eat. She didn't particularly like making those trips to the liquor store, but she begrudgingly did it. She was still holding out hopes I would one day visit her church.

The bruising on my face had finally disappeared, and I was pleased there were no permanent scars to remind me of the brutal beating I received. Although the physical marks were gone, I was still emotionally battered. I was terrified to go out of the house for fear of running into one of my tormentors. But I couldn't stay inside forever. I needed to find a job.

I picked up the phone and tried Gina again. It could be just bad timing on my part that I wasn't able to get in touch with her. She didn't have an answering machine on her phone. She hated using them, and I didn't have her cell number. Short of driving back to Atlanta, I had no choice but to keep on calling her. I thought about calling Merlin at work since he'd changed his number, but I dismissed the idea. He wouldn't want to hear from me, and I didn't need any more rejection in my life.

"Hello?"

I wasn't expecting to hear a male voice answering Gina's phone. "I'm sorry, I must have dialed the wrong number."

"Who are you trying to reach?" He sounded totally sexy to me.

"I was trying to reach Gina Meadows."

"You've got the right number, but she's sleeping right now."

Confused, I looked at the clock. It was one o'clock in the afternoon, and Gina was an early riser. At least, she was when I stayed with her.

"Oh, I'm sorry. May I ask with whom I'm speaking?"

"This is her husband."

"Her what? Are you kidding me? When did this happen?" I screeched. The man chuckled good-naturedly.

"Yes, I know. We've been getting that a lot lately. We didn't tell anyone—we just did it."

"I guess I should say congratulations."

"Thanks. Should I have her call you back, uh..."

"Yes, please tell her Cojo called. I've been trying to reach her to see how the baby is doing."

"Ah, I should have known it was you, Cojo. I thought your voice sounded familiar."

"Excuse me? Do I know you?"

"Yeah, it's me, Gavin."

I dropped the phone like it was on fire. It rolled off the sofa and onto the floor. I had been drinking, but I was by no means drunk. My mind had to be playing tricks on me. I snatched up the phone, clutching it to my ear. "Gavin?" I whispered. I felt like I was having an out-of-body experience.

"I know, right? Shocker," he laughed as if he thought it was funny. Even through the phone I could feel his swagger and confidence. He was so totally different from his brother.

"Did you say you and Gina got married?" I was still whispering for some stupid reason even I didn't understand.

"We sure did. It was best for the kid."

"Aw, hell no! You mean you're the baby's father? That's disgusting. I don't believe you. She would never marry you. I want to talk to her. And when did your ass get out of jail?"

"If you would stop screaming at me, I'll tell you."

I bit down on my lip to keep from cussing his ass out. I thought he was fucking with me, and I didn't appreciate it one bit. If this were true, then I had fucked up my marriage for nothing.

"Fine. I'm listening."

"Don't say it like I owe you an explanation. You were a married woman when we were fucking around."

I thought I was done hurting, but obviously I was wrong. His words were as powerful as any weapon. "That was low, even for you." I was ready to hang up the phone, but for some sadistic reason I couldn't let go. Even though he wasn't saying anything I wanted to hear, his deep voice was sending sonic waves of pleasure to my vagina. I wondered if he somehow tricked Gina like he'd fooled me.

For some reason, I wanted to give Gina a pass. She seemed to commiserate with me as I moped around her apartment after I had lost the baby. Was that all part of this plan, too? Making sure she was the only one carrying Gavin's baby? It pained me to think that the whole time I was staying with Gina, she was probably laughing at me. I thought we'd moved past the I hate you stage and had formed a friendship, but this was like the ultimate fuck-you. It was bad enough she ruined my wedding; now she was responsible for ruining the little bit of peace I had left.

"Look, that was mean. I'm sorry. I never planned on talking to you about us getting married. I figured if Merlin didn't have a problem with it, why should you."

I gasped, "Merlin knows about this?"

"Of course—he was at the wedding. He even gave us your wedding ring since I didn't have time to get one. Gave me his wedding ring, too. That was sure nice of him."

"Is it just me, or are all of you fucking crazy? This is some Jerry-Springer-type shit." I was so upset I was panting over the phone.

"Get over it, Cojo. Gina and I weren't actually related. She was a woman who raised me—that's it. Now we have a kid together." It sounded like I had struck a nerve with him. Maybe it was the Springer reference that had hit home.

Instead of twirling strands of my hair like I normally did when I was nervous or in deep concentration, I had begun pulling them out. The tingling in my scalp allowed me to stay focused. I had so many questions they were tripping to get out of my mouth.

"But you told me you hated her. How do you go from hating someone to fucking them?"

"Come on now. You know for a man one thing doesn't have anything to do with the other. If it makes you feel any better, we were drunk when it happened. I was trying to tell you this when you came to visit me, but you ran out before I could do it. Gina didn't even know we did it until she started putting the pieces together."

"Are you saying you raped her?" I almost wished it were true.

"No, it wasn't rape. For it to be rape, she would have had to say no. She didn't say anything because she was unconscious."

"That only makes it ten times worse, Gavin. How could she marry you after what you did?"

"I never said I was proud of the way things went down. I apologized to her, she accepted, we got married for the sake of our baby."

"Do you love her?" Even though it was none of my business, I had to know.

When Gavin didn't answer right away, I assumed he wasn't going to answer me. However, after a few more seconds he did. "I don't know how to describe what I'm feeling right now other than immense pride in the knowledge we created a beautiful baby boy who deserves two loving parents. For most of my life, I gave the two people I care for the most, Gina and Merlin, hell. I asked for their forgiveness, and believe it or not, they gave it to me."

I wanted to scream. They were all apple pie and forgiveness, but what about me? Where was my forgiveness? Why couldn't I pick up the pieces of my life and go on? "Ain't that special. This sounds like a twisted bedtime story where everyone gets to go to sleep dreaming about sugar canes and lollipops. Well, what the fuck? Did any of you think about me? Shouldn't I be able to skip off into the sunset happy, too?" My anger was like venom dripping from my lips.

"I can't speak for anyone else but myself. I'm sorry for what I did to you and my brother. He's forgiven me and I hope you will, too."

"In your dreams! You ruined my life, and I lost my baby because of you."

"Hold on now. I've done a lot of fucked-up things in my life, but that one I will not take responsibility for. I didn't ask you to come visit me in jail. You did that one on your own."

I groaned in pain. It seemed like he was going out of his way to hurt me. He was pretty much saying that I killed my own child, and it was more than I could take. "How dare you! I was thinking about leaving my husband for you."

"Were you really? I don't think so. Why would you give up everything for me? I didn't have anything to offer you. I think you liked this dick, but that's about it."

"You son of a bitch."

"I get where you're coming from. You want some closure. I understand it. While I was in jail, I had a lot of time to think about the mess I'd created in my life. It's like I told my brother—you two should have never gotten married."

"You told Merlin that?" I felt like someone was standing on my lungs—I couldn't breathe.

"Yes I did, but not because I didn't think you were a good enough woman. You were each other's first; therefore, you had nothing to compare it to. If I didn't turn your head, someone else would have. Especially with him being gone and all."

"That's not true. I loved Merlin. He was my life."

"But you just said you were thinking about leaving him for me. You can't have it both ways, Cojo. If you loved him like you say you did, you wouldn't have let me fuck you the second time."

"I, uh… I can't deal with this. You got my head all messed up."

"Like I said before. I'm sorry for what this has done to your life. Everyone else has moved on. It's time you do as well."

"Are you speaking about your brother, too?" My head was pounding almost as hard as my heart.

"I think he has. He seems happy. Look, I can hear the baby fussing, so I have to go. I'll tell Gina that you called."

I couldn't even say goodbye. I just ended the call. I was only trying to find out about the baby. I didn't need to know all the rest of that shit. I stumbled through my tears into the kitchen to pour myself another drink. Just thinking about Merlin being with someone else was literally killing me. It was almost as difficult as it was for me thinking about Gavin lying next to Gina every night.

My hands shook as I held the glass up to my lips. I was drinking entirely too much. I knew it, but I felt powerless to do something about it. If this was all I had to look forward to, why was I even bothering to keep on fighting?

28 GINA MILLS

I could not stop staring at the ring on my finger. It had been a long time coming, but my last name was now officially Mills. Although it didn't happen quite the way I'd planned it, it still happened. Now, I just had to learn how to deal with it. Although living with Gavin wasn't new to me, I was having to learn how to deal with him. I could no longer treat him like an errant child; I had to approach him not just as a man, but as my man.

When we first got home from the hospital, I was still unclear how this relationship was going to work. Was he going to sleep in his old bedroom, or would he be sharing mine? My apartment was small, big enough for one, but now we were going to have to think about getting something bigger.

I wasn't the only one confused about our relationship. I felt like Gavin was also struggling with it. He went from being very assertive and authoritative, to passive compliance, and sometimes it confused me. I wanted him to pick a side and stick to it. I had no problem with him taking the lead. I had been running shit for years, and a sister was tired. Like the day he moved the bassinet out of my room and into his.

He didn't tell me he was going to do it—he just did it. But when he didn't join me in the bed that night, I couldn't figure out what I was supposed to do. He still had to bring Jaylen to me for feeding, so what was the point in moving it?

I tore my eyes from my ring finger and went in search of Jaylen. From the heaviness in my breasts, I knew it was time for him to nurse. Gavin was doing an amazing job of keeping the baby quiet so I could rest, but I knew it wasn't going to last. He was going to get tired of being Mr. Mom. I found them both on the sofa sleeping. I couldn't help but to smile at my two men.

"Hey, what are you doing awake? What time is it?" Gavin looked down at his sleeping child as he carefully lifted Jaylen off his chest.

"It's still early, but I know he'll be waking up any minute to eat."

"What a life; this boy has got it made." He handed me the baby and stretched.

"You should stop holding him all the time. You're going to spoil him."

"I know. I didn't intend on falling asleep with him in my arms. I was watching television and he was being fussy, so I moved him so you could get some sleep. Next thing I know..."

"You've been very good with both of us, but you've got to get your rest, too." I was a little uncomfortable baring my breasts in front of Gavin, but just holding Jaylen made them ache to be emptied. It was like I was trained to drop milk like a vending machine when he was near me. Almost on cue, without even opening his eyes, his tiny lips started sucking in air.

"Look at him. That little nigga is whipped," Gavin said, laughing. His eyes were slightly closed and very sexy to me.

"I'll say one thing; he's got a healthy appetite."

"He just likes those titties." Gavin licked his lips, and I had mixed emotions about it. On one hand, it was almost vulgar, but on the other, it turned me on. I hadn't had sex since I conceived the baby, and even then I didn't remember it. Physically, I wasn't able to try it yet, but mentally I was ready.

"He doesn't see them the same way you would. To him I'm just a food source."

"I should hope not. At least not yet." For some reason Gavin looked amused. I wasn't going to touch it. I felt like we were still toeing this imaginary line in the sand.

"Why don't you go lie down and get some more sleep while you can."

"I'm good. I just want to watch."

His eyes were purely lustful, and it made me feel all sloppy inside. I didn't know if it was supposed to be this way, or if I was being overly perverted.

"Did I hear the phone last night?"

"Uh, yeah. You had a call from Cojo." Gavin sat up and picked up the remote like he was suddenly interested in the television.

"Really? Is she alright?" I hadn't heard from Cojo since she left my house a couple of months before, so I was really surprised she'd called me. It made me feel nervous too because Gavin had expressed an extreme amount of interest in her at one time.

"I guess. She said she was checking on you and the baby."

"Oh, that's sweet. I'll give her a call later today. Did she leave a number? I'm so bad about keeping up with folks."

"It's on the caller ID."

Gavin was being rather tight-lipped, and it made me hypersensitive. He seemed to have lost interest in me and the baby. "Did you tell her about us?"

"Yeah, I told her."

I felt an overwhelming sense of dread and shame. "How did she take it?"

"About the same way Merlin did at first, but I don't think she's going to come around like he did. She's a little peeved."

"Why? Does she still want you?" My antenna was up and firing on all cylinders.

"I wouldn't say all that. I mean, I tried to apologize for the pain I caused in her life. I just don't think she wanted to hear it."

"Why do you say that?" Jaylin had fallen back to sleep. I pulled my nipple out of his mouth and placed him over my shoulder, gently patting his back.

"Because, man, she was talking all crazy. I guess you need to call her. She's upset because we've all made up, and she's sitting on the sidelines."

"Oh Lord. I can't deal with no drama today. It's not my fault she packed up her bags and left. If her marriage were important to her, she should have stayed and fought for it."

"Well, she may need some time to come around anyway."

"Gavin, you weren't mean to her, were you?"

"I wasn't mean per se, but I didn't sugarcoat it either. I fucked up when I slept with her the first time, and maybe even the second. But her coming to the jail and all, I can't take credit for that. She wanted to say it was my fault she lost the baby."

"Ugh, maybe I should call her."

"And say what? There is nothing that you can do to fix this, Gina. I've apologized; let it go."

"She doesn't have anybody, Gavin. The least I can do is listen to her."

"You do what you want to do. She's looking for closure. I gave her mine."

I felt better knowing that Gavin had clearly ended whatever there was between him and Cojo. It hurt my heart to know she was all alone. I'd been there before, and it didn't feel good. However, with the way my emotions were swinging, I wasn't the one to be trying to offer someone some advice. I didn't even know what was going on in my own household, so I damn sure couldn't help her with hers.

"Maybe I'll call her tomorrow."

"Good idea. I don't want her upsetting you or the baby. Babies can sense when their mommas are stressed."

I looked at Gavin strangely. How would he know these things? I couldn't believe how supersensitive and caring Gavin was acting. He was doing everything that his father had not done in all the years we'd been together. I liked it, but it also terrified me.

I went to put the baby in his bed before I ended up doing the same thing his father did, which was fall asleep with him in my arms.

"You getting back in bed?"

"Yes," I whispered as I backed out of the room.

"I think I'll join you."

For a moment, I couldn't move. It wasn't something we discussed—it just happened. I got into bed and Gavin got in beside me. I turned over trying to pretend like this happened every day. My breath was coming fast and heavy, but if Gavin noticed he didn't say anything. He rolled over on his side facing the door.

"Nite."

"Good night," I exhaled as we drifted off to sleep.

29 CANDACE JAMISON

I got up early and prepared a breakfast fit for a king. Merlin was still snuggled deep in the covers. It was hard leaving him when he was looking so luscious, but I knew he would be hungry after the workout we'd given each other.

Over the past few weeks, Merlin had been acting differently. He was moody and unpredictable. I was trying really hard not to take it personal, given all that was going on in his life, but it wasn't easy. For the most part, he kept me at a distance. I felt like Merlin had compartmentalized his life, and I was trying to figure out which slots I fit into. He would make general comments about his family, but he wouldn't tell me how he really felt. This confused me because I thought we were closer than that.

When he came over last night, we watched some television and went to bed. He didn't act like he wanted to talk, so I didn't fill him in on my news. The only place we actually came together was in bed. It was the only place where he wouldn't hold back.

Merlin walked into the kitchen smiling. "I woke up and you were gone. What's all this?"

"I thought you might be hungry so I threw a few things together."

"Oh, I'm hungry alright, but this is not what I was looking for when I woke up." He walked up behind me while I was standing at the stove and wrapped his arms around my waist, sending tiny waves of pleasure through my body.

"You'd better be careful. I got hot grits in my hand."

He backed up with his hands in the air. "You ain't got to tell me twice. I do respect the grits." He took a seat at the table with silverware in hand.

"Did you want coffee or juice?" I was enjoying the way he was acting this morning. He was behaving more like the man I'd fallen in love with.

"Actually, I want both, but you don't have to wait on me. I can get it myself."

"What if I want to wait on you? You don't let me take care of you like a woman should."

"That's because I believe couples should take care of each other, and there shouldn't be any set role for a man or a woman."

"Oh, I agree with you, but sometimes I just want to pamper you and today is your day."

"Bring it on then. But don't forget once you feed the stomach and my mind, you might have to feed something else." He gave me this sexy ass grin.

"I think I can handle whatever you throw at me."

"I know you can." I set the plates in front of him and he started loading the eggs, potatoes, pancakes and bacon onto his plate. "This all looks good, babe."

"It's just a little something, no big deal. Hey, I've been meaning to tell you about my talk with the commander. He called me yesterday to let me know we don't have anything to worry about with regards to my ex. He's alerted the first sergeant too, just in case he comes around again trying to stir up trouble."

Merlin put down his knife and fork as if he'd lost his appetite. His voice was no longer playful, making me regret even bringing it up. "How much did you have to tell him?"

"I told him the truth; that I was seeing you, and my ex might be causing a problem. But I didn't make it so much about you; I made it more about me. Like I told you, he's a friend, and he knows what I went through with that man."

"I don't have a problem with your telling him about me, unless it causes him to ship my ass to Siberia."

For a second, my feelings were crushed. I wanted a man who was willing to go to Siberia for me and back. I tried to push past that pain. "He wouldn't do that. Technically, we aren't in violation, but it was better to be honest about it just in case it becomes a problem down the road."

"Good. I don't think I'd be able to handle it if I lost you just when we're getting close."

"Aw, you can be so sweet sometimes." I wanted to leap in the air and fist pump God. That's how good I felt.

We finished the rest of the meal in a comfortable silence. I wanted desperately to get back to the playful banter we were having before, but I didn't know how to get there. I should never have brought my ex into the early-morning conversation. Merlin gathered the dishes and carried them to the sink.

"I've got those, babe."

"No, you cooked. I don't have no problem with doing the dishes."

"I know you don't, but you don't have to do it." He was going to make some lucky woman a wonderful husband, and I prayed I would be that woman.

"I got this. Besides, with all this food I have to move, or I might end up back in bed."

"I could handle it," I said suggestively. I had no problem at all mixing it up in the sheets again with this sexy ass man.

Merlin flicked me with some soapy water. "Cool it down, woman. I'm trying to concentrate. We've got plenty of time for the other stuff later."

"Okay, I'll be good. What do you want me to do?"

"How about getting your fine ass into the shower. I wanted to get some shopping done today."

I felt my eyes glaze over as I went into an almost trance-like state. Even though I knew it was much too soon, I had visions of wedding rings dancing in my head. "Shopping," I chanted like it was a hypnotic mantra.

"Oh Lord, did I utter some magic word or something? You looked like you checked out for a minute," Merlin said, laughing.

I was embarrassed at being busted. Nothing spoke couple more to me than shopping together. I detested going to the mall alone. "Uh, I was thinking about this pair of shoes that have been calling my name at Macy's." I said the first damn thing that came to my head. I never shopped Macy's for shoes; DSW had much better deals.

"I had something different in mind, but we can stop by Macy's if you want to."

"No, I'm good. Let me go ahead and get my shower so I'll be ready. Unless you want me to wait and we could take one together."

"Woman, get out of here before you have us spending the day together in bed."

"Hey, sounds like fun to me."

"Woman, you are insatiable."

30 MERLIN MILLS

"You ready?" I was standing by the door for what seemed like an eternity waiting for Candace to come out of the bedroom. I couldn't understand what was taking her so long when she started getting ready before I did. Typically, she was a no-nonsense type of woman, but today she was being extra. She'd changed her clothes at least four times, and it was starting to work on my nerves.

"I'm coming now." She rushed out of the bedroom wearing this gorgeous red strapless dress I'd never seen before. She honestly took my breath away.

"Damn girl, when did you get this little sexy number. You've been holding out on a brother. You're about to make me say forget shopping and let's find something else to do."

"I take that as a compliment. Thank you. I've had this dress, but we've never gone anywhere together so I could wear it."

"Are you kidding? We've never done anything together?" I don't know why this came as such a big shock to me, but it did. I had this beautiful woman and I'd yet to show her off. I didn't mean like an owner shows his horse or dog, I meant as a man who's proud of his woman. *I was going to have to do something to rectify this situation immediately*, I thought to myself.

190

"You keep on wearing stuff like this, I'll book us two tickets to the moon."

"I don't want to go to the moon, silly, but dinner and a movie might be nice. I'd even like to go dancing one night."

"I can do all of those things. We've been trying to keep our relationship on the low at work and I didn't even realize we were doing it at nighttime, too." I held open the door for her and waited for her to lock up. Then, I trotted to the car and opened the door for her.

"You look pretty good yourself." I had put on a freshly starched pair of jeans and a white button-down shirt with some Dockers. I wasn't on the same level as she was, but I'd be the first to admit we made a striking couple.

"Thanks."

"What are we shopping for anyway?"

"A boy. I haven't brought my nephew anything, and I was hoping you could help me pick out the perfect gift. Then I thought I would take you around there to meet my family."

"You're taking me to officially meet Gina and Gavin today?" She sounded more than a little worried.

"Relax. It's no big deal. You already know about them, so don't stress over it."

"Yeah, but do they know about me?"

I adjusted the buttons on the air conditioner. It suddenly felt warmer in the car. "Well, uh, not exactly." There was no sense lying to her about it since she would find out anyway.

"What's that supposed to mean?"

"I think they know I have someone, but I haven't come out directly and told them who I was with. I made the mistake of hiding who I was with from my family before, and it cost me dearly. I don't want us to get too far involved without all of us getting to know each other."

"I don't know, Merlin. I really do want to meet them, but I don't know if I want to do it in this red dress. Gina might think I'm a hooker."

I laughed out loud. "Are you kidding me right now? Didn't I say you looked gorgeous?"

"You said the dress was gorgeous. But seriously, Merlin, maybe I should put on something that covers up more of me. You know how important first impressions are."

"Nonsense; if I know Gina, she will be asking you where you got that dress from. You're fine. Now I'd be lying if I said I wasn't worried about how my brother will react to you. That nigga, he's the dog of the family." I continued to laugh, but Candace looked to be near tears.

"You're serious about changing clothes, aren't you?"

She nodded her head yes and I turned the car around. Even though I didn't think it was necessary, I couldn't take her somewhere knowing she was uncomfortable.

"Baby, thank you. I promise it won't take me more than five minutes to change dresses and my shoes."

"It's okay. I'm not mad. I want you to be comfortable." I pulled up to her house and parked while she ran inside. If I lived to be one hundred, I didn't think I would ever understand women. They obsessed about the small stuff that we didn't give a shit about. I was prepared to sit for another twenty minutes, but true to her word, she was in and out of the house within five minutes. Her second dress was also cute, but a little more conservative.

"You feel better?"

"I really do. Thanks. I'll save that little number for another time."

"I'm going to hold you to it, too. You still look nice though. Are we ready to go?"

"Yes. We're ready. Do you have any idea what you want to get for the baby?"

"I don't have a clue. I'm assuming they have the basic things like the car seat; well, they had to have that to bring the baby home. But like the stroller, crib or whatever you call that bed they sleep in, they might have those things."

"Bassinet."

"Yeah, that thing. What else do they need?"

"Are you thinking clothes, furniture, a survival kit or diaper bag?"

"What's a survival kit?"

"Ear plugs, booze, vibrator…"

"That's enough. We won't be getting that. What else?"

"Instead of getting them something they might need now, you could get them something they would need in the future."

"Like what?"

"A walker, highchair, swing or a playpen."

"You're pretty good at this. You must have done this before."

"No, not really. It's just commonsense to me to get something for the future if you're unsure of the past."

"The future it is. Now where do we go to get it?"

"We're bound to find something at the mall in one of the department stores. Hell, we could even go to Walmart really. That might even be the best option because if she doesn't want or need it, she can take it back and get virtually anything in one place."

"I don't mean no harm, but I don't want my first gift to my nephew to be from Walmart, no matter how logical it sounds. Let his parents be practical. I got the cool job of being the uncle."

"I hear you. That's your prerogative. Well damn, if you're thinking like that, get him a cell phone, iPad and a MAC and be the bomb.com."

"I said cool, not stupid. He won't need an iPad until next year."

"Oh Lord, this poor child is going to get spoiled rotten. Just remember—if you create a monster you're going to have to feed the monster."

"I hear you. I was only joking with you. I don't think Gina or Gavin would let me do those types of things, even if I thought they were the right thing. To a certain extent, we were materialistically spoiled. My dad brought us things because he didn't want to spend time with us. I doubt very seriously my brother is going to be like that."

"I should hope not. It really doesn't take a lot to please a child. They get spoilt when they start going to school and competing with the other children whose parents were just like your dad."

"I know that's right. Hey, you know what, you don't talk much about your mom and dad. Do y'all get along?"

"My dad died when I was little, but my mom and I talk a couple of times a week."

"I'm sorry to hear that. I'll bet you were a daddy's girl."

"I sure was. I still miss him, too."

"Have you told your mother about me?"

Candace shifted in her seat, obviously uncomfortable.

"That's okay if you haven't. I understand."

"She knows all about you. We don't keep any secrets. She knows me better than I know myself sometimes."

"Wow. Then I guess I'll have to pull out a suit so I can get to meet her, too."

"You can meet her whenever you want, and I promise you won't have to pull out a suit to do it. It won't impress her one way or the other."

"Oh yeah? What will?"

"The way you treat me. That's all she cares about."

■■■

"You got everything?" Candace shouted. She was lingering by the car, but she didn't fool me. I could tell she was nervous. I didn't blame her; I was too. The first time I ever brought someone home to meet Gina was the last time I brought someone home period. It went horribly, and I didn't know what I would do if this visit went the same way.

Candace finally closed and locked the doors. I waited until she was standing beside me before I rang the bell. I sent Gavin a text telling him we were coming. I didn't want to interrupt anything.

"Hey, bro. What's all this?" Gavin asked when he opened the door. I pushed the larger boxes at him and waited until Candace had gotten inside before I made the introductions.

"We just wanted to drop off a few things we picked up from the store. Where's Gina and the baby?"

"She's coming. When I told her you were bringing company, she decided they needed to change."

I was about to say something about Candace's wardrobe antics before I saw the look on her face and changed my mind. I could tell she didn't want me to mention the amount of times she changed clothes as well. "Gavin, this is Candace. Candace, this is Gavin."

"Nice to meet you," Gavin said with a twinkle in his eye. I was waiting for him to say something slick, but he kept a civil tongue in his head.

"I know y'all are sick of hearing this but wow, you two do look just alike."

I groaned aloud because I didn't warn Candace about saying it ahead of time. I braced myself for Gavin's backlash.

"He wishes he looks as good as me," Gavin boasted.

195

I looked up at him in surprise as I wondered for about the hundredth time who he was. I kept expecting him to flip out on me.

"Whatever, negro. Y'all got something to drink? I could use a beer." I grabbed Candace's hand and walked her into the living room. Her hand was warm and moist. I squeezed it to let her know things would be okay.

"Does the baby sleep through the night yet?" Candace asked.

"Heavens, no. The little nigga is up about every two hours."

"Oh my, you both must be exhausted," Candace said.

"We're alright. We're taking it in shifts. She does the feeding and I do the cleanup."

"You trying to tell me you're changing diapers? I don't believe it," I said.

Gina walked in carrying my nephew. "He's changing them. Trust me, it shocked me, too."

I felt Candace's hand tugging on my pants legs. I stood up and pulled Candace up with me. "Gina, this is my lady, Candace. I think you may have seen her before, but I can't recall if I actually introduced you two."

"If you did, I don't remember it either." Gina looked Candace up and down like she was taking inventory. I felt her almost shivering next to me. "I just love that dress. Where did you get it from?" Gina said with a smile.

"Thanks, I think I got it from Marshall's, but it's last season though."

"Pity, I'd like to have one just like it."

"I have to admit I have an addiction to shopping. If I see one like it, I'll be sure to pick one up for you."

"Honey, you don't have to buy it, just let me know where to get it. I'd really appreciate it."

"You heard it, Merlin; I have a reason to go shopping now."

Gavin walked back in carrying two beers. I noticed that neither he nor Gina joined us. I could understand why Gina was abstaining, but it did surprise me that Gavin was. Already this visit was turning out better than I'd hoped.

"Gina, we got you a few things for the baby. We hope you like them." I made it a point to let Gina know the gifts were from both of us. I really wanted them to like and accept Candace. I honestly didn't know what I would do if they didn't. Although I hated the way Gina acted with Cojo, I couldn't ignore the fact she was right about her.

"Can I hold Jaylen?" Candace asked.

I wasn't sure how well this was going to go over with Gina, and I tensed up waiting for her response. She had a tendency to say exactly what was on her mind, regardless of how it might come out.

"Sure, just be careful and support his head. He's such a good baby, hardly ever cries."

I wanted to walk outside and make sure I was in the correct house. I stole a look at Gavin, and he just smiled and winked at me. I couldn't get over how different they both were or how at ease they were with each other. It was like they'd been together for a very long time. It wasn't at all weird to me either.

Gina tore into the boxes like a kid at Christmas time. "Merlin, you shouldn't have done all of this. How did you know we needed these things?"

"It was all Candace. She suggested we get the things Jaylen would need down the road since you probably already had everything he needed for right now."

"That's one smart lady you got there. I hope you don't plan on letting her get away."

At first, I almost got offended by Gina's remark. I took it as if she were suggesting I was the one who messed up with my first wife until I realized I was still sensitive about it. Then, I smacked myself in the forehead at my own naivety. I had prepared myself for Gina acting an ass in front of Candace. I didn't really prepare myself for what would happen if they actually liked each other.

"I'm trying to hold on to her. I know she's definitely a keeper."

"Yeah bro, if y'all hurry up and get married, we can raise our children together."

Candace was blushing. "Can you guys not talk about me like I'm not sitting here listening?"

"I'm sorry, babe. I didn't mean to make you feel uncomfortable. I don't know what has gotten into my family. I didn't expect them to call me out."

Gavin chuckled. "Don't be talking about us like we can't hear you either."

Candace gave Jaylen back to Gina after she got up off the floor with the gifts. "Candace, have you ever been married before?"

"Yes, but it didn't work out." Candace hung her head as the smile slipped off of her face.

"Do you have any kids?"

"Come on, Gina, this isn't an inquisition."

"Boy, you brought her over here so I could get to know her. How else am I going to do that unless I get to ask her questions?"

"It's all right, Merlin. No, Gina. I've never had children, but I would like to one day."

"Sounds good to me. What about your parents, have they met Merlin yet?"

"Gina," I hissed as if she would head my warning. I already knew I couldn't control what came out of her mouth, so I didn't know why I was trying.

"Merlin and I talked about his meeting my mother today. She knows about him already; we just have to make the time to go see her."

"That's good. Don't wait too long. I might even have taken to Merlin's first wife if he'd brought her around sooner. Oh dear, I'm sorry. I didn't mean to bring her up."

"It's okay, Mrs. Mills; I know about her. I'm fine with it."

I didn't know if I wanted to choke Gina or kiss her. Candace never wavered. For all of her nervousness, she handled Gina like a pro. I liked that I didn't have to run interference with her. It felt good to have all the people I cared about in one room, but I couldn't help but wonder what was going on with Cojo.

31 GAVIN MILLS

Two Months Later

Gina was going back to work, and I was a little anxious. In most cases, the men go to work and the women raise the children. Our case was a little different. For now, Gina was going to work, and I was going to take care of Jaylen. It wasn't a decision that we made lightly. Of the two of us, Gina had the better-paying job, but that wasn't the deciding factor. We decided that I should be the one to raise our boy to be a man. It was a huge responsibility, but I was up for it.

My anxiety came from how Gina would look at me after working all day. I didn't want her to regret her decision to marry me or to think she was still raising me.

"When you get home tonight, we're going to have to go through some of this mail that is stacking up on the living room table."

"What mail?" Gina had just finished pumping milk into bottles. I could tell she was already having separation anxiety, and she hadn't walked out the door yet.

"I haven't opened them, but you got those two certified letters yesterday. You just tossed them on the table and I'm sure they're important."

"Damn, I forgot all about them. Can you deal with it? I feel like I'm losing my mind. I just don't want to go back to work and leave my baby."

"I know, but it needs to be done. I got Jaylen, you know that, right? If I went to work too, we'd end up spending more money with daycare, and they wouldn't give our child the individualized care we would."

"That's not the issue. I know you can take care of him even better than I can. I just don't want to miss anything with him. He's holding up his head now and smiling. Will you promise me you'll record it if he does anything else new?"

"Of course I will." It made me feel better when she acknowledged I was completely capable of caring for our child. I didn't start stressing about it until she started walking toward the door.

Gina looked at her watch. "I have to go." She picked up Jaylen and gave him several kisses on his face and neck as tears streamed from her eyes. I hated to see her cry, but I couldn't fix it. She placed Jaylen back in his crib. I opened my arms and she came to me. I kissed away her tears as her hurt became my hurt.

"You'll call me if anything comes up?"

"I sure will. I'm going to try to keep him up today so he can sleep longer at night."

"Okay, but I don't want him cranky when I get home from work. That's when I'll want to play with him."

"Fine, then I'll make sure he gets a nap before you get home. Don't worry about anything. I've got this. If there's anything else you want me to do, send me a text."

Her shoulders were shaking as she sobbed, and the only thing I could do was hold on to her. We were in such a comfortable place where everything fit. Much better than I imagined and it was a little bit scary. I wasn't used to things going right for me, and more than anything, I didn't want to mess up.

"Let me go before I pick up the phone and tell them I quit."

I practically pushed Gina out of the baby's room to the door. I knew how hard this was for her. I didn't even like going to the store without them, so I completely understood how she was feeling.

"Go before he wakes up and makes it harder for you. We'll be fine and no crying while driving! We can't have you getting into an accident." She nodded her head.

Gina still had tears on her face as I closed the door behind her. I was powerless to help her with that, but I could make sure everything in the house was okay when she got back. I was really curious about these certified letters. In my experience, nothing good came by certified mail.

I went to get them. When I opened the first letter, I almost called Gina and told her to come back home. Rather than alerting her prematurely, I decided to call the number and find out exactly what it meant.

"Hello, may I speak with Mr. Ambrose?"

"May I ask who's calling?"

"Gavin Mills."

"Hold on please and I will see if he's in."

I was placed on hold for less than a minute.

"Mr. Mills, thank you for returning the call. I'd almost given up hope of getting in contact with you."

"My...the letter was addressed to my...uh...Gina Meadows, and she asked me to find out what it was about."

"Yes, the letter was addressed to her, but it actually concerns you and Merlin Mills. Are you able to get in contact with him?"

"Yeah, sure. What's all this about?"

"I would prefer to discuss this in person if I can. Can you ask your brother to come in with you to meet me?"

"I'll call him but if we come, I'm going to have to bring my son. He's a newborn, and I don't trust him with sitters."

"Well, congratulations. By all means bring your son. What I have to say won't take long. Just phone my secretary and let her know when you can come in, and I'll make myself available."

"Okay, I'll see if we can get there today."

"Thanks, and I will see you both soon."

I hung up the phone and called Merlin. He didn't answer, so I sent him a quick text asking him to hit me back. Thankfully, he called right back.

"Hey, what's up?"

"I know you're busy at work, but Gina got this certified letter from a lawyer and she asked me to handle it. I called and the dude said it concerns both of us."

"Us? What is it?"

"I have no idea. He wants us to come to his office as soon as possible. Seems like he's been trying to get in touch with us for a minute."

"Where's his office located at? If it's not too far, I could meet you there on my lunch hour."

"Hold on, let me get the envelope. I think it's in Cobb County."

"Text me the address and I'll meet you there at noon."

"Will do. I'm bringing Jaylen with me because Gina went back to work today."

"Oh man, I know that was hard on both of you."

"It really was. But let me call this guy back and let him know we're coming. I wish he would have just told me over the phone instead of making us drive all the way over there."

"I know that's right. Maybe it makes the dude feel important when he can inconvenience someone else."

"Yeah, whatever. I'll see you at noon." I hung up and called the lawyer back letting him know we'd be there. I was about to get off the phone when I remembered the second certified letter which was from a different attorney's office. I was beginning to feel like this was some type of scam, so I had a little bit of attitude when I made the second call. '

"I need to speak to Mr. Ayers."

"This is he. May I ask who's calling?"

"My wife received a certified letter asking her to contact your office. I want to know what this is about."

"What is your wife's name?"

"Gina Meadows."

"Hold on and let me pull her file."

I assumed his ass was so busy he couldn't remember who he sent out letters to, but I doubted it since he was answering his own phone.

"Thanks for holding. Sir, I appreciate the phone call, but this matter is regarding your wife. Do you have a number where I could reach her or could you please have her call my office?"

I was really irritated now. Gina asked me to handle this, and it looked like I wouldn't be able to. "I'll ask her, but she's going to be pissed, especially if I can't tell her what this is about."

"I understand. Please tell her it is very important I speak with her."

I didn't even bother to say goodbye. I'd relay the message; what she decided to do about it would be strictly up to her. If I was going to meet Merlin at noon, I had a lot to do. I was still practicing getting out of the house with the baby in a timely fashion. Something almost always went south when I'd tried it before. Hopefully things would be easier this time around.

32 MERLIN MILLS

I was waiting for Gavin outside of the lawyer's office when he and Jaylen got there. He looked stressed, and I struggled not to laugh at him to his face.

"I could use a little help here," he said as he bent in the car to unstrap the car seat.

"Are you having a bad day or something like that?"

"No, but there are a million things you need to have when you travel with a baby. I should have made a damn list because I had to turn around like three times. It's annoying, and I don't see how Gina does it."

"Maybe you should sit down and watch her prepare. I'm sure she had a little practice and that's why she's so good at it."

"You might be right about that one, because I think I've brought everything but the damn stove."

I grabbed the diaper bag which was stuffed to the gills, and the blanket from the passenger seat of the car. "You really think you're going to need this blanket? You got enough clothes on him plus a hat. It's like ninety degrees out here."

"But we're going into an office building, and we don't know how long we'll be sitting in there. They like to keep those places cold so folks don't fall asleep."

"I can't disagree with you. Come on, let's see what this is about so I can get back to work, and you can get this little man back home before all hell breaks loose."

I approached the secretary while Gavin took a seat. His face was still broken down into a grimace. I said a silent prayer that this lawyer didn't start no mess which would mess up our day.

"We're here to see Mr. Ambrose. I'm told he is expecting us."

"Your names, sir?"

"Merlin and Gavin Mills."

"Fine, sir. Would you take a seat? I'm sure he will be with you shortly."

A short time later a short, balding white man came out into the foyer to greet us. I grabbed the diaper bag while Gavin grabbed Jaylen. We followed him down a short hallway to his office.

"Thank you both so much for coming in to see me."

I said, "What's this all about?"

"This is about your biological mother, Tabatha Fletcher. I've been appointed the executor of her estate, which has been in probate since her death."

I exchanged looks with Gavin, who seemed to be as surprised as I was. We had only learned she was our mother shortly before her death, so we were surprised there was any mention of us at all.

"Our mother left a will?"

"No, she didn't, but she did have some insurance policies, which need to be disbursed. Technically, both of you were entitled to the money when you reached the ages of twenty-five. However, for whatever reason, it doesn't appear as if those policies were cashed in or converted."

"Wow," Gavin and I both exclaimed.

"Excuse my frankness, but how much money are we talking about?"

"You are each entitled to receive fifty thousand dollars minus taxes, of course. In addition, there is the matter of her life insurance policy, which designates Gina Meadows as guardian for you two. Since you're both of legal age, there is no need to have Miss Meadows administer those funds."

"Get out of here. Is this some kind of joke?" I was angry because if it was, it wasn't funny. Tabatha had plenty of time to tell us about these policies if they existed, and she didn't. I didn't believe it.

"I assure you it's not a joke. I understand your time is precious and so is mine. Now, if I could get your signatures, I will have my secretary cut the appropriate checks. You have the option of having my office calculate the taxes or paying them yourself. I would recommend your letting us handle this part of the transaction since we are more familiar with these types of taxes, but the decision is yours."

"I don't mean no harm but if those checks are real, I would prefer to take mine right to the IRS and let them calculate the taxes for me. That way if someone messes up, it will be them," Gavin said as he scooted to the edge of his seat.

I had to agree with my brother as he made a valid point. Besides, I'd like to see a check for fifty thousand dollars just once in my life with my name on it.

"Me, too. We'll take care of the taxes."

"Mr. Mills, you have a son; you might want to consider taking out a policy on him, much like your mother did for you. As a representative of—"

"Uh, Mr. Ambrose, I'll be sure to discuss this with my wife, and if she agrees, we'll call you. How about that?"

"Again, that's your prerogative. I'll be right back."

Mr. Ambrose left us alone in the office. I was so stunned I didn't know what to think.

"Man, is this shit crazy or what? Gina can stay home now if she wants to. This is great."

"I'm speechless. I guess Tabatha loved us after all. I'm also glad she didn't give us the money sooner, because I think we would have both blown it."

Gavin said, "I know I would have. I probably would have killed myself with it. It's coming at the perfect time now. Oh, snap. Dude, Gina got two letters from an attorney; I wonder if Tabatha left her something, too?"

"Hold up, man, something ain't right. I thought when you killed yourself you weren't eligible to receive insurance benefits."

"Nigga, she ain't getting no benefits—she's dead."

"You know what I mean. Most policies have a clause in there that cancels the policy in case of self-inflicted death. I ain't trying to take this money if they're going to come and ask for it back."

"Well, the policy she had on us can't be cancelled. Right?"

"Right."

When Mr. Ambrose returned, I stood up. "I have a question about this life insurance policy. I was under the impression that my mother may have killed herself. Wouldn't that void the life insurance policy?"

"Yes, it would. Believe me, our firm has conducted its own investigation in conjunction with viewing the coroner's report. Your mother couldn't have administered the fatal injection. Therefore, her death has been classified as murder and the terms of the policy are enforceable."

Mr. Ambrose handed us both a check.

Gavin leaped up from his chair shouting, "Holy shit, man. This checks for one hundred thousand dollars! I thought you said fifty thousand."

Mr. Ambrose laughed. "Fifty was for the insurance policy on you—the other fifty is for her life insurance policy. Here is my card just in case you might be interested in purchasing a policy of your own."

"Thanks. Come on, Gavin, let's get out of here before he changes his mind."

I put the envelope containing the check in my pocket and quickly walked out, completely forgetting to help Gavin.

"Oh, you gonna leave your brother hanging now that you got some money?"

I looked around surprised. "My bad, bro." I was slightly embarrassed when I walked back and got the bag. My mind was already a light year away.

"Dude, this check changes everything for me, man. You just don't know."

I nodded my head in complete understanding. I might not have a child, but hey, who couldn't use one hundred thousand dollars? "Gina is going to flip out when you tell her. I almost want to be there to see her face."

"We can go right now if you want. She didn't want to go back to work anyway."

"Don't do it on the job, man. You don't need anybody all up in your business. I've got to get back to work, but I'll holla at you tonight."

"You know, when I found out that Tabatha was our mom, I was really upset with her for not telling us. This feels good to know that she really did care about us." I put the bag in the car while he strapped in Jaylen, who had managed to sleep through the entire thing.

"You ain't even lied. We should find out where she's buried and at least put some flowers on her grave."

"True that. All right, man. I'll call you later. I'm going back to work and photocopy this damn check before I cash it."

"I know that's right. I'm gonna make a copy of mine, too. It will be something that I can share with my son. We don't have a lot of pleasant memories to pass down. This will be one of many."

33 COJO MILLS

As hard as it was to do, I broke down and called my parents. I dreaded making this call to admit how messed up my life had become, and that I needed help.

"Mom," I couldn't get out anything else as sobs escaped my mouth and shook my body.

"Cojo? Is that you?" I could hear the concern in my mother's voice, and it only made me cry harder. I heard my father in the background asking my mother what was wrong.

I cursed my damn luck. I had purposely timed my call to miss my dad. I wanted to just tell my mother and let her fill Dad in the particulars later. But that wasn't my luck. My father must have taken the phone from my mother.

"Pumpkin, what's wrong with you that has gotten your mother all upset?"

I immediately felt ashamed and contrite. "I didn't mean to make her upset, Daddy," I said between sobs. I felt like I was two and was about to be punished.

"Then what's all that crying for. Can't nobody understand you when you're talking like that. Take a minute and get yourself together. Count it on down."

My father was forever the drill sergeant. I didn't want to do a fucking countdown. I wanted to have a full-fledged meltdown with my mother. Damn. "One." I reached for my glass and turned it up.

"Two, three." I took several deep breaths and another sip.

"Are you better now?"

"Yes, sir. I'm good."

"Now, what is the problem?"

I started sniveling again. "Can I talk to Mommy?"

"Your mother is upset. You can talk to me."

Fuck the glass, I grabbed the bottle and turned it up. If I was going to have to talk to him, I needed it. I never told my father I was getting married, and now I had to tell him I was divorced. "I'm in trouble, Daddy. My marriage is over. I don't have a job, and I need money."

"Let me get your mother for you."

I held the phone away from my ear and looked at it, wondering what the hell happened to the 'you can tell me' he'd just uttered.

"Sweetheart? Have you been drinking?"

Leave it to my mother to zero right in on it. "Mom, if you went through what I've been going through, you would have one drink, too."

"Sounds like more than one to me."

"Mother, do you want to hear what's going on or are we going to talk about whether or not I had a drink?" I knew that she knew I was fucked-up, but I wasn't about to admit it to her or anyone else.

"I want to hear what has you so upset. Did I hear you say your marriage is over?"

"Yes, Merlin and I are divorced."

"Sweetheart, no. How could you be divorced? Marriage is work. You can't just give up. You're not a quitter. Whatever the problems are, you have to work through them."

"Mom, it's over and done with. I moved back to Alabama."

"Oh my goodness. How? When? Why didn't you tell me?"

"I honestly thought we could fix it, but after I lost the baby—"

"A baby! Oh James, she lost a baby! And she said she's divorced."

My mother was no longer talking to me; she was talking to my dad even though she had me on speakerphone. This was the reason why I wanted to call when she was at home alone. My gut instinct was to hang up the phone. They were going to go back and forth like I didn't even exist until they decided what I should do. I just wanted to tell her to call me back when they figured out.

"Mom!"

"Why are you yelling at me?"

"Because you were talking to Dad like I wasn't on the phone. I didn't want to tell you any of this. But like I was saying, I moved to Alabama thinking I had a job, and it didn't work out, and now my rent is due and I'm about to be put out." I said it all very fast before I lost my nerve or she interrupted me again.

"Oh my. I think you need to talk to your father."

"Fuck!"

"Oh no, you didn't just cuss at me, young lady! You might be going through some things, but that doesn't mean you can disrespect me. I'm still your mother."

"Jesus, Mom. Do you know how hard it was for me to call you? I'm in trouble and I need your help! I don't need to be going back and forth between you and Dad. Can you just make a decision to help me on your own for once? Please?"

It was like the line went dead. I didn't even hear her breathing. "Hello?" I whispered. I had stepped so far over the line it wasn't even funny, and I knew it. I wanted to blame it on the booze, but I was finally saying what was on my mind. My mom let my dad run her. It was like he'd strapped a saddle on her, and she just trotted around like a show pony. She taught me to be my own woman except when it came to them.

"Are you done?"

"I'm sorry. I just don't know what else to do."

"You could come live with us."

"No, Mom. I can't just pack up and travel half way around the world. That's not going to fix anything. I want to make it work here. I only need a couple of month's cushion so I can find myself a job."

"What if you can't find a job? Then what?"

"I'll find a job. It's not like I don't have any skills." This was a little bit harder than I thought it was going to be. I knew I was going to have to grovel a little bit, but she made me doubt myself. I might have found another job by now if I'd actually tried to look for one.

"I don't know, sweetheart. I don't like your being there all by yourself. What if I come and stay with you for a couple of months?"

"Huh? What will that do? My rent will still need to be paid. I'll need to pay my other bills and food. With you here, those things would be doubled."

"I don't think I like your attitude. I haven't heard from you other than a card on holidays, and now that I do—I get attitude."

"I'm frustrated, Mom. I wanted to handle everything myself. I didn't want you or Daddy to have to worry about me. Especially since you weren't all that thrilled about my getting married in the first place."

"You're right about that. I told you that you were rushing things. I should have followed my gut and made you move back home with me."

"We were happy for a while; we just couldn't get past losing the baby. I think he blamed me, or maybe I blamed myself and took it out on him. Either way, it's over." This was about as much responsibility as I was willing to fess up to in the whole mess. All the extra stuff she didn't need to know.

"That's preposterous. What woman would go through the trouble of being pregnant only to lose the baby? That boy is a fool."

It didn't bother me at all that my mother was slaying Merlin. They didn't have a relationship, and the odds of them ever talking again was nil to none.

"I can't focus on who was right or wrong, Mom. I've got to move forward."

"So why did you leave Atlanta? I still can't believe you didn't tell me about any of this. It's so unfair of you to be unloading all of this on us at one time."

"I had to leave. I was hurting so badly, I didn't want to run into anybody that knew me. The only friends I had were friends of Merlin and me as a couple. I didn't want them to choose." I decided to ignore her last statement completely.

"That's pretty noble of you, but I don't know if I would have let some lowlife motherfucker run me off my job or away from my home."

It was official—my mother was pissed. When she started calling folks motherfuckers, I knew it was on. I could hear my dad in the background trying to give his opinions. "Your dad says he has connections in the army, and he can have Merlin squatting in his helmet for the rest of his career."

"Mom, no! That won't change anything. I just need some help."

"Fine, your father and I will wire you some money right now. I'll send you a text where you can go pick it up."

"Thanks Mom, and thank Daddy for me, too."

"Take care of yourself, honey, and never be afraid to call us. We're your parents and we love you."

TINA BROOKS MCKINNEY

"I know. I won't forget again. Thanks." I was emotionally drained when I hung up the phone. It took a load off my mind that my shit wouldn't get put out on the sidewalk, but I needed to get busy and find myself a job. I couldn't keep hiding in the house drinking myself to death.

I turned up the volume on the television looking to pass some time before I had to go get the money. I went into the kitchen and put some ice into a glass and refreshed my drink. Driving to pick up my money was out of the question. The last thing I needed was for me to get a DUI on top of all my other troubles.

Walmart had a twenty-four-hour money service. I sent my mom a text telling her that information. Then, I called Rozz. Saturdays were big days in the church for her. I didn't ask her if she was going that day, because I already knew.

"Hey girl, what's going on at the church this evening?"

"We're not having services tonight. The bishop wants us to go support one of his friends who has started his own church. They're having an open house tonight, and I don't know if I'm going or not."

"I don't believe it. You've been in church every Saturday night since I moved here. Why wouldn't you go?"

"First of all, I don't go to church every Saturday. I go when I want to because I enjoy it. Secondly, I'm very particular where I worship. The devil is alive and very busy. Everybody that speaks the Word doesn't necessarily know the Word."

I was trying to get a sense of her mood. I wanted her to run me to the store later, and I believed the only way I was going to get her to agree would be if I did something she wanted to do first.

"So what are you saying? You don't like the bishop's friend?"

"I'm not saying that. I've never met the man. I just need to pray on it before I make up my mind."

It was a good thing Rozz was on the phone and not in my living room, because she would have caught me rolling my eyes.

"Oh, okay. I was going to ask you if I could go with you tonight. I think I'm finally ready."

"Yeah, right. Do you know how many times you've told me that?"

"It's true this time. I've done everything my way, and I've failed. Now it's time to try something different."

"I guess God has given me my answer about going tonight. He must want me to go to this service. I'll pick you up at six."

"Cool. I'll be ready."

"Uh, Cojo, have you been drinking?"

"See, forget it. I don't need this right now."

"Wait, I didn't mean any harm, but you know. I don't want you going if you're going to embarrass yourself or, uh, me for that matter."

"Like I said, forget it. It was probably a bad idea anyway. If God wants me to go to church, he'll send a car and take me as I am. You act like I'm going to get out in public and act a fool."

"You're right. I'm sorry. God is sending the car. I'll see you at six." I was smiling when I ended the call. If sitting through a couple of hours at church got me what I wanted, I could do it. It might even do me some good and give me a sense of purpose.

I took my glass and went into the bedroom to try to decide what to wear. I had never been to a revival before. We didn't do them in the Catholic church. Our worship tended to be more subdued. I chose a pair of summer slacks and a short-sleeved top. I laid the clothes on the bed and went to take a shower. Then I was going to take a nap so I'd be ready for the festivities.

■■■

Rozz arrived promptly at six. "You look nice."

"Thanks, so do you." I had brushed my teeth about a hundred times, and damn near used the entire bottle of mouthwash trying to get the smell of alcohol off my breath.

"The service doesn't start until seven; I thought we'd get there early so we could get a good seat."

I almost groaned out loud. I didn't plan on sitting front and center at the service. I really wanted to sit closer to the back, just in case I needed to slip out. "Do you think we have time to run into Walmart? I could use some breath mints."

"You can get some at the gas station; I need to fill up."

"What, and pay those gas station prices? I can run into Walmart while you're filling up. This way we could kill two birds with one stone."

"Fine. Just don't go shopping while you're in there. I don't want to be walking in the church all late drawing attention to ourselves."

"I'll be done before you are. I promise." My mother had sent a text letting me know the money was there. I just hoped the line for customer service wasn't that long. I could have waited until the next day to pick up the money, but I would feel better knowing I had the money in hand. I had no idea how much money she had sent either. I just hoped it would be enough to take the pressure off.

Rozz dropped me off in front of Walmart, and I really did run inside. It felt like God was smiling on me because there was only one person ahead of me in line. "Thank you," I mouthed as I genuflected. The cashier was fast and it was my turn in line.

"May I help you?" the cashier asked with a smile.

"Yes, I'm here to pick up some money my mother wired to me."

"Do you have your identification and confirmation code?"

"Yes, I have them." I slid the information over the counter and quietly patted my foot. I kept looking at the door praying that Rozz hadn't finished with her gas purchase.

"Thanks. I see it. Is the address on your license correct?" The cashier entered some things into the computer.

"Yes, everything is correct."

My heart was racing when I saw her counting out money. I stopped counting when she passed two thousand. My mother had hooked me up. Now I could take my time and find the right job, without rushing to take the first thing that came along. The cashier handed me the money in an envelope.

"I need your signature next to the x." She pushed some forms to me, and I quickly signed them and collected the money.

"Will you need anything else?"

"No, thank you." I stuffed the envelope in my purse and ran back outside just as Rozz was pulling up. Perfect.

"See, that didn't take long at all. What's the name of this church anyway?" I asked.

"Mt. Pious Church of Deliverance and Salvation."

"That's a mouthful. I sure hope they got the air conditioner cranked up. It's hot as hell out here."

"Cojo, we're going to church. Please temper your words."

I had gotten what I wanted, so there was no need for me to eat my words. "Are you going to lecture me all night? Because if you are, I'll go home."

"Wait, I…uh…wasn't trying to lecture you. I just thought it was inappropriate to say hell right before we go into church."

"Child, please. Hell is in the bible. And most of the hell-raisers will be sitting next to us in the pews."

"I sure hope I don't live to regret this," Rozz mumbled to herself.

Even though I heard what she said, I didn't respond. As much as I didn't want to be there, I still needed to get my ass back to the house. I wasn't trying to spend any of my money on a cab either. I was going to sit my happy ass in the back of the church, so I could slip out and sip on the flask I carried in my purse. The Lord was just going to have to take me as I was.

We still got to the church early, but not as early as Rozz intended. She went through the door like a woman on a mission. I had to grab her arm before she got away from me.

"I'm just going to sit back here. You know, and get a feel for the place."

"You sure? I see my bishop up front and I wanted to go say hi." Rozz looked to the front of the church with longing in her eyes.

"Girl, do you. This is your element. I don't mind being back here by myself."

"Okay. I'll check on you later." Rozz had clearly walked into her type of environment surrounded by the sanctified sinners. I could smell them from where I sat. I even saw a few of them turn their noses up at me, but I didn't care. I wasn't there to please them. I wasn't the one they had to worry about because I'd probably never come to that church again.

It wasn't a bad building as churches went. The air worked, and that was most important to me. If they were going to be whooping and hollering, I at least wanted to be cool. The congregation got to its feet when the music started playing. There was an air of expectation in the room that was almost palpable. I knew something was about to happen, but I didn't know what as I struggled to get to my feet too. I was already starting to feel a little sleepy, and the service hadn't even started yet.

A slow clamor arose as the choir entered from the side doors in flowing purple robes. The brown faces next to the rich robes lifted my heart. I just hoped the choir sounded as good as they looked.

We stood during the introductory song, but I didn't mind; it was a foot stomper. The choir was on point, and the church showed its appreciation with their shouts and applause.

"I just might enjoy this," I said out loud, but not loud enough to be heard over the thunderous clapping and foot shuffling. I had to give it to black churches—they knew how to rattle the rafters. The doors at the back of the church were pushed open and in walked a vision of fineness in black. His bald head glistened from the globed lighting. I couldn't help but take inventory of everything about him. I hadn't seen a man as handsome as he was since my Merlin. I felt my thong slip between my butt cheeks.

"Amen," I shouted as I waved a bible I'd grabbed from the pew over my head as if it were my own. That man could take me in the church.

34 MERLIN MILLS

I went back to work, but my head wasn't in the game. It was a good thing I only had to push some papers around to look busy because I would have failed miserably at anything else. I pushed back from my desk and threw my pen down on it. With purposeful strides I walked down the hall to Candace's office. Now that the word was out about us dating, I tried not to spend too much time in her office. I stopped short of her door and knocked.

"Come in." Candace's work voice was nothing like her at the house one. It got me every time I heard it. She had to sound hard. It came with the territory. As a leader of at least one hundred men, she commanded respect.

"Hi." I didn't step into her office. I just stood in the doorway at attention. Even though she wasn't my commanding officer, she was still an officer, and it didn't matter if I was fucking her seven ways till Sunday, she got saluted.

"Hi, yourself."

"I would like for you to go home and put on that red dress you showed me the other time. With no underwear, please."

"Say what? Fool, come in here before the entire office hears you." She was trying very hard not to laugh but was failing miserably.

I smiled. "Did you hear what I said?" I asked when I got closer.

"I heard you," she answered seductively.

"I'm taking you out to dinner tonight." I turned to leave but turned back around. "No panties; we're not remixing Keith Sweat tonight either. I want your hair up. To me, it's sexier like that." I walked out and closed her door.

I couldn't stop smiling. I was already thinking about how to make this night extra special for us. A dozen roses weren't enough. I wanted to buy out the entire store. I called the florist we used on base to send flowers to the families of the soldiers who didn't make it home.

"Hey, Gene. This is Lieutenant Mills. I need to place an order for some flowers, but they have to be delivered in a few hours."

"You're cutting it a little close, aren't you buddy?"

"I know, but I just decided what I wanted to do. Trust me, if you can do it, I'll make it worth your while."

"What do you need and where do you want it to go?"

"How many roses you got in the store?"

"Are you kidding me?"

"I'm dead serious. Can you pack them all up in your van and take them to Chops Lobster Bar in Buckhead? I need them there by seven. So if you can't do it, let me know, and I'll get somebody else."

"Are you kidding me? I'll close up shop right now and start filling out cards. What do you want them all to say?"

"Hold on before you start agreeing to this. There are specific colors that I need. I've given it a lot of thought and I need pink, white and red roses only. Do you have all of those colors?"

"Yeah man, I got them."

"Great; put Candace Jamison's name on all of them. I've reserved a corner table at the restaurant. I want her to see these pink and red flowers with her name on them everywhere she walks, and I want the white ones for our table."

"She must be some special chick you going all out like this."

"Believe me, she is. I want her to be the envy of every woman in that restaurant. Can you make this happen for me?"

"Consider it handled, dude."

"Send me an invoice through *PayPal* and I'll take care of it right away. Just make it nice, man. Do me proud."

"Oh, it's going to be nice. I might even wait around to hand her the first bunch myself. This sounds too good for me not to be a part of it."

"I appreciate that, but if you can't stick around, at least leave one dozen at the check-in so she'll walk in carrying them."

"Oh, I'll be there. I can't miss this. Shoot, I'm a romantic at heart, and you're about to make a smooth player move."

I'd been thinking of doing something nice for Candace ever since I took her to meet the family. She was my rock, and I was ready to see if we had what it took to make it on the next level. I wasn't ready to go out and buy a ring, but I wasn't running from the idea either. We would just see what happened.

The money was a blessing, but it wasn't the reason for my actions today. It was time I completely moved on with my life, instead of hovering on the outside of a relationship with Candace. It wasn't fair to her, and it wasn't fair to me either.

After work, I drove home to get dressed. I hadn't been there in days. It almost didn't make sense to keep my apartment since I spent so much of my time over at Candace's, but I respected her too much to shack with her.

I chose my clothes carefully. Candace had never seen me in a suit. I wanted her to be as wowed with me as I was with her. Everything needed to be perfect because she deserved it. Candace and I both got the raw end of the stick when it came to the people we chose as our mates. She was as committed to her relationship as I was, and her man threw it all away. I needed someone I could trust with my heart, and I believed she was the one. I couldn't go through another breakup because the first one almost did me in.

My brother said I should have experimented more with women before I made a commitment. I wasn't that guy. I had seen what it did to Gina, and I never wanted to inflict that type of pain on anyone. I took one more glance in the mirror and at my watch. I was ready to go.

On the drive to her house, I had more butterflies in my stomach than I cared to acknowledge. It was ridiculous to me, especially since Candace and I were already dating. But those butterflies flew away when she answered the door.

"Oh my goodness. How is it that you look even better in that dress today than you did the first time?"

"I'm glad you approve. It was, after all, a special request." Candace was blushing, which made her even more beautiful in my eyes.

"As much as I would like to stand here and stare at you, we should be going because we have a seven-thirty reservation." I held out my arm for her to take, and she did with a flourish. If she thought I was being a tad bit corny, she didn't say it.

"When I told you that you didn't have to wear a suit for my mother, I had no idea how good you looked in it. So, I'm taking it back. If you ever do meet her, you must wear this suit."

"If that's what you want me to do, then I would be honored to do it."

"So, what's up? I've been trying to figure this out all afternoon. It's not my birthday or a holiday, so what's the occasion?"

"I'm doing a rewind with you, Candace. The way we got together was different, and I think we needed to back this up a bit."

A big frown line appeared on Candace's forehead. "Back it up?"

"Although we're dating, we've never been on an actual date. This, sweet Candace, is our first date. So sit back and enjoy these carefully selected songs I put together just for you."

"Boy, if you don't stop you're going to make me cry."

"There's no need to cry. I could've kicked myself when I realized we hadn't done this. I actually enjoy doing things like this."

"Something about you surprises me just about every day, Merlin."

"I sure hope you mean that in a good way."

"I certainly do."

We pulled up to the restaurant, and my nerves kicked up into high gear when I didn't see the florist's van in the parking lot. I would be really be upset if this part of the evening didn't go as I planned.

I walked around the car and opened the door for Candace, and once again gave her my arm. She made me want to be a better me.

"I made the reservation in your name."

"Uh, okay." She looked at me a little strangely, and I could almost see the wheels turning in her head.

"We have a reservation for Jamison," Candace said.

I was standing behind Candace, so she didn't see me nodding my head yes when the hostess reached for the vase full of pink roses. "Then these must be for you," she said.

Candace's mouth dropped open as she squealed in apparent delight. "Oh my God! Merlin, how sweet." She reached for the roses, but the hostess pulled them back.

"I'll carry them for you to your table. Follow me."

Candace kissed me right on the lips like we were alone instead of in a room full of people who were all watching us. We walked a few steps, and we pass another vase of pink flowers. Candace stopped and put her hands over her mouth as her eyes got bigger.

"Oh look, I think these are for you, too," the hostess again shows the flowers to Candace and puts them on a cart she brought with her. Candace was jumping up and down, and it seemed as if everyone in the restaurant had stopped what they were doing. We gathered five more vases of pink flowers before we got to the first vase with the red roses.

Candace was openly crying as the hostess gathered up another five vases of red roses. The cart was full, and a waiter brought another one to follow us the rest of the way. I had to hold Candace up because she couldn't see where she was going with all the tears.

"I can't believe you did all this for me," Candace kept saying.

I was watching Candace carefully as I handed her my handkerchief to wipe her face. When she saw all the white roses surrounding our table with her mother sitting at the table, she practically went to her knees. This was a crowning moment for me. I had managed to put a lot of elements together in a short amount of time.

"Baby, how did you do all this?"

Candace's mom got up from the table and hugged her daughter. As they sat down, I slipped the hostess a tip and asked her to move the flowers out of the way so as not to disrupt the flow of traffic. I plucked two roses from the vase and handed one each to Candace and her mom.

I walked over to Candace's mother and gave her a hug. She was crying as well. "Thank you so much for agreeing to come on such short notice."

"Young man, this was simply beautiful. I wouldn't have missed it for anything in the world. Thanks for inviting me."

Candace was still crying softly and smelling the roses that surrounded the table. "I just don't know what to say."

I was still standing. "I wanted you to remember our first date for the rest of your life."

"What am I going to do with all of these flowers?"

There were twenty-six vases of red, pink and white roses. "Whatever you want to do with them. You can even donate them to the restaurant if you want to."

"I can do anything I want?"

"Yes, baby. Anything." I saw Gene coming forward with the final bouquet, but Candace didn't see him. I'd already anticipated what I thought she was going to do.

"I think I want to take one from each vase and give the rest to the ladies here tonight having dinner."

"Consider it done, but I've already prepared a bunch for you to take home." Gene handed her the bouquet amidst all the snot and bubbles. I looked around the restaurant, and so many of the patrons had their cell phones out taking pictures and recording the entire parade of roses. I wasn't sure how I felt about it either. We went from being undercover to viral in one date. I didn't want any repercussions behind my pubic display of affection.

"I am so outdone right now. I just need a moment," Candace said.

"Thanks, Gene. You did your thing, man. I really appreciate it," I patted him on the back and gave him a hug.

"No, thank you for letting me be a part of it. I just love it when a plan comes together." Gene also gave Candace and her mother a hug before he left. It was the best thousand dollars I'd ever spent.

"Merlin, you didn't have to do all this, but I am so very glad you did. No one, and I repeat *no one*, has ever shown me this type of affection before, and I will cherish this memory forever."

"That is all that matters, boo. Let me get the waiter; I think some champagne is in order, too."

34 COJO MILLS

Whoosh! My drawers were on fire. It was so hot down below, I had to stand with my legs open just to get some air down there. I knew it wasn't the booze because all the women around me were fanning themselves.

I didn't really pay attention to the congregation before I sat down, but ninety-five percent of the people I saw were all young women. It was like someone ran an ad in Hoochies R Us, and they were all applying for the job. They had their short dresses on with their boobs hanging out, being all extra while the pastor came down the aisle shaking hands.

I scooted over to the end of the pew so I could shake his hand, too. My eyes zeroed in on his manicured fingernails and the empty ring finger. This brother was fine, but I wasn't about to compete for him with all these trailer hoes.

The woman behind me grabbed his hand and stuck it over her heart. *Really, bitch?* I thought to myself as I rolled my eyes. I wanted Pastor Devin's attention too, but I wasn't about to be all obvious about it. I was too much of a lady, and I wouldn't mind being the First Lady of his church.

I locked eyes with Pastor Devin, and it was like the blood of Jesus was flowing through my veins. I started praying real loud. "Hail Mary, father God, I'll holler your name. Protect me from your sins, and yeah I might walk in the shadows of death, but I'm not afraid oh Lord, and give us this bread so I can lay down to sleep. The rod and staff will protect me Lord, and I pray for these sinners. Praised be to hallelujah, amen." You couldn't tell me nothing. I was in my moment as my eyes locked with the pastor.

Instead of shaking my hand, he pulled me into his arms and gave me this tight hug. "Damn, your boobs are amazing."

It was like a record scratched inside my head. "Come again?" I had to be tripping. There is no way he said that to me.

"You heard me. I want to talk to you after the service." He pulled away from me and proceeded to the pulpit.

I couldn't get mad at him for what he said. He was a man of God and he spoke the truth. I did have some amazing breasts. I settled back into my chair and waited for the other heifers to settle down. They were mad because the pastor didn't give them the same attention I got. I could feel their hatred ooze over me like paste.

I didn't want to miss a minute of the sermon, but my liquid courage was running on fumes, so I used the bible to hide my face and took a huge swig from my flask. It tasted so good, I had to stop myself from smacking my lips.

"You should be ashamed of yourself," the woman next to me said.

"Bitch, please mind your business. I'm not all up in yours."

Her face alternated between shock and rage as she gathered her purse and changed seats, which was fine by me. I didn't need her judging me anyway.

Pastor Devan started preaching, and it was like he was talking directly to me.

"Know your own self-worth. Don't wait around for someone to tell you how valuable you are. God knows you on the inside and can see through your facade. So stop pretending.

Some of you ladies are single mothers trying to do everything by yourselves. The Lord didn't mean for you to do this alone. Bring them to me. I will help you raise them in the eyes of the Lord.
Some of you are looking in all the wrong places for the man of your dreams. I'm here to tell you he doesn't exist. You are not equipped to see the man you need. You need guidance."

My eyes were drawn to five people who stood up in the front of the church and appeared to be leaving. One of them was Rozz. I frowned because they were distracting me. She stopped at my pew. "Come on, we're leaving."

"Leaving? Why?" I didn't realize how loud I was until she shushed me. I ducked down self-consciously.

"Because we've seen enough."

"Well, I'm not ready to go. I want to hear what he is saying."

Rozz looked truly torn as she looked between me and the front door. "I can't listen to this. I'm sorry."

"Don't be. I'm sure I can get a ride home. You go ahead, I'm fine." I already knew the perfect person to ask.

"Who? You don't know anyone here."

"Go, Rozz. We're making a scene. I'll call you when I get home. I'll be fine."

"Okay, if you're sure," she whispered as she started backing away from me.

"I'm sure." Although the scowl didn't leave her face, she seemed compelled to follow who I assumed to be her pastor out the door. She reminded me of a sheep following her leader which made me laugh. I couldn't be like that; I had my own mind, and it was time I used it.

■■■

"That was a wonderful sermon, Pastor. I thoroughly enjoyed it." I was gushing inside as I gazed into his eyes.

"Thanks. I was beginning to think you had left without my getting the chance to speak with you."

"I had to hide out in the bathroom until everyone else had left. Those ladies were watching me like a hawk."

"They can be a little overprotective of me."

"If that's what you want to call it. I didn't exactly see it that way."

I was sitting in his office as he took off his black robe. The size of his arms had me mesmerized. "How long have you been a pastor?"

"I got the calling when I was in high school, and I've mentored with several bishops until I had enough of a following to open up my own church."

"That's pretty good. It's nice to see young men preach the word." I wasn't even giving my words a lot of thought. I was still thinking about why he singled me out.

"Would you like a tour of the church?"

Honestly, I could have cared less, but I couldn't form my lips to say that to him. "Wait, I have a problem. I let my ride leave me. Do you think you could give me a ride home?"

"Where do you live?"

This should have raised a flag with me, but I was in such a daze it flew right over my head. Why should it matter where I lived if the only reason why I stayed behind was because he asked me to. But of course, he had no way of knowing that I didn't have a car with me so it kind of made sense.

"It's about fifteen minutes away."

"I guess I can do that. Are you going to share your flask or do I need to pull out my own?"

"Mine is empty, but we can get some more on the way to my house." This dude was cool and he wasn't all preachy. I liked that about him. Not to mention how sexy he was.

"Let me show you my church first." I reluctantly followed him on his tour. My feet were already hurting and I really wanted to lay it down.

"You've seen the sanctuary and my office, but this is where I baptize the little motherfuckers."

I sobered up instantly. It was one thing not to be all preachy, but this was on a whole different level. "Wait, what?" I looked up at the ceiling, fully expecting lightning bolts to come down through it.

"Don't go acting all brand new. I love my congregation, but they can be a bit much. Just because they throwing money on my plate, doesn't mean I should have to fuck every one of them. I should be able to pick and choose which ones I favor. Much like I did you." We had stopped beside a small bed which was located next to the baptismal.

I might have been slow on the uptake, but I finally got it why Rozz and her friends had left. This wasn't a man of God—he was a wolf in sheep's clothing. Preying on people's vulnerabilities. "This is nice and all that, but I think we should be going. It's getting late and all." I had made a huge mistake. Why couldn't I have seen it before it was staring me in the face?

He sat down on the bed and undid the buttons on his shirt. "You want to leave right now, before you've gotten a chance to see everything?"

My eyes followed a trail of fine hair down his chest to his navel. My knees shouldn't have gotten weak, but they did. Was it so wrong that I get some attention? I was in my prime, and it just wasn't natural to deprive my body. My mouth started watering.

"Come on. You know you want to suck this dick." He unbuttoned his pants. The imprint of his dick was strained against the fabric of his pants.

He wasn't even lying; I did want to suck it. It was like I was in a trance, but at the last second I pulled back, because something about this man was making my flesh crawl. "I don't think so. I really need to be going."

"Then I guess you need to find your own way home. Ain't nobody got time for no tease. I could have had any one of them hoes up in here, and I chose you."

"I'm sorry I disappointed you." I practically ran out of that church, and by the time I got to the street I was panting. I felt like I'd just faced Satan himself and escaped unscathed. Which only reinforced my beliefs about more sinners being inside the church than outside.

Dodging a satanic bullet was one thing, but being alone in the dark in unfamiliar territory was another. It was a bit daunting at first. I hated to do it, but I was going to have to call Rozz and beg her to come get me. I reached for my phone, and I realized I'd left my purse inside the church. Not only that—my money was in that purse! I went into full panic mode.

"Fuck!"

I rushed back to the church and beat on the door like a crazed person. I could not believe this was happening to me. I just couldn't. I needed that money to pay my rent. It was my lifeline, and I was sinking fast. I knocked on the door for a full five minutes before Pastor Devin answered. He had this evil smirk on his face that caused a shutter to race down my spine.

"Did you change your mind about this dick?" His pants were still undone and sagging off his narrow waist. This time, there was nothing remotely seductive about it. All I felt was revulsion.

"No, ah, I left my purse inside. I need to get it." Instinctively, I knew that I couldn't let him know how much my purse meant to me.

"Really? I don't recall you having a purse."

"I had it. You have to remember it too, because you asked me about the flask I had in it."

"Oh, that's right. You can look inside for it, but you need to hurry up. I've made some other plans." He rubbed his crotch suggestively.

I pushed past him and ran over to the pew I'd been sitting on, but my purse wasn't there. I sprinted back to his office and saw it sitting in the chair across from his desk. I exhaled as relief rushed through my body. I snatched my purse up and stomped out of the church. I was so relieved about getting my purse back I decided against calling Rozz. I figured a walk would help me clear my head. The last thing I wanted was to be standing out in front of the church like a desperate hoe when the pastor left. I was happy I didn't get him to drive me home because I didn't want that bastard to know where I lived. He didn't have to worry about my coming back to his house of sin again.

35 GINA MILLS

Getting back into the workflow mode was hard for me. I no longer cared about anything outside the four walls of my apartment. Inside those walls, I had everything I needed. Including a husband whom I was beginning to fall in love with. It was hard to believe, especially considering how much I hated him when he was growing up, but it was true. My feelings had completely changed, and I'd started to see him in a different way. For me, our little arrangement for the sake of our child was becoming much more.

As I put my key in the door, my breasts started to ache. It was feeding time. I fulfilled a need for my son whom no one else could, and there was no feeling like it in the world. It was difficult to describe, but it was very fulfilling. I mattered to him if for nothing else than for my boobs. On the other hand, Jaylen was so much more to me. He gave me a purpose I never had before.

"I'm home." I sounded like a sitcom actress from the eighties. I giggled feeling like a schoolgirl. Gavin came out of the kitchen drying his hands on a dish towel.

"Hey, boo. How was your day?" Gavin gave me a long hug, and I didn't want to let him go.

"Long. I missed you guys." I was dying to tell him I missed him as well, but I was scared. These emotions I was feeling were so foreign to me, I didn't know how to process them.

"We missed you, too." Gavin pulled me over to the sofa to sit down.

"Where's Jaylen, he must be hungry. My boobs feel like they're about to pop."

"You might have to pump them because our schedule got a little messed up today. I just put him down about half an hour ago."

I immediately got scared. "Is everything okay?" I didn't doubt Gavin's ability when it came to taking care of our child, but that didn't mean something didn't happen out of his control.

"Relax. Everything is fine. I just had to make a run and it threw off the schedule."

"Ah man, that sucks. He's going to be up for most of the night."

"True, but when I tell you what happened today, it's going to seem like such a small price to pay."

"Why? What happened?"

"Remember those letters I told you about this morning?"

"Yeah."

"One of them I was able to handle. The other one you have to do it yourself because they wouldn't talk to me."

"I don't know what a lawyer would want with me. I don't owe nobody any damn money."

He pulled a folded piece of paper out of his shirt pocket and gave it to me. "What's this?" I didn't feel like playing any guessing games. I wanted to take my clothes off, get a glass of wine and relax.

"Look at it."

I was about to get pissed, but I suppressed it. I didn't want to ruin what was left of my night. I unfolded the paper that actually turned out to be a check. "What the hell is this?"

"It's ours. Tabatha had taken out an insurance policy on Merlin and me for one hundred thousand dollars. We should have gotten it years ago, but she never told us about it. On top of that, she had a life insurance policy on herself for one hundred thousand dollars, and we were named as beneficiaries. Is that not insane or what?"

"Get the fuck out of here. Do you mean you both got a check for this amount?"

"Yup. We'll have to pay taxes on it, but as far as I'm concerned there will still be enough money so you don't have to go back to work right away, unless you want to."

"Are you serious? Well, I'll be damned. Wait, what do you mean I don't have to go back to work?"

"Just what I said. I saw how you were this morning, and I don't ever want to see that look on your face again."

I shook my head back and forth. "This is your money, Gavin. I can't ask you to do that."

"I told you, woman; this is our money. Don't you get it? We're married. What's mine is yours, and I should hope you feel the same way."

"This might be true for most normal married couples, but we're…different."

"I wish you would get that out of your mind. We might have started differently, but we're the same. Or at least we can be, if you'll let it happen."

"You really mean it?"

"Give me time, I can show you better than I can tell you." He leaned forward and kissed me like a man kissed a woman. It left me breathless because I wasn't expecting it. I knew my feelings for him had changed, but I didn't know he was feeling the same way, too.

"This is really unbelievable. When I found out that Tabatha was your mother, I thought she was the coldest and most heartless bitch I'd ever met. She really fooled me. It's good to know she truly did care about both of you."

"We thought the same thing. But you know what? If Tabatha had told us about the policy a few years ago, we would have blown the money. Now, we're both more responsible and can use it wisely."

"I just don't get it. She killed herself. How were they able to pay out her policy?"

"Trust me, we asked the same question. She must have thought about this very carefully. She had to have our father inject her with the drugs, and then she probably injected him."

"I guess so."

"I think you should call that attorney tomorrow about the other letter you received. Wouldn't it be something else if our dad had a policy too and his lawyers are contacting you?"

"I seriously doubt it. Your father was a selfish son-of-a-bitch, and even if he did have a policy, chances are his new wife would be the beneficiary on it."

"Well, it wouldn't hurt to call the office and find out. It would blow my mind if he did. Either way it works out, the choice is still yours about going back to work. I know this money won't last us a lifetime, but it will hold us over until Jaylen gets a little bit older."

"I'm so happy right now I just don't know what to say. Going into work today was probably the hardest thing I've ever done. I made a promise to myself I wouldn't come home whining and crying about it. I was just going to suck it up no matter what."

"Well, now you don't have to. I'm not saying you have to quit, but at least you have a choice."

I heard Jaylen stirring on the baby monitor. "I'm going to go see about him."

"Okay, and I'll go warm up our dinner."

"Do you think we can get a bigger place?"

"Absolutely." Gavin pulled me to my feet and kissed me again. I wanted to rip his clothes off and show him what I was feeling, but it was going to have to wait till later.

"I wish the lawyer's office was still open, but you can best believe I will be calling him first thing in the morning."

"Are you going to go to work tomorrow?"

Despite my best efforts to keep a smile on my face, it faltered. "I can't just call them and say I won't be back. It wouldn't be right, and I don't want to burn any bridges. I'll talk to my supervisor in the morning to see what we can work out. I'd be willing to do it part-time, or from home like I did while I was on maternity leave. Just knowing I don't have to do it will make all the difference in the world."

"Whatever you decide to do, babe, is cool with me. You'd better get your son before he brings the roof down. Those days of him being a quiet baby are over. He showed me today what he was working with. He's got a set of lungs on him."

"Aww. He's crying more?"

"I don't think he's crying because he wants something. I think he's figured it out that when he cries, it gets our attention. It's like he's training me instead of the other way around."

"That's too funny. Let me go get him. I'll be back in a minute."

36 COJO MILLS

Rozz was right about one thing. God had been talking to me, and I hadn't been listening. She heeded the warning about Pastor Devin when I didn't. Had I listened to her, I would have been at my house, chilling in my bed, instead of hoofing it to the house. It was a good thing I realized I didn't have my purse before I got too far away from the church. It would have been tragic if I'd had to walk back. I wouldn't have been able to get in my car or my apartment.

I decided to concede the fact I was being stupid and call Rozz. She would probably be a little mad at me for not listening to her when she asked me to leave. But I felt like she would still come and get me if I asked her to. I wouldn't know until I did. She might even welcome the opportunity to come get me, just so she could say I told you so. I pulled the phone out of my purse and made the call. The worst thing she could do would be to tell me no.

"Cojo, are you all right?" Rozz sounded like she'd been sleeping.

"I'm sorry, did I wake you?"

"That's okay, is everything all right?"

"Yes and no."

"Are you home yet? You sound out of breath."

"No, not yet. I'm walking."

"What the hell do you mean you're walking? I thought you said you had a ride."

"I thought I did, but I guess I was wrong."

"Where are you? Do you know how far our apartment is by foot?"

"I'm on the same street where the church was. It's dark though so I don't know the name of the street."

"How do you even know if you're going in the right direction?"

"It's the same way we came, so I think I'm good."

"Why didn't you ask the pastor to give you a ride?"

"It's complicated."

"I knew it. I had a bad feeling about that dude. Let me throw my clothes on; I'm coming to get you."

I wasn't even going to front and tell her I would be fine. Being out alone, and at night, is never a good thing. Especially when I didn't even know where I was. "Thanks, Rozz. From now on, I'm going to stop being so hardheaded and listen to you."

"I hope so. This is not only dangerous, but it's dumb, too. I can't wait to tell my pastor what his friend allowed to happen. Keep your keys in your hand in case you need them as a weapon. I'm on my way."

"I'm on the right-hand side of the street about two blocks from the church."

"Okay, see you in about ten minutes."

"Thanks, bye." I pulled my keys out of my purse and held them in my hands. I didn't even have time to feel the relief that Rozz was coming before someone hit me over the head causing me to fall—face forward onto the sidewalk. My forehead connected with the cement with such force, I could feel every piece of sand in it. My phone and keys flew from my fingers.

My head hurt so badly, it hurt to think. "What the fuck?" I rolled over on my back hoping to see my assailant. It was a man.

My attacker snatched the strap of my purse and began wrestling it from me. I tried to hold onto the thin strap, but had to let go when he stomped on my chest. His brutality took my breath away. "It ain't worth dying over it, bitch."

When I still didn't let go, he kicked me in the head. I tried to see his face, but my vision was doubled, and I couldn't figure out which face to concentrate on. "Please," I begged before everything went dark."

I woke to Rozz screaming my name and shaking me. My head felt like someone was playing a bass drum inside of it. I reached up to touch it, and my fingers were covered with this sticky substance. I groaned. It was so tender to the touch.

"Thank God you're okay. Should I call the police?"

"My purse." The sound of my own voice made my head hurt worse.

"Can you sit up? I don't see your purse. All I found were your phone and keys."

I let Rozz pull me to a sitting position. It felt like my entire world shifted on its side. "Did you see anybody near me?"

"No. I drove past you, and when I got to the church, I turned around because you weren't answering the phone."

"Damn, I don't know what I'm going to do."

"We're going to get you off this sidewalk first. Did you fall?"

"Hell no, I didn't fall. Someone hit me in the back of my head and took my purse." I started crying, which only made the pain intensify.

"I'm calling the police."

"For what? They're long gone now. At least I have my keys and phone."

She helped me to my feet and into her waiting car. I put on my seatbelt and rested my head in my hands.

"I can't believe you tried to walk home. What happened that you couldn't get a ride?"

"That dick of a pastor asked me to stay after service. But he wasn't interested in helping me to salvation; he wanted to help himself into my pants."

"Are you kidding me?"

"He's got a bed right next to the baptismal. I wouldn't be surprised if he didn't use it as a hot tub. How did you know he was no good?"

"I just got a feeling. Then my pastor confirmed it. I wish I would have insisted you come with me."

"I wouldn't have listened. I'm just so stupid."

"Do you think you need to go to the hospital? Your head isn't bleeding anymore, but I can see it starting to swell."

"This street was empty when I talked to you. I didn't see anyone, and I was paying attention. I swear; I wouldn't be surprised if it were that crooked ass pastor had something to do with this."

"Cojo, are you sure? That's a pretty bold accusation."

"I can't be sure—I didn't see the guy's face. The pastor was angry when I left, so I wouldn't put it past him."

"I think we should call the police anyway."

We'd just gotten to our apartment complex. Rozz came around to my side of the car and helped me inside.

"And tell them what? Do you realize how stupid I will sound telling them about a pastor? They wouldn't believe me anyway. I'm not even sure you believe me."

"You're coming to my apartment. I don't want you to be alone. You might have a concussion, so I want to keep watch on you." She didn't address whether she believed me or not. I don't blame her; it was a harsh thing to think given his so-called calling.

I didn't want to go to Rozz's apartment. More than anything, I wanted to take something for my headache, and fix myself a drink. "I'm going to be alright. I'm just mad at myself for getting into this situation. I'm making some appalling choices. I realize it. I'm going to take a nice hot bath and relax."

"I don't want you to be alone."

"I'll be fine. I'll even give you a key to my apartment so you can come and check on me if you want to."

"Okay, if you're sure, but I don't like it."

"I'm sure. I wouldn't be much company anyway if I came to your house."

"I'll check on you later then before I go back to bed."

I closed the door behind her and went into the kitchen and fixed me a strong cocktail. Hennessey was my truth serum, and there were a number of truths I needed to face. I took three Advil's and ran a hot bath. I didn't even want to look in the mirror because I already knew I looked a hot mess. This was becoming a common occurrence, and it felt like it wouldn't be long before my face just stopped healing itself.

This was the third major beating I'd had in the last six months. First, my husband beat me up for sleeping with his brother; the thugs, and now this. Hell, even Gavin kicked my ass around a little bit when he kidnapped me. I knew my body couldn't take much more of it. I put my glass and my phone on a stool next to the tub before I got in. I brought the phone just in case Rozz decided to call rather than come down so I didn't have to get out of the tub.

The warm water plus the booze calmed me. I was just about to close my eyes when I received a text. It was from my mother.

Hey, baby. Just checking to make sure you received the money we sent you.

Thanks, Mom. I got it. It's in my—" I stood up so quickly I dropped my phone in the water without finishing my response. I had forgotten all about the money which was in my motherfucking purse! I immediately started crying. I didn't know what I was going to do without the money, and I couldn't ask my parents to step in again.

"Oh, Lord! What have I done?" I wailed. My heart felt like it sank right to my feet. I fished my phone out of the tub rethinking my decision not to call the police. I was hoping the thief would take my wallet, but not pay attention to the envelope with the money in it. My phone was dead, and with it, any connection with my mother.

I had to be realistic. There was no way the thief was going to ignore the envelope since it had MoneyGram written right on the outside in big blue letters. Once they found out I had less than twenty dollars in my wallet, they would search for anything else of value. The envelope was too thick to put in my wallet so it was out in the open. Getting it back wasn't going to happen.

I walked into the kitchen and snatched the remainder of the Hennessey. I had fucked up good this time. I also grabbed the bottle of Ambien the doctor had given me after I lost the baby. Distraught, I poured the remaining pills into my hand. I couldn't recover from this mistake. There was not point trying.

I swallowed the pills with the Hennessey and got back into the tub. There was no point leaving a note. It was better no one knew the bitter details of my life. Other than my parents, there was no one else who really cared whether I lived or died anyway. I was sick of fighting the inevitable. I just hoped things would be better for me on the other side.

It didn't take long before the drugs, booze, and a possible concussion knocked me out. It wasn't an unpleasant way to go. My water had cooled, but I pretended I was swimming in a pool. Besides, I didn't have the energy to do anything about it anyway. Instead, I reached for my glass, knocking it to the floor. For some reason, it was funny to me. I giggled myself to sleep.

"Cojo! No!" I heard Rozz's screams sometime later, but I couldn't open my eyes even if I wanted to. I hated that she had to find me naked, but she'd get over it. I wanted to say goodbye and tell her what a good friend she'd been, but I just couldn't find the words. It was really cold now.

37 CANDACE JAMESON

"Captain Jameson," I said as I answered my phone at work. Merlin and I had a fantastic weekend, and I was still basking in the glow.

"Captain Jameson, my name is Amber Rose, and I'm calling from Good Samaritan Hospital in Opelika, Alabama. I'm trying to get in touch with Merlin Mills."

I had a bad feeling in the pit of my stomach. "Lieutenant Mills is in the field. May I ask what this is in reference to?" Merlin wasn't a bit more in the field than I was, but I wasn't about to tell her.

"It's of a personal nature. Can you get a message to him?"

"Based on the need, yes I can."

"He is listed as the emergency contact person for Cojo Mills."

My gut was rarely wrong. I felt it the minute she mentioned my man's name. "Has something happened to his ex-wife?" I made it a point to let Amber know that Merlin was no longer married to that trick, and she was no longer his responsibility.

"She's in the hospital. Can you get a message to him?"

I feigned concern. "Is she okay?"

"She's in a critical condition. So we are trying to reach her next of kin."

Shit. I wanted to tell the lady to keep on dialing, but my conscience got in the way. I didn't want Cojo to die; I just wanted her to go away. I sighed, "Fine. I'll make sure he gets the message. Is there a number he should call, because I know he will have a lot of questions?"

"Yes, the number is…"

I listened while she recited the number. As much as I wanted to take it down wrong, my fingers refused to cooperate.

"Thanks for your assistance."

I didn't feel like it was necessary for me to lie and tell her she was welcome because she wasn't. Every fiber in my body told me to ball up the note and throw it away, but that wouldn't be right. I wasn't trying to piss off God for doing something so mean as to not tell Merlin. Besides, I knew that every relationship had a test, and I felt this was ours.

I picked up the phone and dialed his extension. "Could you come into my office for a minute?"

"Of course, Captain."

A few seconds later he knocked on my door and came in. "Missed me?" He was all smiles, but it faded when he took in my somber expression. "What's wrong?"

"I took a message for you from a hospital in Alabama. Cojo is in a critical condition there. You were listed as her emergency contact."

"Oh shit, are you serious?"

I was watching him carefully trying to determine if he still loved her. We didn't discuss her anymore, and I hated that we were going to discuss her now. His facial features remained the same, but it was anyone's guess what he was feeling on the inside.

"The call seemed pretty legit. They left a number." I pushed the piece of paper across the desk. The longer it sat there without his picking it up, the more I wanted to snatch it back and destroy it.

"What do you think I should do?" He took a seat. I wasn't sure if it was because he wanted to ask my opinion about it, or if he felt unsteady.

"If you knew how hard it was for me to give you this message, you wouldn't ask me." I expected him to ask me why they were calling him, but he didn't.

"I can understand. I would feel the same way if the situation were reversed. Let me rephrase the question, what would you do if you were me?"

"Merlin, I can't be a part of this decision. You have to do what feels right for you. If something, God forbid, happens to her, I can't have you blaming me for telling you not to follow up with this. Then she gets to be immortalized, and I'm the bad guy."

"I would never do that. Ultimately, I know this is my decision, but your opinion matters more to me than anything."

"I appreciate that more than you know. This is going to be difficult for both of us. I can't honestly tell you I want you to go. I also can't ask you to stay."

"Can you just dial the number to see if it's real? She hasn't tried to contact me in any way. It seems weird that she would try now."

I shrugged my shoulders and dialed the number. I put the call on speakerphone. I already knew the number was legit as it was the same number that appeared on the caller ID.

"Good Samaritan Hospital. How may I direct your call?"

Merlin said, "Patient information, please. I'm checking on a Cojo Mills."

"She's listed as critical. Immediate family members are allowed to visit during the hours of ten to eleven or two to three for no more than fifteen minutes at a time."

We might as well have been talking to a machine for all the warmth this lady had in her voice.

"Thanks."

I disconnected the call. While Merlin was no longer her family, they still had the same last name. Things would be a lot simpler in my mind if she had taken back her maiden name when the divorce became final, thereby ending the connection.

We sat there staring at each other in silence. I assumed he had a lot on his mind. I know I did. I couldn't help feeling like things between us would go very badly if he went to Alabama. We didn't know her condition. If she'd been in some type of accident that left her paralyzed or something else dreadful like that. I knew Merlin well enough to know that he would sacrifice his own happiness to take care of her. But how could I tell him my fears without him thinking ill of me?

Merlin broke the silence first. "Her family is overseas."

He didn't have to say it; I knew he'd made his decision. I felt my heart break into tiny pieces and there wasn't anything I could do about it. "I understand."

He stood up and came around the desk. He attempted to kiss me, but I turned my head so his kiss landed on my cheek. I felt tears burning at the back of my eyes, but I refused to let them fall. I had to be strong, if not for myself, but for him. "I'll call you when I know something."

I didn't say anything as he walked out the door. I wanted to run after him and beg him to stay, but my pride wouldn't let me. I was the better woman, but did I do everything I was supposed to do? I was conflicted.

I managed to get through the rest of the workday by keeping to myself and staying busy. I kept my door closed, and instructed my secretary to take appointments for anyone who dropped by without one. When my day was done, I grabbed my purse from my desk and turned out my light. I needed to talk to someone who knew Merlin even better than I did.

I drove to Gina's house praying she would be home and receptive to my visit. When I was last there, she acted as if she really liked me. I hoped my coming by unannounced wouldn't be misconstrued. I needed to talk to her not as her son's girlfriend, but woman to woman.

Gina answered the door, and I fell into her arms crying. It was not how I intended on saying hello. I held it together all day, but the moment I saw her kind face, I lost it.

"What's the matter, honey?" Gina asked as she pulled me inside. She led me over to the sofa with her arms still wrapped around me.

"Is something wrong with Merlin?"

I couldn't speak so I just shook my head.

"Did you two have a fight?"

Again, I shook my head.

"Honey, I'm plumb out of suggestions then. You're going to have to tell me."

She didn't rush me and gave me time to get myself together. I really appreciated it too because I was one big snot ball. Most of which ended up on her blouse. When I could finally speak, I pulled away. "I got a call from a hospital in Alabama. They said Cojo was in the hospital in a critical condition and they were looking for Merlin.

"Oh, Lord. I do hope she'll be all right. I didn't like her in the beginning, but towards the end, we became friends."

This bit of information didn't make me feel any better. I began to regret my decision to bring his family into this.

"Did you tell Merlin about this call?"

"I didn't want to, but I did. I feel horrible about it, but she scares me. She had such a hold on him."

"You love him, don't you?"

I couldn't lie even if I wanted to. "Yes I do, with all my heart."

"I could tell when I met you, and he might not have told you yet, but he loves you, too."

"How do you know?" I began to feel slightly hopeful.

"I know him, remember."

"But why do I feel like I did the wrong thing. I don't want to lose him."

"It's a slippery slope you're standing on. On the one hand, you have to trust your man to make the right decisions. On the other, you can't be no fool with it either. Where is he now?"

"He already left to go to Alabama."

"As he should. She doesn't have any other family here. He needs to find out what's wrong with her and help her if he can."

"But what if—"

"There are no what ifs. He's doing the right thing. If she were to die, he would carry the guilt in his heart for the rest of his life."

"Then why does it feel so wrong to me?"

"You should have gone with him. He didn't need to go there alone."

"If he wanted me to go, why didn't he ask me?"

"How would that sound if he asked you to go see about some other woman? You should have offered to go. Instead of preparing yourself for if she dies, you'd better be getting things ready if she lives."

What she said made a lot of sense to me. "But they said only family members can visit her."

"Then you sit your happy ass in the waiting room. You don't want to see her anyway. Let him know you're there for him. That's all that matters."

Everything became crystal clear to me then. I jumped up from the sofa and rushed to the door. "Gina, thank you. I've got to go. I'll call you as soon as I know something."

"You be careful driving. If you get tired, pull over. If something were to happen to you, Merlin would kill me."

"I will, I promise. Thanks again."

38 MERLIN MILLS

I left work and drove straight to Alabama. A drive that would normally take three hours, I managed to do in less than two. My need for speed had nothing to do with Cojo. I wanted to get there so I could get back.

It hurt me to my heart when Candace wouldn't kiss me before I left. I wasn't stupid enough to believe it had anything to do with how she felt about me. The whole situation was messed up. My responsibility for Cojo was over. I just wanted to assess what was going on so I could get back. However, I hated walking into the unknown.

I parked the car, and after stopping at the front desk for directions, caught the elevator to the critical care unit on the third floor. I didn't feel anything as I walked toward her room. I paused for a moment before pushing open the door.

My heart lurched when I saw her battered face. She looked to have been in a car accident. For a moment, I felt some compassion for her. Her eyes were closed, but she didn't appear to be hooked to any life-saving devices. She wasn't alone in the room, as a petite woman was sleeping in a chair near the bed. I had no idea who she was. I didn't want to disturb her, but she seemed a likely source for information. I cleared my throat.

The woman jumped as her eyes focused on me. She smiled and pointed to the door. She clutched her bible as I followed her out into the hallway. "You must be Cojo's husband, Merlin. I didn't know who else to call. My name is Rozz." She extended her hand to me. Her handshake was warm and firm.

"I'm her ex-husband. Nice to meet you. Did she have a car accident?"

Rozz looked uncomfortable. "Do you want to go sit down in the waiting room?"

I really didn't want to appear rude. But I wasn't sure what my role there was supposed to be. Obviously, Rozz cared for Cojo or she wouldn't be sleeping in her room. So what was I doing there? "Okay."

She led the way again, and I reluctantly followed. I didn't know what Cojo was telling people about us. I wouldn't intentionally put her on blast, but I wasn't about to take the blame either.

"She wasn't in an accident. I think she tried to kill herself. I'm the one who found her."

I was not expecting this news. Cojo was a very strong woman, and I couldn't understand what had happened to her to push her to that point. "Wow. What's going on with her? We haven't spoken in months."

"I know; she told me."

I bristled as I waited for the barrage of insults that I felt would be coming. When they didn't come, I visibly let my guard down. "Were you and Cojo old friends?" I remembered Cojo used to live there before moving to Atlanta.

"Yes we were, although we didn't keep in contact much after she moved. I used to send her cards on holidays, but she didn't really return them. We hooked up again when she moved back here, but things aren't going so well for her here."

"Why?"

"I'm not trying to throw her under the bus, but she's been drinking pretty heavily and making what I consider to be very bad choices."

"I'm sorry to hear that. When did all of this happen?"

She laughed nervously. "What day is it? I've sort of lost track of time."

"It's Monday."

"I found her on Saturday. I've been with her ever since."

"I'm glad she had someone like you in her life." I meant that. I no longer felt any ill will toward Cojo. I attributed my change of heart to Candace.

Rozz said, "I wish I could have done more. I tried to get her involved in my church, but she resisted me. For whatever reason, she felt like God was done with her." She looked quizzically at me as if I was going to elaborate on why she could feel that way.

I could fill in some of the blanks, but I wasn't about to go into the details of my personal relationship with Cojo, especially since Cojo obviously hadn't. "She had some bad experiences in the church as a child. What are the doctors saying? Is she aware of what's going on?"

"The doctor said physically she is out of danger. She was lucky. Another few minutes and she wouldn't have made it. Mentally, I'm not so sure. "

"Why do you think she tried to kill herself and what happened to her face?" This wasn't making any sense to me.

"She told me she was robbed. We'd gone to a church service earlier that night. I didn't like the message, so I asked her to leave with me. She refused, saying she'd gotten another ride home. I feel guilty about it. I shouldn't have left her there alone, but I couldn't listen to that false prophet. She called me later and said she was walking home. I went back to get her and I found her beaten, lying on the sidewalk."

"Damn. I'm sorry, excuse my language. Did you call the police?"

"She didn't want me to do it. She'd been drinking." Rozz shrugged her shoulders.

She said this as if it explained everything. It still wasn't making any sense. "So you took her home, then what?"

"I tried to get her to go to my apartment so I could watch over her because I thought she might have a concussion, but Cojo is very stubborn."

"You don't have to tell me," I said, laughing.

"Of course, you would know that, too. She said she was going to take a hot bath, and she gave me a key to her apartment to check in on her. When I did, I found her in the tub with a bottle of prescription drugs beside her and a bottle of Hennessy."

"I don't understand what's going on with her. When we were together, she hardly ever drank unless she was upset about something."

"That's not the case now. She's been drinking non-stop."

"Is she aware of what's going on?"

"She's been going in and out. She knows she's in the hospital, but she isn't talking much."

"I think you should go home and get some rest. I'm going to be honest; I don't know what I'm supposed to do here. I probably should get in touch with her parents. They need to know."

"I understand. Maybe she'll tell you what's wrong since you obviously know her better than I do. I am going to take you up on your offer though, because I could really use a shower and a nap. I feel so disgusting."

"You've been a good friend. I'll see what I can find out, but I don't know if she will talk to me. We weren't exactly on speaking terms."

She pressed a phone and some keys into my hand. "I have a feeling she will speak to you. I can tell she still has feelings for you. I'll come back to stay with her after I've rested for a bit."

"Don't get me wrong. I care about her as a person, but all that other stuff—it's done." That was all I was willing to say about our relationship. I just didn't want Rozz to have any false perceptions about my being there.

"I understand. I'm under no illusions about you two. Cojo made it perfectly clear to me that she messed up and it's over. Just try to get to the bottom of her troubles. The doctor said they are going to be transferring her to the psych ward for evaluation. It's standard procedure."

"Damn. She's going to hate that. I'm going to call her parents, and I'll stay with her for the night. After that, I may need to head home."

"Thanks again for coming. You seem like a good guy; I just wish we would have met under different circumstances."

"Me, too. Get some rest now and I'll see you in the morning."

"My number is in her phone. Don't hesitate to call me if you need me."

"Thanks, I will."

I was nervous going back inside the room. Rozz had given me a lot to think about, but it didn't change how I felt. Of course, I had some empathy for her, but I wasn't compelled to do anything extra for her.

Cojo's eyes were open when I went back inside. I hated to see her all banged up. It took me back to that awful day when we had a physical fight. In the heat of the moment, I put my hands on her, and I still regretted it to this day.

"Hi." I didn't know what else I was supposed to say to her. I felt like I didn't even know her anymore.

Cojo's eyes filled with tears and what looked like remorse. "You shouldn't have come."

I couldn't have agreed with her more. I felt out of place and useless in this situation. "Someone from the hospital phoned me. I hope you feel better than you look." She cringed. My words sounded much harsher than I intended them to be.

"Just barely."

"That didn't come out at all how I wanted it to. I was trying to be funny."

"I know. You look good."

I felt really uncomfortable. I wasn't trying to get personal with her. "I haven't spoken to the doctor yet, but I think I should call your parents."

She started to cry then. Instinctively, I wanted to go to her and comfort her, but I didn't want to give her any mixed signals. "I can't face them now."

"Why? What's going on with you?" I allowed her time to get herself together. I didn't know if she was going to answer me or not.

"My life is falling apart. Everything about it sucks. I just don't want to be here anymore."

"So, you're telling me that when you get out of here you're going to try this again?"

"I, uh…"

"That's not cool, Cojo. Things can't be as bad as you're making them out to be." I was struggling with this conversation. I didn't want to believe karma was kicking her ass, but it seemed to be true.

"They are. I'm miserable here. I don't have a job, and I'm running out of money."

"So, this is about money then?" I was growing impatient. I didn't want to be there, and it showed on my face.

"No, it's not only about money; it's a culmination of everything. I thought this place would bring a new beginning for me, but I hate it here."

"Damn it, Cojo, so you move. When did you become this cowardly person? If you don't like your life, change it. Why the hell did you move here in the first place?" I didn't intend to lash out at her, but she was pissing me off.

"Because I didn't want to risk running into you! I have to live with what I did to us every day. Seeing you would only make it more difficult for me."

"It was rough in the beginning for me too, but I've moved on. You should, too."

"I heard that you and your brother made up and that he and Gina were together. I didn't realize you'd moved on, too?"

I knew I was over her when it didn't bother me to hear her talk about my brother. A short time ago it would have driven me insane. Now, I could care less. Gavin and I were in a better place, and his life had turned around. "You've lived all around the world. I still don't understand why you came here."

"I knew a little about the area and it was the first place to offer me a job."

"What happened with that?" She squirmed in the bed. It felt like I was pulling teeth with her.

"It just didn't work out."

"Did your drinking have anything to do with it?"

"Rozz can't hold water in a bucket."

"She wasn't throwing you under the bus. She obviously cares about you. You should be glad you have her as a friend."

"I'm glad, but she can't fix me. Nobody can." She started crying softly. I felt sympathy for her as a human being going through a struggle, but that's where it ended.

"Why won't you let your parents help you? You and your mom used to have a great relationship."

"I just got around to telling them briefly what happened to us. They sent me some money to help with my rent and whoever did this to my face stole it. I couldn't tell them I'd been so careless. Mom already wants me to move in with them. I just couldn't."

It was an ah-ha moment, and I felt like I was getting to the crux of the matter. I could actually help her out a little bit financially, but the question became did I want to. "You should get some rest. We can talk some more later when you wake up."

"You're staying?" She looked hopeful.

I needed to nip this hope I saw in her eyes in the bud. "I'll stay until Rozz gets back. Besides, I want to talk to the doctors too before I head back to Atlanta."

Cojo turned her head away from me. I'm sure it wasn't what she wanted to hear, but I wasn't trying to give her any false hope. I walked out into the hallway to make several phone calls. Candace didn't answer, so I left her a voicemail letting her know I arrived safely. As I was driving here, I'd come to a decision about our relationship. I was ready to move on to the next level and ask her to marry me.

I took the short walk to the waiting room and made the call I'd been dreading. I used Cojo's phone and called her mother. She answered right away.

"Cojo, are you okay? I've been worried sick about you." The phone call dropped out before I could answer. I tried to make the call again, and I didn't get a signal, so I used my phone.

"Mrs. Winfrey, it's not Cojo, it's Merlin. I was using her phone but it died."

"I was wondering what happened. I kept calling her back…"

"I hate to be the one to tell you this, but your daughter is in the hospital. I'm told she tried to kill herself, but she's okay."

"What? Not my baby, she wouldn't do something like that. What did you do to her?"

"Me? I didn't have anything to do with this. I haven't seen or spoken to Cojo in months. She told me you knew about the divorce."

"She told me. I just think young people give up too easily. Marriage is not a cakewalk; you have to put in the work."

"It wasn't that simple. I don't know what she has told you; that's none of my business. She didn't want me to call you, but I felt you needed to know. She needs help, and I feel like if she doesn't get it, she will do it again. The next time she might not be as lucky as she was this time."

"I can't believe this. Cojo is not that type of person. Where did we go wrong?"

"It won't do any good playing the blame game. I'm going home in the morning. Her friend Rozz is here, but I think she's going to need you, too. Rozz said they would be transferring her to the psych ward as a precaution."

"If I get the first flight out, could you at least stay until I get there?"

I sighed. I really didn't want to see her mother, but I agreed to do it. "I'll be here."

"Thank you." She hung up on me, presumably to make reservations.

I walked back to Cojo's room to wait for the doctor. I had a feeling it was going to be a long night. If I thought money would solve Cojo's problem, I would gladly give it to her.

From speaking with her, I knew this would only be a Band-aid. She needed help.

39 GINA MILLS

It took me a couple of days to schedule an appointment with the attorney who sent the letter to my house. Gavin believed it would result in a financial windfall, but I was a lot more pessimistic. Ronald wasn't the type of man to prepare for the future, and he damn sure didn't think of anyone but himself. Unless he discovered a way to claim the money in the afterlife, I seriously doubted this was the reason why the attorney contacted me.

It was easier for me to believe Ronald had somehow obtained a loan in my name, and now someone was expecting me to pay for it. If this was the case, they had another think coming. I wasn't paying one damn cent for anything Ronald was connected with. I didn't care if it sent my credit score up in smoke.

Gavin offered to come with me to meet the lawyer, but I told him it wasn't necessary. It wasn't because I didn't want him to know the details of the conversation, rather I didn't want him to see me act the ass if the discussion went to the left. My whole demeanor had changed since we'd had a child, so I didn't need him having flashbacks on how vicious I could be.

"Miss Meadows, Attorney Ross will see you now."

I followed the receptionist into a large conference room. I felt a little silly sitting at this big table, as if we were about to discuss something of mega importance that couldn't be handled in a smaller room.

"Thank you for coming, Miss Meadows. I hope you didn't have any difficulty finding our offices."

I wanted to tell the bitch I was married now, but decided not to because it would raise more questions than I wanted to answer. "No, it was fine. Can we just get to the point?"

"Right, of course. As you know, Mr. Mills is deceased, and there are some matters that still remain to be settled regarding his estate."

"I don't care what your records may say—I don't owe shit."

"Excuse me?"

"I'm not trying to talk ill of the dead, but Ronald was a conniving bastard. He'd pimp out his own mother if he thought she would bring a profit."

"Miss Meadows, I assure you I wouldn't know about any of that. I never met the man. I was hired to settle his estate. Now, may I continue?"

"I'm sorry. If you only knew what this man put me through, you would understand why I flew off the handle. I raised all his children. Stayed faithful to him for over twenty years, and he treated me like scum on the bottom of his shoe."

"I understand."

Her remark made me hotter than fish grease. I hadn't begun to tell her all the humiliating things Ronald had done to me, so she couldn't possibly understand. However, I was getting ahead of myself and decided to remain quiet so I could get the hell out of the office. "I'm sorry, go on."

"Mr. Mills died intestate, meaning without a will. Most of his assets went to his wife of record."

"Which should have been me. Did you know I was the one who found the house he was living in? I did all the work, met with the builders, picked out the furniture, all that stuff because he said we were finally going to get married. I showed up ready to move in only to find out he'd moved some other bitch in. He's lucky I didn't kill his black ass."

"Oh, my. I…um…wow. I'm so sorry this happened to you, but unfortunately, it is irrelevant. The house, vehicles, and any other personal effects he had went to his wife."

"Then what the fuck did you call me for? I don't need you to rub my nose into the shit." I started to get up, pissed because I had wasted my time coming out to the office. It was not like I'd tried to get anything from the bastard or his stinking wife.

"Miss Meadows, could you please sit back down. There are still a few other matters which need to be disposed of." Attorney Ross's face was bright red as I reluctantly sat back down. She probably wasn't used to a real bitch like me.

"I'm so sorry. The man drove me batty. It would be just like him to reach back from hell to fuck with me."

"This won't take long if you allow me to continue." I could tell I was getting on her nerves.

"Go ahead, please; I'm done."

"Mr. Mills named you—"

"I done told you I am not paying shit. I don't owe shit; I ain't got shit, and he ain't worth shit."

Instead of getting mad, Attorney Ross started laughing. She laughed so hard she was having difficulty breathing, but I didn't find a damn thing funny.

"Miss Meadows, I assure you I am not trying to get money from you. Mr. Mills had a life insurance policy from his job that named you as a beneficiary. You are also named on his

401K plan. While his wife is entitled to his assets, she cannot claim the proceeds of those two accounts because of his living designation. She did try to contest it, but the judge ruled in your favor."

I was stunned into silence. It seemed like no one had ever ruled in my favor, and I didn't know how to react to it.

"Are you with me, Miss Meadows?"

"I'm listening."

"The insurance policy was for one hundred thousand, and the value of the 401K is two hundred and fifty thousand." Attorney Ross pushed some forms to me.

I sat stunned for several minutes. It would be just like Ronald to pull this sort of prank on me. My hands were shaking when I picked up the paperwork and tried to read it. The only thing I saw was the amount of the check. "Are you shitting me?"

"I absolutely am not. I just need your signature on these forms, and the check is yours. I do wish to advise you to consult with your tax professional about the ramifications of such a large disbursement. If you don't have a tax professional, I will be happy to recommend someone to you."

"The only thing that man ever gave me was a hard way to go. I'm going to sign these papers and get out of here before you figure out a way to get all of it back. Thank you very much." I signed the papers and waited until she had made copies of them and the check.

"Have a nice day, Miss Meadows.

"You, too. Thanks."

Instead of driving home after leaving the attorney's office, I drove to work. Despite Gavin's urgings to quit, I continued working because I knew his money would not last long with all of us spending it. Knowing I didn't have to work made it easier for me to go in. Everything had changed now. I walked into my supervisor's office and placed the check on her desk.

"Rose, it's been nice working with you, and I hate to do this to you on such short notice, especially since you held my job while I was out, but I have to go."

"Girl, if someone gave me a check like this, I'd go, too. I wouldn't even have come by the office; I would have called you on the phone."

"Thanks for understanding. You've been good to me. If it had been anyone else, I probably would have done the same thing. You take care of yourself."

"You too, Gina. I'm so happy for you. Lord knows you deserve it."

"You're right—I do. Take care."

40 CANDACE JAMESON

I spent the night in the hospital waiting room stretched out on two chairs. I didn't think I would be able to sleep, but I surprised myself. After about thirty minutes, I fell into a deep sleep. Luckily for me, there were no other visitors sharing the space with me. My dreams were of Merlin and what I would say to him when I finally saw him. At first, I thought about letting him know I was there, but I decided against it. I didn't even answer his repeated phone calls to me. I wanted him to deal with the situation at hand first.

Merlin was standing over me when I woke up. "Hey, you." He was smiling.

"Hi." I sat up slowly and stretched. I was trying to make it seem completely natural for me to be there as he sat down next to me. He looked tired, and my heart ached for him.

"How long have you been here?"

"Since last night."

"I've been calling your phone. Why didn't you answer me? I was beginning to get worried."

"I didn't want you to worry about me. I just wanted you to concentrate on why you were here. How is she?"

"She tried to kill herself."

"Oh no! Did she say why?" I knew it was wrong, but I didn't necessarily care for Cojo. However, if she attempted suicide, she must have been in a great deal of pain, and I wouldn't wish that on anyone. I just hoped she didn't leave her pain on my man's heart.

"She's had a string of bad luck. I don't want to call it karma, but it sure looks like it. She's a mess."

"I'm sorry to hear that."

"I don't want to talk about her right now. I've phoned her parents against her wishes. She's going to need someone, and I already let them all know that I'm not the one."

"You did?" His words could not make me happier.

"I told her I'd moved on. I didn't tell her I was in love with someone else because I had to tell you first. I love you, and you would make me the happiest man alive if you would agree to become my wife." He slipped down on his knees in front of me.

I started to shake my head yes, but a little nagging voice in the back of my head stopped me from committing. "Does this have anything to do with Cojo?"

"Of course not, baby. I've been trying to get up the guts to say it before. I wanted to do it at dinner, but then I invited your mom, and now this happened."

"Then my answer is unequivocally—yes. You already know I love you."

"Whew, this is such a load off. I'm sorry I didn't get a chance to pick out your ring, but I thought we could do that together."

"I could not care less about all that. You know I'm not a materialistic person anyway."

"Yes I do, but I want to put that ring on your finger. I want the world to know you belong with me. Would you like a big ceremony, or shall we keep it small considering we've both been down that path before?"

"I'm a simple kind of girl. We can just go to the courthouse with our families."

"Perfect. As soon as we get home we can make the arrangements. Now, are you going to tell me why you're here instead of stretched out in your own bed?"

"I came to support my man. I spoke to Gina, and she said it was okay to be supportive, but not to do it at a distance. She convinced me that it was okay to let you know I stand with you."

"Remind me to thank Gina when I see her! She's a wise woman."

"She sure is. She told me not to be no fool and to come get my man."

Merlin got up and sat in a chair, pulling me into his lap. I felt his dick pushing through his pants. I kissed him thoroughly, liking the way he held me. Never before had I felt so loved or so safe. "I sure wish we were anywhere else besides this hospital. Then I would show you what to do with that thing poking me in the butt."

"Woman, say the word and we can leave right now!"

41 MERLIN MILLS

"Merlin, are you sure you're ready to do this?"

"I thought I was, bro, but the way my knees are shaking I'm not so sure. I don't remember being like this when I married Cojo."

"Getting married isn't like riding a bike, man. Just because you've done it before doesn't mean it's going to feel the same or be the same."

"I understand all of that. Hell, I don't want it to feel the same. Remember, the last time didn't work out too well for me." I felt a frown slip over my face.

"You're right, but Candace is a different woman. It's also a different kind of love," Gavin said confidently.

"What makes you so sure she's so different?" I froze as panic set in. Gavin had fucked my first wife. Was he trying to tell me he'd test driven my future wife too? I guess he could tell by the look on my face that I was about to lose whatever semblance of peace I had left. I got up and started pacing the room, getting more and more agitated with each step.

"Nigga, would you sit your ass down! You're wearing the crease out of your slacks."

I reluctantly took a seat as my foot tapped nervously on the floor. "You still didn't say why you thought this was different."

"First of all, you've changed. You're not the young and naive little boy you used to be. You've gotten a chance to know what makes you happy. Candace has also been through this before, and she knows what she will and won't accept in a relationship. Knowing that you both have tolerance levels that won't be compromised, makes this relationship stronger from the get-go."

I'm just looking at my brother like he'd started talking in a foreign language. He was never the sharpest tool in the shed compared to me, so why was he coming off so profoundly wise all of a sudden? He wasn't this relationship guru, but for some strange reason, I trusted his assessment.

"I want her to be happy almost as much as I want to be happy. I guess that's where this fear comes from. I keep thinking I'm going to fail her."

"And as long as you both keep each other's happiness in the forefront of your minds, you both will be fine."

"That's it, who the fuck are you?"

Gavin laughed long and hard. "Relax, bro; it's me. This isn't rocket science. Any moron can figure it out, even me."

I just shook my head and smiled. "I still don't understand if everything is so right, why am I so nervous? You weren't like this when you married Gina. You were like a rock. How's that possible when you've never been married before?"

"Honestly? I think it was the baby. Seeing him made all the difference in what I had to do. I was determined to be a better father to my child than our father was to us. When I made that decision to do better, the rest was easy. The other thing that helped me was that I'd seen Gina at her worst, and I'm enjoying seeing the best of her."

I was really amazed. I never thought I would see the day when Gavin would care about anything other than himself.

"You really do love her, don't you?"

"Yeah, man. It's legit."

"That's great, man. I'm happy for you. I hope we will be as blessed in our marriage as you appear to be."

"You will."

"I hope so. When I divorced Cojo, I was done with putting my heart on the dotted line. Candace showed me that love isn't supposed to hurt. She gave it to me in small doses, so I didn't get scared and run off. She was slick with it. I didn't realize I wasn't done with love and all into our relationship until I saw Cojo again. I knew for certain I was ready to move on then."

"Wait, were you still holding out hope that you two would get back together?"

"I don't know how to describe what I was feeling. I'm not a quitter. Sometimes it would fuck with me that I walked away from it."

"Come on, man. You didn't fucking walk away by choice. I can't let you carry that all by yourself. You two might have still been together were it not for me. I feel bad about it, but every time I see you look at Candace, I can't help but to think this is the way it was meant to be."

When I thought about it that way, I started to relax a little bit. Cojo and I were happy in a juvenile sort of way. We were playing grown-up for the most part. We might have rushed into marriage because her mom wanted to move Cojo away, and Gina couldn't stand Cojo. My relationship with Candace felt more mature and sincere. I didn't want to marry her to keep her; I was marrying her because I wanted to.

"All right, man, I'm ready now. Candace probably thinks I'm not coming."

"Candace is okay. It's Gina who is sending me about one hundred texts asking what's going on," Gavin said, laughing.

"Then we should not keep our ladies waiting any longer."

Getting married in Vegas was Candace's idea, and I quickly jumped on board. It was the perfect solution to our needs. We could have the no-fuss wedding that we both wanted, and a mini-vacation all rolled up in one. Having Gavin and Gina come along with us was an extra bonus. Candace had even arranged to have her mother babysit Jaylen. So far, everything was working out perfectly.

As we stepped off the elevator, I spotted my bride standing next to Gina in the lobby. My eyes locked in on the swell of her breasts as they pushed up against the bodice of her white dress. Even though I had become used to seeing her in civilian clothes, she continued to take my breath away. I smiled as I walked over and took her in my arms.

"You look beautiful," I whispered in her ear.

Candace blushed. "Thank you, baby. You're looking handsome as well."

"Ahem, is she the only one you see?" Gina pretended to clear her throat as she folded her arms across her chest pretending to be mad.

I felt the tips of my ears burn. I had gotten cold busted. "I'm sorry, Gina. It's not like I didn't see you, but damn, do you see this woman right here? You can't hold that against a brother."

"It's alright. I'm not going to bust your chops about it this time. She should be the only one you're looking at today. Besides, I don't need you to tell me I look good. I've got my own man to tell me that." Gina held out her hand to Gavin, and he pushed me to the side.

"You got that right. My baby be looking good, too!" Gavin gave Gina a big kiss, tongue and all. "It don't matter at all what some other dude says about my wife. She knows I give her flowers every day."

"Come on, y'all. I don't want to wait another minute to make this lady my wife." I took several deep breaths and grabbed Candace's hand. Just touching her calmed my nerves, and I knew everything was going to be all right.

42 COJO MILLS

When the nurse told me that my mother had been waiting to see me, I flat out refused to see her. I couldn't see past the shame and guilt I felt to consider how she must be feeling. She had flown halfway around the world to see me, and I was acting like a dick about it. Knowing that I was wrong didn't make it easier to see her. It wasn't that I didn't love my mother; I just didn't want to hear her say I told you so. Or, to see pity in her eyes. Things would have been easier for me if I *had* been able to kill myself.

For my own safety, I was transferred to the psych ward. At first, I was freaking out about it. I didn't think I was crazy, but I recognized I needed some help. I didn't want to die, but I didn't know how I was going to go on living.

The nurse came into the room pushing a cart. More drugs. Yippee. The best time of the day as far as I was concerned. I watched her as she took my vitals and recorded them into her laptop. I didn't care about all of that. The only thing I wanted was in the little plastic cup. She poured some fresh water and ice into my cup and handed me my pills.

"Thanks." Sick or not, I still had manners.

"Your mother told me to tell you she's going home."

I immediately felt overwhelmed with fear. What was I thinking? How could I punish my mother for the dumb things I did?

"Is she still here?"

"Yes, she's in the waiting room."

"Can you get her for me, please?"

"I sure will as soon as I finish my rounds. Do you want me to send in an aide to help you spruce up a little bit?"

I hadn't given a thought as to how I looked in days. The nurses kept me bathed, but I was so sure my hair had to be matted. I was in desperate need of a perm, and I couldn't remember the last time I ran a comb through it. "I could use a brush or a comb."

"Good. I don't think I could tell your mom no again. It's going to be okay."

I could care less about her opinion. She didn't have to walk in my shoes, nor did she know how much my life had changed. I put my head back on my pillow and tried to quiet my mind so the pills could work. Getting myself worked up before I saw my mother wasn't going to help anything. I'd almost drifted off to sleep when the aide came in with the comb. By then, I didn't have the strength to do my own hair. She pushed the button that lifted my head higher and attempted to comb my hair.

"Wait, you're hurting me." She was yanking on my hair like she was combing a doll's hair.

"I'm sorry. I don't know what else to do with it."

"Just leave the comb. I'm sure my mother will help me."

"Do you want me to go get her now?"

"Please." The aide nodded her head and left the room. I sensed her relief without her saying a word. I felt my anxiety level begin to rise, but I fought against it.

As soon as I saw my mother's face, I started crying. Her eyes showed all the concern she must have been feeling as she rushed to the bed and took me in her arms.

"Oh, baby. I've been so worried about you."

"I'm so sorry, Momma. I can't believe I was so selfish to keep you away from me."

"Shush, that's not important now. Are you okay?"

It was an oxymoron. I was in a mental institution, and I'd tried to kill myself. "I'm better now that you're here." I wasn't lying; I actually did feel better.

Mom pushed me back and stared into my eyes. I tried to look away, but she turned my face so she could really see me. "What happened, baby?" Tears were streaming down her face, too.

It was like a floodgate had opened inside my heart and head at the same time. The words began spilling out of my mouth. I told her everything starting from the day I slept with Gavin until I tried to end my pain. My mother listened quietly, and if she was shocked by my confessions, she didn't let it show on her face.

"After all that, can you still love me?"

"Are you kidding me? You haven't told me anything that would cause me or your father to love you any less."

"I feel so lost, Mom. I was hurting so badly, and I felt like there wasn't anyone whom I could turn to. What am I going to do now?"

"For starters, we need to get you out of here. The doctor said there is no need for you to stay if you aren't a danger to yourself. That part is all on you, sweetie."

"But where will I go? My furniture is probably going to get put out on the street. All that money you sent me is long gone."

"I don't want to force anything on you, baby. If you want to stay here, I'm sure we can work out something."

I shook my head no. "I can't stay here. The only good thing in this place is my friend Rozz."

"She's a sweet girl. I remember her from when you were younger."

"She is. I was never a good friend to her. I realize that now."

"Trust me, she doesn't hold it against you. She's been here practically every day since I've been here."

"Where is Daddy? Did he come with you?"

My mother got up off the bed and went to sit in the chair nearest the window. She looked extremely uncomfortable, and it made me frightened.

"Honey, your father loves you, but I thought it was best that I made this trip alone."

"Is he ashamed of me?" The thought ran through me like a knife.

"Of course not. You see, your father and I haven't been together in a couple of years. We're still friends, but we've grown apart."

"Mom, why didn't you tell me?" I didn't know how I felt about the failure of my parents' marriage. I went through a range of emotions. Shock, disbelief and finally, sadness.

"I guess for some of the same reasons why you didn't feel like you could confide in me. I was ashamed."

"But he was there when I called you. I spoke to him."

"I know. When you called, I realized just how miserable we both were. At first, neither one of us were willing to admit it. We spent so many years living apart, it wasn't until after he retired that I accepted the fact I didn't even know him. We were just going through the motions."

"Wow. I can't help but wonder if knowing this would have made a difference to me."

My mother nodded her head in agreement. "In hindsight, it might have saved us both from a lot of grief. Then again, it might not have made any difference at all. That's just how life is, honey. We all have to live and learn, and part of that process is making mistakes. How we recover from the mistakes makes all the difference."

"Do you think Daddy has found somebody else?" I couldn't bear to think of my father loving someone else. This hurt me almost as much as knowing that Merlin had found someone.

"I hope he has, sweetheart. I don't have any ill will toward your father. He's a good man and a great father."

"How you can you say that? Doesn't that make you feel like less of a woman?" This was probably the most candid conversation that we'd ever had.

"Me? Why? I'm still a good woman. Just because I don't want the same things as my husband does, doesn't change me. We were married for almost thirty years. In that time, we probably spent a good five years together. During that time, I've changed, so it's only natural he's changed, too."

"Do you have someone else?"

I saw the sadness in my mother's eyes, and it made my heart hurt more. I never once considered how solitary her life was when I was a child. I always thought she was happy.

"No, dear. Not yet. I hope to meet that special someone someday."

"Do you think it's possible?"

"What are you trying to say? I'm still a beautiful woman. I've got some good years left in me, too."

I chuckled a little bit. "That's not what I meant, Mom. I was asking you if you still believed in marriage and finding the perfect mate?"

"Of course I do. I'm not done and neither are you!"

"I want to move back to Atlanta, Mom."

"I don't think that's such a good idea. What about all those bad memories that chased you away the first time? None of that stuff has changed."

"I understand, but like you said, I've changed. I know Merlin has moved on, and Gavin too for that matter. He has a wife and a baby now."

"Have you thought about what you are going to do if you run into either of them?"

"There is nothing to do. I think I will always love both of them for very different reasons. Just like you will always have love for my dad. Besides, Atlanta is a big place. We'll probably never run into each other again."

"Are you sure about this?"

"About as sure as I can be about anything. I won't know unless I try it. Right?"

"You have a point there." She didn't seem entirely convinced.

"Besides, I'm pretty sure I can get my old job back if they have any vacancies. At least it's worth a shot."

"What would you say about my moving to Atlanta with you? We could get an apartment large enough for both of us and help each other out."

"You would do that for me?"

"I'm not doing it for you; I'm doing it for us. I liked Atlanta. I just didn't want to continue living there by myself after you and Merlin got together."

"Mom, just because I got married didn't mean I was going to stop spending time with you."

"You were starting a new life, honey. You and Merlin didn't need me sticking my nose in it. I also thought it was time I spent some time with your dad, doing what he liked to do, which was travel."

I was surprised. "I thought you were the one who liked to travel so much? You sure did pack up our bags often enough."

"I did it to be close to your father. But even though we were in the same space, we still weren't connecting. His attention was elsewhere. At the time, I didn't want to see it. When we were together all the time, I couldn't deny it. It doesn't upset me anymore; I'm good.

"If we get an apartment, Mom, I can't live in it like I'm a child again."

"I wouldn't expect you to. We'll split the bills just like roommates do. You respect my privacy, and I'll respect yours."

It sounded good to me, especially since I didn't have a whole lot of other options to go with. "I can live with that."

"What about your drinking? Is this something you're going to need help with?"

"I think I can get it under control on my own. If I see I can't, I promise you I'll be the first person to admit it."

"I can live with that, too. We're going to make it, honey. I think we'll do just fine."

For the first time in months, I had hope. I didn't feel like such a failure either. "So what do I need to do to get out of here?"

"I'll speak with the doctor and let you know. In the meantime, we need to think about what to do with your stuff."

"With the exception of my clothes, I don't care. The stuff I took from the house I shared with Merlin are toxic to me. I should have known it would be, but I kept hoping we'd patch things up again. Now, I don't need those reminders from my past."

"Sounds like a plan to me. I still have some things in storage. Whatever else we need, we'll get after we both get jobs."

I couldn't stop smiling. Things were beginning to look up for me at long last. It wasn't perfect, but it was something. "I'm so glad you didn't leave without us talking. I was wrong to keep you away."

"I wasn't going anywhere. I was lying. I was going to wait here until I wore you down."

"You were faking me out?"

"You're damn right I was. Don't make me have to do that again either. If something is going on with you, I need to know. There is nothing that we can't accomplish together. Do you get that?"

"Yes, ma'am. I got it. But that also applies to you. You can't keep things from me just because you're trying to protect me. If I've learned one thing through this whole ordeal, it's that honesty is the best policy."

"I'll second that! Now let me go see if I can chase down that doctor. The sooner I get you out of this looney bin the better I'll feel."

"I know that's right. We've got some packing to do. The hot-mess-express is headed back to the A."

ABOUT THE AUTHOR

Tina Brooks McKinney began her writing career as a dare. As an avid reader, writing was the next step for her. Armed with a very active imagination and a story to tell, Tina penned her first novel All That Drama. Readers fell in love with Tina's no-nonsense characters and her comedic style of weaving a story. Since then, Tina has written ten novels and two novellas. Her titles include, All That Drama, Lawd, Mo' Drama, Fool, Stop Trippin', Dubious, Deep Deception, Snapped, Got Me Twisted, Deep Deception 2, Snapped 2: The Redemption, Betta Not Tell, Catch Fire, Catch Fire 2, Undone, Outdone and Done.

A wife and mother of two, Tina uses real-life situations to both entertain and inspire her readers. You can find out more information about her by visiting her website.www.tinamckinney.com or drop her an email at tybrooks2@yahoo.com. She would love to hear from you.

www.ingramcontent.com/pod-product-compliance
Lightning Source LLC
Chambersburg PA
CBHW021511240626
47154CB00002B/593